Abigail Henry Feels Fine

A Novel by Neva Bell

Cover Design by Barbara Schwenzer
        olibeebees@gmail.com; IG: @olibees

For Jeff.

He told me he never wants to see his name in any of my books. Unfortunately, he did not say "over" after his instructions. According to Stewie from *The Family Guy*, this means his request never existed.

You're welcome.

Over.

Chapter One

Do all moms call at the worst possible time, or just mine?

I struggle to hold a giant down comforter in my arms as I balance my cellphone between my shoulder and ear. "Mom, I really can't talk right now."

"Abigail Henry! I'm so sick of hearing you say that."

"Can I call you back in an hour? I'm in the middle of something."

"Are you on a date?"

I roll my eyes. "It's 2 p.m. on a Thursday. No, I'm not on a date."

"Of course you're not," she tsks. "It won't kill you to get out more."

I softly smack my forehead against the doorframe of the bedroom I'm trying to finish decorating. "I'm at the Warner house. I really need to go."

"Fine. But for the record, I think you should call Adam. The two of you were such a cute couple."

"Let it go Mom. We broke up ten months ago."

"He was such a good catch."

"No he wasn't. He was a jerk."

"But he was so tall," she insists.

"Yes, because height is the most important characteristic in a partner."

"Don't you want tall children?"

"Good-bye Mom." I end the call before she can give any more advice on my love life.

1

I chuck my phone on the plastic-covered loveseat that was delivered this morning to the Warner mansion. The beautiful royal blue chesterfield will remain covered until the room is completely done to avoid any spills or mishaps. It was custom built and cost more than my first year of college. The last thing I need is a stain.

I wrangle the Egyptian cotton flat sheet onto the new mattress of Mrs. Warner's antique wood-framed bed and carefully tuck the pillows into their new cases. I smooth the top of the white down comforter and smile to myself. Perfect.

I am one day away from finishing what has been the largest project Interior Motives has undertaken. My best friend Elle and I started our interior design business right after college on a wing and a prayer. Our earliest jobs were for friends and family, but then we expanded to commercial businesses. I never thought we'd be working in a high-end residence like the Warner mansion.

When Mrs. Elizabeth Warner reached out to us, we nearly fainted. Everyone in Columbus knows Elizabeth Warner. Not only is she the former CEO and owner of the largest computer company in the United States, she also serves on the board of several charities and is an active socialite.

We were initially hired to do a kitchen remodel, but our projects expanded to the foyer, two bathrooms on the main level of her home, and her master suite. The project has taken six months to complete, largely because some of the high-end textiles and materials Mrs. Warner wanted are manufactured in foreign countries.

Next stop – the master bathroom. It is gorgeous. I sit on the edge of the new jacuzzi tub we installed and take it all in. Mrs. Warner wanted "crisp and clean", which to her meant everything had to be white. I was able to convince her that touches of gray add a little pop, but maintain a clean look. Despite the fact that her walk-in shower can hold ten people if she tries, and her closet looks like a retail shop, Mrs. Warner is surprisingly humble and gracious.

"Do you ladies want one?" she asked when she saw Elle and I drooling over her handbags.

2

Shocked, I turned her down.

"I have so many, I don't use half of them. Here," she grabbed a vintage Louis Vuitton and handed it to Elle, "this will look nice on your shoulder." She glanced my way, then back at her collection. "And for you my dear, a classic Prada. You can't go wrong with Prada."

"Mrs. Warner," I protested, "we can't accept these."

She waved me off. "Take them. I'll forget they were here in a week."

"Are you sure?" Elle asked as she posed in front of the closet mirror checking out her new bag.

I threw her a look, one reminding her we were on a job.

"I don't have any daughters. Let me spoil you girls a little."

We walked out that day with new purses, new to us anyway, and have left with several other gifts during the course of our employment. Chocolates from Anthony Thomas Candy, cookies from Cheryl & Co., and trinkets from Mrs. Warner's various business trips.

I'll miss her, I realize as I reminisce. Not just because of her generosity, but also because of the conversations we've had these last few months. She's a deep thinker, a rare find these days.

I catch a glimpse of myself in the new mirror we installed. My makeup looks good considering how much manual labor I've done today, but I detect faint purple smudges under my green eyes. I'm exhausted, mentally and physically, and it shows.

I run my fingers through my blonde hair, fixing a tangled section. The curls I made this morning are holding strong.

"Why do you straighten your hair just to curl it?" the infamous Adam asked me one morning when we were still together.

"I have to straighten the wavy sections so they're smooth, then I can add the curl."

He shook his head. "That makes no sense."

"You make no sense," I muttered under my breath when he walked away.

A few weeks later, we were over. It had nothing to do with my hair and everything to do with the fact that he's an ass. A tall ass.

I sigh when I think of my conversation with Mom. I need to start dating again so she gets off my back. I've been too busy with this project to even think about dating. My business is too important and I don't want any distractions.

Still, it's been almost a year since he and I split. It's probably time to get back in the game.

My reverie is broken by the click-clack of tiny nails on the marble floor. I smile, my favorite four-legged friend is paying me a visit.

"What are you doing in here Otis?" I scoop up Mrs. Warner's teacup yorkie. I've become particularly fond of this little guy. I kiss his head. "I'm going to miss you, Otis." He licks my cheek in response.

I walk through the master bedroom with my furry friend, closing the door behind me. I pause on the other side, realizing my part of this job is over. I've closed the door on this project. Literally.

I'm hit with a wave of mixed emotions. I'm excited Elle and I were able to see this project through. I'm super proud of the work we've done. And I'm also a little sad to be done with what turned out to be my favorite job so far.

"Mrs. Warner?" I call out as I walk down her beautiful staircase. "Mrs. Warner, are you home?"

I search the main level of the house without any luck. "Where is your mommy, Otis?"

I'm about to give up when I spot Mrs. Warner outside one of the living room windows. She's in her backyard digging in a flower bed. I open the sliding glass door and step out into the October air.

"There you are Mrs. Warner, I was about to call in the troops."

She smiles up at me, her brown eyes shining in the sunlight. "Hello dear. Just doing some last minute fall planting."

4

I look around and admire her landscaping. "I didn't know you handle the yardwork."

She laughs. "I wish. The landscapers do most of the work, but I like to plant the tulips myself. They're an excellent lesson in patience."

"Oh," I say simply, not sure how to respond to her insight.

"Have you come to tell me you're done?" Mrs. Warner asks.

"Yes and no. My part of the project is done, but Elle will be here tomorrow to handle the last delivery."

Mrs. Warner stands and brushes dirt off her knees. A tattered gray baseball cap covers her short brown hair. This is the first time I've seen her in a flannel shirt and jeans. She's usually dressed in business casualwear, even on the weekends.

She heads for the house. "Before you go, I have something for you."

"You do?"

"Yes. It's in my office."

I follow Mrs. Warner inside, curious what she has for me. We say "hello" to June, one of Mrs. Warner's house cleaners, as we pass by. She is sweeping dust bunnies into a dustpan.

June wags a finger at Otis. "This is your fault, Mister," she scolds before giving his head a pat.

"How are you June?" I ask while trailing behind the speedy Mrs. Warner.

"Wonderful. You?"

"It's my last day."

June frowns, her blue eyes saddening. "Really? Already?"

I laugh. "It's been six months."

She shakes her head. "Time does fly, doesn't it?"

"Absolutely." I wave before Mrs. Warner and I turn a corner. "I've got your number. We'll get together for lunch sometime."

"You betcha."

5

I smile. This is June's signature catchphrase. Whenever I asked for her help, her response would be, "You betcha." She knows Mrs. Warner's house, and tastes, like the back of her hand. She's worked for Mrs. Warner since the house's completion in 1985.

"If it wasn't for June, I would have sold this place years ago," Mrs. Warner admitted the day we met.

"Really?" I asked surprised.

She nodded. "Yes. This is too much house for me. June keeps me sane."

I quickly learned why. June is not only a reliable person, but she's always good for a laugh when you need a mental health break. A sturdy woman in her sixties, she has ten grandchildren to keep her occupied when she isn't bailing out Mrs. Warner.

I follow Mrs. Warner through her first floor. While Elle and I put our stamp on the place, the bulk of it is Mrs. Warner's original vision. She chose wisely back then, picking timeless décor that will withstand any trends that come down the line. Beautiful bamboo flooring, white crown molding, and expensive woodworking somehow accommodate the modern touches we added.

"It won't be the same around here without you," Mrs. Warner notes as she approaches her office doors.

I blush. "Aw, stop it. You'll probably enjoy not hearing my heels clacking through your house."

Mrs. Warner laughs. "I always know when you're coming."

She pushes open the white six-panel doors leading to her office. It is one of the rooms in her expansive house we did not touch. It is essentially a contemporary version of a library. The double doors open to a large room with built-in bookshelves on every wall. Like her master bathroom, the walls are painted white and are adorned with brightly colored artwork. Most of the white shelving is taken up by books, but modern art sculptures and family photographs are tucked in various spaces. My favorite is a photo of her and her two boys in orange life vests smiling as they balance in a raft after a trip down a river in West Virginia.

6

"The boys had a ball, I almost had a heartache," she told me when I admired the picture for the first time.

Her boys were young then, probably no more than ten and twelve. They are in their thirties now with children of their own. I've never talked to Mrs. Warner about her ex-husband, but I know from the local papers it was a messy divorce.

Mrs. Warner walks over to her massive glass desk holding her fuchsia laptop and several desk organizers filled with stacks of paperwork. Her tortoise shell glasses rest in the center of the desk waiting to be used. A simple white box with a pale pink bow sits on her white leather chair.

She hands it to me with a smile. "Just a small token of my appreciation."

I set Otis down on the floor and take the gift box. "You didn't have to do this."

"I know, but I saw it and it made me think of you."

I pull the ribbon and lift the lid. I laugh. "This is perfect." Inside the box is a white coffee mug with the phrase "Like a Boss" written in gold script.

"Remember the day you had to explain what 'Like a Boss' means?"

I giggle again. "I do."

A few months back, I wore a grey tank top with "Like a Boss" scrawled across it in pink. I don't usually wear tank tops on the job, but it was a hot July day and I was installing flooring in the master bathroom.

"Mrs. Warner, you are the embodiment of living like a boss," I explained to her.

"How so?"

I wiped sweat from my brow with a wet paper towel. "Well, a boss is someone who owns who they are without any fear. They get the job done."

"Ah, I see." She paused. "I like it."

I turn the mug around to see my name written on the back in pink script. "This is awesome Mrs. Warner. Thank you."

I attempt to put the mug back in the box, but my hand suddenly trembles and I almost drop it. Mrs. Warner reaches out, prepared to catch my gift. Luckily, I'm able to grasp the handle and return the mug to its box in one piece.

"Is your hand still acting up?" she asks with a frown.

I flush with embarrassment. "Yes."

"You need to see a doctor about that."

"I have."

"And?" she presses.

"He referred me to a neurologist."

Her eyes widen. "A neurologist? Oh Abby…"

I put my hand up. "It's nothing to worry about. I went to see the neurologist last week and I'm having an MRI done tomorrow just in case."

"An MRI? Of your wrist?"

I pause. "Of my brain."

Mrs. Warner's brow furrows. "Abby, this sounds serious."

Her reaction is exactly why I'm not telling anyone about my doctor appointments. I'm freaked out enough as it is.

"It's probably something silly like early stages of carpal tunnel."

"Carpal tunnel isn't any fun either," Mrs. Warner points out.

"I know." I sigh. "I just hope they give me a diagnosis soon. It's frustrating for sure."

"Any other symptoms?"

I hesitate. There have been. Several actually. Dizzy spells. Using the incorrect words at times – like microphone instead of microwave. But I don't want to tell Mrs. Warner all of this.

Instead, I say, "I'm fine Mrs. Warner. No need to worry."

"Well, keep me posted."

"I'll keep in touch," I promise.

"Good."

I reach out and give her a hug. "Thank you so much for this opportunity."

"As soon as I saw Ruth's salon, I knew you could handle the job."

Ruth Jones owns the newest and chicest spa in town. She also happens to be a sorority sister who was willing to give Elle and I first crack at designing her business. She was a pain to work with, Ruth is the perpetual taskmaster, but it was worth it. In addition to Mrs. Warner's job, we get calls regularly from Ruth's clients who are impressed with our work in the salon.

"It was a big risk on your part, and we truly appreciate it."

"Prepare yourselves. When everyone comes to my holiday party in December, you'll get referrals. I've kept the renovations hush-hush so my guests will be surprised." Her eyes light up. "You and Elle must come to the party! Then I can introduce you to everyone."

Wow. Anyone who's anyone comes to Mrs. Warner's holiday party. It's one of the biggest social events of the season. Elle and I could make a ton of contacts there.

"Mrs. Warner, please don't feel obligated…"

She waves me off. "Nonsense. You're coming. I'll send the invitation to your office."

After another hug and a final good-bye, for now, I walk out her massive front door. My white Toyota Corolla is parked in her circular driveway right next to her black Porsche Boxster.

"It was a silly indulgence," she told me one day, "but I love driving that car." A small smile crossed her lips.

It's hard for me to imagine Mrs. Warner with her pedal to the metal, screaming down an empty highway. Then again, this is a woman who took her two young boys white-water rafting.

I start my car and shake out my right hand. It is numb from the trembling episode inside Mrs. Warner's office. I open and close my fingers, making a fist over and over again. My hand feels like it has gone to sleep, but I don't have the painful tingling sensation that usually comes with it.

I nearly jump out of my skin when my phone rings through the car speakers. I catch my breath before answering.

"Hey Elle."

Elle's familiar voice fills my car. "What's up chica?"

"Getting ready to leave the Warner house."

"Just now?"

"I wanted to make the bed before I left. It looks fantastic."

"I told you I would handle it tomorrow."

"I know, but I had to see it for myself."

Elle chuckles. "Of course you did."

"So what's up?"

"Your doctor appointment is tomorrow at 8:30 a.m., right?"

"Yes, but you don't have to go. It will take at least an hour and you have to be here for the delivery."

"The furniture isn't coming until ten. I'll meet you at the doctor's office, then head to Mrs. Warner's when you go back for the MRI."

"You sure? I can go by myself."

"Forget it sister. I know how nervous you get about these things. I'm going."

No point in arguing with her. Once Elle gets an idea in her head, she sees it through come hell or high water. It's one of the many things I love about her.

"Do you know where the office is?"

"Corner of High and Juno. Will you need a ride after?"

"No. I won't be on any medications."

"Okay. I'll see you in the morning."

"Sounds good. Oh, and Elle?" I say before she hangs up.

"Yeah?"

"Thank you."

***

The next morning, I'm nervous driving to the medical facility where I'm getting my MRI. I hardly slept a wink last night. I don't know what to expect aside from the information my neurologist, Dr. Harris, gave me last week.

"You'll have a set of scans done without contrast, and then you'll do another set with contrast," she explained while taking notes in my file.

Dr. Harris is young for a specialist, her brown hair shows no sign of grey, but she is incredibly knowledgeable. I was expecting a doctor's coat paired with the typical white sneakers I've seen doctors wear in the past. She walked into the examining room in a navy blue wrap dress with four-inch nude pumps and an oversized pearl necklace.

"Contrast?" I asked her.

"It's a dye they inject intravenously."

"I'll need an I.V.?" Fear started setting in at that point. An I.V. makes everything seem more serious.

My nerves must have been apparent.

Dr. Harris looked up from my file. "There may be slight pain when the I.V. is placed, but you won't feel anything when they inject the dye."

"How long will it take?"

"You'll probably be in there an hour."

"An hour?"

She nodded. "It takes a while, so make sure you use the bathroom before you go in."

Seated on the edge of the examining table, white paper crinkling beneath me, my heart sank. I looked down at my hands, the culprits in this situation. "Am I okay?"

Dr. Harris walked over and touched my shoulder. "I can't predict the outcome of the MRI, but let me ask you this."

I gazed up at her, tears in my eyes.

11

"Are you still living and breathing?"

"Yes," I whispered.

She smiled. "Then you're okay."

Working extra hours at the Warner house and calling new clients has kept me busy the past few days, but now it's game time. I can't avoid thinking about it any longer.

I calm down a little when I pull into the parking lot for the medical facility and see Elle's grey Volkswagen Passat. I park my car next to hers and take a deep breath before stepping out. She's waiting next to my trunk by the time I open my car door.

I plaster a smile on my face. "Good morning sunshine! Glad to see you made it on time."

"Yeah, yeah, yeah," she grumbles. "I bought you coffee, so you're not allowed to give me any shit."

I laugh as I take my coffee from her. "Thank you."

She cocks an eyebrow. "Seriously? You did your hair and makeup for an MRI?"

"Hey, not all of us roll out of bed looking like a supermodel."

Elle is one of those lucky women who doesn't have to try. She gets more attention in jeans and a t-shirt with zero makeup and a sloppy ponytail than most people who put in an hour's worth of effort before they leave the house. She can eat most men under the table, but somehow maintains 125 pounds on her 5'8" frame.

"You ready for this?" she asks as we walk in.

"I guess so."

"I did some research online last night. Does this place have an open or closed MRI?"

I shrug. "No clue."

"Do you get to choose the music?"

"The music?"

She nods. "The music they play during the testing."

"I have no idea."

"Maybe you can sleep the whole time. God knows it looks like you could use the rest."

"Thanks a lot." I bump her with my shoulder. "It would be nice, but I can't fall asleep."

"Why not?"

"I can't move, and if I fall asleep, I might move."

"Ah, gotcha."

I check-in with the receptionist, then take a seat in the waiting room next to Elle.

I change the subject. I'm about to spend an hour in an MRI machine, I don't want to spend my morning talking about it too. "Judy Smith called yesterday. She wants to meet with us next week to discuss her new office."

"Judy Smith? Chiropractor, right?"

"Yep. She's opening a new office in Gahanna."

"That could be cool." Elle picks up a *Cosmopolitan* magazine and starts flipping through it. "Did you hear back from Scott Wilson?"

I frown. "I have not. It's been two weeks. He probably gave the job to someone else."

"Good. I didn't want to work on his house anyway. Creeper."

"Elle!"

"Well he was." She shivers. "He looked at me like he wants to wear my skin."

"Eew. Wear your skin?"

"*Silence of the Lambs*...Buffalo Bill..."

I shake my head. "You're crazy."

"You didn't get bad vibes from him?"

"I did," I admit with a sigh.

"The thought of working alone in his house freaks me out."

Before I can agree with her, a nurse pokes her head into the waiting room. "Abby Henry."

13

Elle and I exchange a glance, then stand. "Will you walk back with me?" I ask.

"Of course."

We follow the young nurse down the hallway. "We'll start off in room three."

She steps to the side and lets us walk into the examining room first. Elle and I take seats in blue chairs pushed against the wall as the nurse sits in front of a computer on the opposite side of the narrow room. An examining table sits to my left. I should probably be on it, but I've sat on enough examining tables lately.

"I'll take your blood pressure and temperature before having you change into a gown. Did you remove all body piercings?"

"Yes."

Elle can't help herself. "Even the one, you know... downstairs?"

The nurse looks over her shoulder at me.

I glare at Elle. "I don't have a piercing downstairs."

The nurse chuckles. "No judgment."

"Can you behave yourself please," I hiss at Elle under my breath.

She smirks in response.

Given my nerves, I expect my blood pressure to be through the roof, but it's normal. No fever either. Looks like I have no excuse to avoid the MRI.

Elle says her good-byes when it's time for me to change into the hospital gown.

"You've got this Abby." She gives me a hug. "Call me when you're done, okay?"

I nod.

The room is eerily quiet as I change into the pale green gown. My bra comes off, metal underwire, but I decide to keep my panties on. Knowing my luck, I'll accidentally expose my backside at some point.

I struggle with closing the gown. Do the ties go around the front or the back?

Once I've tied all the strings into double knots (just in case), I slip my feet into the grey socks the nurse provided. I sit on the examining table, my feet swinging back and forth gently. I glance around the room and feign interest in the posters on the wall. One poster catches my eye. An anatomical drawing of a brain hangs above the scale. Is that what mine will look like? Or will there be something on mine that shouldn't be there?

Thankfully, the nurse returns and doesn't leave me alone with my thoughts for any longer. "You ready?"

I hop down from the table. "Yes."

We make small talk as we walk down the hallway to the MRI room. Casual banter about the weather, the OSU football team, and our lunch plans. My heart skips a beat when I see the MRI machine. It is closed, not an open MRI like I was hoping for. I didn't visit the facility's website because I knew if it confirmed the machine was closed, I'd stress even more.

The thought of being placed in a closed tube inside this hulking machine of cream plastic isn't pleasant. It would be easier on me if there were more openings.

A young man in green scrubs is laying a white sheet on the table. "Perfect timing," he says with a smile.

He looks like a Ken doll. Brown hair perfectly combed with a hard part off the center. Nicely built and shiny white teeth. If I wasn't so nervous, I'd be excited to shake his hand.

"Tim Greene, your technician for the day."

"Abby Harris, your reluctant patient."

He laughs. "All my patients are reluctant, but it's a piece of cake. Promise."

I sit on the table as Tim rattles off information about the exam. Most of it I already know.

"In a few minutes, I'll walk into the room over there." He points to a small room behind a pane of glass. "The bed will

15

slowly enter the tube and you'll hear a series of beeps. That's the first set of images."

"Okay."

"If you start to feel antsy, look in the mirror on the cage, you'll be able to see your feet."

"The cage?"

"Yes, the birdcage." He holds up a plastic contraption. "I'm going to place this on your head like a helmet."

"Uh, no one said anything to me about wearing a birdcage on my head." Panic creeps in. What the hell have I gotten myself into?

"It's not heavy, it's to help keep your head steady while you're in the machine. Even the slightest movement can throw off the results."

My heart thumps as he puts the cage on my head. I don't like this. I don't like this at all.

"Take a deep breath Abby," Tim says softly.

I try, my breath shaky.

He buckles the chin strap of the cage. "Too tight?"

Yes.

I shake my head. "No, it's fine."

"If we start the test and you can't handle it, let me know," he says with warm eyes. "Even if you're halfway through and start to lose it, tell me. I'll be able to hear you. I'll slide you out."

"But if you slide me out, you won't get the test results the doctor needs, right?"

He nods. "Right. You'll have to come back and start over."

"Okay. I'll try my best to stay in there."

"You'll do great." He helps me lay down on the table. "Do you want a blanket?"

"Yes, please. This hospital gown is a bit drafty."

He walks over to a cabinet and comes back with a thin, white blanket. My mind automatically returns to my brief hospital stint

16

when I had my appendix removed fifteen years ago. I was huddled under two of the very same white blankets, scared to death.

"Be brave my dear," my grandmother whispered in my ear before they wheeled me back to the operating room.

I can still smell her Chanel No. 5 perfume. Her smile wide, her blue eyes sparkling in the special way they always did when she showed me affection. God I miss her.

"I'm scared Grandma," I admitted, tears in my eyes.

She took my hand. "I know you are, and that's okay. Life can be scary sometimes." She kissed my forehead. "But you are a strong little girl, you're going to be just fine. And I'll be here waiting for you when you wake up."

"Promise?"

"Promise."

Her words ring in my ears as the nurse returns to place the I.V. in my arm. I squeeze my eyes shut, not wanting to see her do it.

"You'll feel a slight pinch," she warns me.

As promised, I feel a prick like a bee sting in the crook of my elbow. I'm not surprised she went for this location, I have a prominent vein there and most nurses go for it.

"She's all set," the nurse tells Tim. She turns to me with a smile. "Good luck."

I nearly groan. I'm going to need it.

Tim turns on the machine and I slowly slide into the MRI tube. "I'll see you in thirty minutes to inject the dye," he calls in to me before walking away.

"Wait…"

Tim steps back into my line of sight. "You alright?"

"Do I get to pick out music?"

He smiles. "I usually play The Beatles or The Rolling Stones, but most people can't hear it over the machine."

"Oh, okay." Dang. I was really hoping music would calm my nerves.

I lay staring up at the tube waiting for something to happen. I'm twiddling my thumbs and moving my feet while I still can. I nearly jump out of my skin when Tim's voice comes over the speaker.

"I'm about to start Abby. Lay as still as possible."

I came prepared with a list of items to think about while I lay here. Potential clients... my new house... whether I want to dye my hair again this winter...

All of the sudden, the machine comes to life. A series of clicks and beeps echoes in the tube. They remind me of the sound effects for an old school Atari game.

It's happening, my brain is being scanned and captured. Weird. Is Tim seeing my brain right now on his screen? Can he see if there's a problem? Will he tell me if there is?

My heart rate increases, nerves setting in.

Deep breath, I tell myself. But not too deep, could mess up the imaging.

Back to my list of topics. Christmas gifts. Christmas is two months away, but no time like the present. I giggle to myself – no time like the present. Pun intended.

After mentally walking through Macy's picking out gifts for my family and Elle, I move on to my future hair color. I don't get the permanent dye, just the temporary color that washes out in a few weeks. I don't dislike my natural color, but every once in a while a girl needs to...

"Abby," Tim interrupts my vanity. "I'm going to slide you out now so I can put the dye in. You'll feel the table start to move."

The dye is the part I'm dreading the most. I'm not sure why. The nurse did an excellent job putting in the I.V., so the worst of it is over. But I've never had dye injected before. What if I have some odd, one of a kind reaction to it?

A few minutes later I'm back in the tube, dye coursing through my veins. What if something happens to me in here and Tim doesn't realize it? What if the machine breaks and I'm stuck in this tube?

18

My heartbeat accelerates again. I'm not claustrophobic, or at least I've never freaked out about confined spaces. But have I ever truly been in a confined space like this? What if I'm claustrophobic and I didn't know it?

The machine kicks on again, drowning out Mick Jagger with its loud beeps and clicks. No, no, no. I want to hear the rest of *Honky Tonk Blues*. I don't want to be in here for another thirty minutes.

I close my eyes, a single tear sliding down my cheek. I don't want to do this anymore. I want out.

Be brave my dear...

My grandmother's words rise within me. I glance up at the mirror on the birdcage and see my toes snuggled under the blanket. I'm tall enough that my feet and lower legs are outside the tube. In the distance, Tim stands on the other side of the glass wall looking down at a computer screen.

You're okay, you're almost done. In half an hour, you'll be back in your car and this will be behind you. You'll be so mad at yourself if you don't get through this.

I repeat these mantras to myself over and over until the machine goes quiet.

"All done Abby. I'm sliding you out now."

I did it!

I smile as the table slides out of the MRI tube. I'm proud of myself. I talked myself down and got through it.

"Nice job!" Tim says as he helps me sit up.

"I'm not going to lie, I had a freak out moment in there."

"Most people do."

"Really?"

He nods. "Oh yeah. I had a guy leave yesterday because he couldn't handle it."

Tim walks me to my examining room so I can change. "Your doctor will call you with the results."

"How long will it take?"

19

"It's usually two or three days."

"Ugh. That's too long."

He smiles. "Good luck to you Abby."

There it is again – luck. I'm not sure luck has anything to do with my health, but I'll take whatever positivity I can get.

I relish the sunshine when I step outside. The fall air is crisp, but I have a newfound appreciation for it after being in that MRI tube. Once in my car, I call Elle over Bluetooth.

"Hola chica. You all done?"

"Yes, thank God. It was awful. How are things at Mrs. Warner's?"

"Great. The furniture is here and I'm getting everything set up."

"Want me to come over?"

"Nope. You go home and rest."

"Rest? I just laid down for an hour."

"Pick up some yummy food, go home, get in your pjs, and binge watch the new season of *The Crown*. You know you want to."

"Yeah, I kinda do," I admit.

She laughs. "Alright, you go get some R and R, and I'll get back to work. Later chica."

"See ya."

I follow Elle's advice and get lunch from a local Chinese restaurant on the way home. I'm thrilled I found a good Chinese food place close to my new house. It will come in handy on long workdays when I don't feel like cooking.

I pull into the driveway for my small craftsman home I bought last month. Although it needs a ton of work, I absolutely love it. As soon as I saw it, I knew I had to have it. The first thing I'm going to do is paint the brown exterior a beautiful blue and the shutters a bright white. I want a bold, red front door with a wreath hanging on it by Christmas.

"Oscar, I'm home!" I yell when I walk in.

My grey and white striped cat saunters down the stairs to greet me. Oscar wasn't too fond of our new digs when we moved in, but he's gotten used to it. I think the two-story cat house I bought helped.

I set my lunch down on the coffee table and head upstairs to put on some comfy clothes, dodging boxes along the way. Most of my belongings are still packed. I spend my days organizing and cleaning someone else's house. By the time I come home to mine, unpacking is the last thing I want to do.

I smile when I walk into my bedroom, the one room in my new home I've finished. Walking into it is like a breath of fresh air. I installed new hardwood flooring throughout the house before moving in and I painted the walls in my bedroom a beautiful light grey. I handmade an upholstered headboard with cream fabric and cream leather buttons. I bought soft pink bedding from my favorite home goods store despite the ridiculous price tag. This is my first home and I want to love everything I put in it. No settling. I've done enough of that in my life.

I change into black sweatpants and a cozy grey sweatshirt, pour myself a glass of wine, and dig into my lunch. Inevitably though, my mind wanders back to my MRI. Waiting for the results is going to be torture.

Chapter Two

"Judy, this is fantastic!" I gush as I survey our new client's office space. "The view of the pond is to die for."

Judy smiles. "Isn't it? I've been practicing for almost twenty years now and I'm finally in the space I've dreamed of being in. My clients will love it."

"Did you buy or lease?" Elle asks.

"I own it. It's mine."

Elle nods with approval. "Good. You can do whatever you want to it."

"Exactly. Plus, this area is booming. I'll make my money back, and then some, when I sell it."

Judy gives us a tour of the entire space. "This used to be a fertility clinic," she explains. "They were in here for three years and they kept the place up nicely. The layout is already perfect for what I need."

I take out my pen and small notepad. "Tell us how we can help you." I flex my fingers, trying to get the blood flowing. It does little to dull the tingling sensation.

"I want something modern, yet cozy. A clean look, but not sterile. The surfaces of the furniture should be materials that are easily sanitized. And no carpeting."

"Color palette?" Elle asks.

"Soft tones. Again, I want my clients to feel at ease."

I tap my pen on my notepad. "Are you okay with pops of color in your decorations?"

"Yes, that's fine."

I examine Judy's outfit closely while she and Elle discuss the types of artwork Judy prefers. I can tell a lot about a person's home décor style by what they wear. Judy is dressed professionally, but I note that her black pants are flat front, not pleated. She wears ballet flats instead of heels, and she opted for an easy to wash and wear sweater as opposed to a blouse. Her choices are very much what she is telling us she wants in her office. A professional appearance that is comfortable and easy to maintain.

As we're wrapping up the consultation, my cellphone buzzes in my purse. I typically ignore calls when I'm with a client, but I'm waiting to hear from the doctor's office. I glance down at the screen in my open bag and see "Dr. Harris" on the caller ID.

"Excuse me for one second. I have to take this call."

Elle looks at me meaningfully, then focuses her attention on Judy. "How about your personal office space? What would you like to see in there?"

My heart is racing as I step outside the glass door. This is it.

My voice shakes when I answer. "Hello?"

"Hi, is this Abigail Henry?"

"Yes it is."

"Hi Abigail. This is Nancy, Dr. Harris's nurse."

"Hi Nancy."

"Dr. Harris would like for you to come by the office this afternoon."

Uh oh. "This afternoon?"

"Yes. Are you available at two o'clock?"

"I can be."

"Excellent. I'll put you on the schedule."

"Nancy," I pause, "can you tell me the results of the MRI?" It's a longshot, but I had to ask.

"I'm sorry, I can't. Dr. Harris will go over the results with you this afternoon."

I frown. This is not good. "Okay."

"Dr. Harris also suggests that you bring someone with you to the appointment."

My stomach drops. "Bring someone with me?"

"Yes."

When Nancy doesn't elaborate further, I mumble, "Yeah, okay. I'll bring someone."

"Great. We'll see you at two."

I hang up and stand perfectly still for a moment. Everyone knows what it means when the doctor tells you to bring someone with you.

Tears well in my eyes. I'm too curious a person to avoid researching my symptoms online. What I'm experiencing is not new to the human experience. I found a lot of people complaining about issues similar to what I'm dealing with. Two main culprits continuously popped up: Lyme disease and multiple sclerosis. I ruled out Lyme disease because I haven't been bitten by a tick. That would require going outside and I rarely spend time in nature. I should, but I don't.

Which leaves multiple sclerosis. I didn't allow myself to go too far down the rabbit hole because it was freaking me out. Now I wish I read a little more.

"Calm down," Elle tells me on the drive to Dr. Harris's office. "You don't know it's MS."

"But I do, Elle. I just know."

"Like the time you were sure you had ovarian cancer because you were spotting in the middle of your pill pack?"

"Not now Elle." I rub my temples. "Please."

"Sorry," she says with a frown. "You know I can't handle this shit. I have to crack jokes. It's what I do."

I smile her way. "I know, and I appreciate it. Thank you for coming with me."

She stops at a traffic light. "No problem. Besides, who was going to go with you? Your mother?"

I groan. Anything but that.

25

Half an hour later a nurse calls us back into Dr. Harris's office. I make mental notes of the waiting room space and the hallway leading to the patient rooms, keeping an eye out for inspiration for Judy's office space.

What do I like about Dr. Harris's waiting room? Is there anything in particular I find comforting like Judy wants?

We walk past the patient rooms and down the back corridor to Dr. Harris's office. The cream wallpaper and tan carpet are nice, but not what Judy is looking for.

"Ah, Abby, come on in," Dr. Harris says after the nurse knocks on her door.

My chic neurologist is dressed in a black sheath dress today. A chunky rhinestone necklace and a stethoscope share space around her neck. Her fingernails are painted cherry red and her hair is pulled back in a french twist.

Elle and I each take a seat in blue fabric chairs across from Dr. Harris's marble top desk. I can't help but admire it.

"Where did you get this desk?"

She smiles. "My brother-in-law custom made it for me."

"Really? It's gorgeous."

"I bought the base at a flea market. He restored it, painted it white, and then installed this desktop."

"He did a great job."

Elle throws me a look that says, "Seriously?"

Dr. Harris clears her throat. "I brought you in today to discuss the results of your MRI. Unfortunately, I have some bad news."

I gulp. "Is it MS?"

Dr. Harris is taken aback. "Actually Abby, it is."

I fight back tears. For once in my life, my paranoid self-diagnosis is right on the money. Elle reaches out and squeezes my hand.

"How much do you know about the disease?" Dr. Harris asks.

"Not much. Just what I read on WebMD."

"Okay, let's start with the basics. MS affects your brain cells. The myelin sheath around your brain cells protects the cells from the infinite number of electrical synapsis that are happening in your brain at any given second. When that myelin is damaged, the brain cell becomes overwhelmed and essentially shuts down. As a result, your body starts having odd sensations or forgets how to do things. We can see this damage on an MRI scan. It shows up as a grey or light spot."

"And I have a spot?"

Dr. Harris frowns. "You have two spots."

"How do you fix it?" Elle asks.

"We haven't come up with a way to fix it completely, but there are medications that can slow or halt the disease. In some case studies, there have been patients who saw improvements in their condition."

"How bad is my condition?"

"MS is a very subjective disease. No one experiences it the same way. Some people have overnight system shutdowns and never recover their lost functions. Others have milder symptoms that are well-controlled with the medications. There are also people who are in a remission stage for years, but are suddenly hit with a bad episode. It's hard to predict."

Elle is all business, a rare occasion for her. "When can she start the medication?"

"There are a few different medication options. The earliest treatments were injections. The patients gave themselves shots every other day."

I cringe. I hate shots.

"But," Dr. Harris continues, "there are oral medications on the market now and my patients like those much better."

Dr. Harris and Elle both look at me, waiting for me to say something. Despite having a good idea of what Dr. Harris was going to tell me, the news is disarming. It's one thing to be pretty sure about something, it's another to have it confirmed.

I have multiple sclerosis...

It's surreal. One of those life moments when you think – is this actually happening to me?

"I know this is a lot to take in Abby," Dr. Harris says softly. "Do you have any questions?"

Questions, questions, questions. Do I have any questions?

"Will the medication stop the tingling?"

"I can't guarantee that it will, but there's a good chance the medication will put your body in a remission phase."

"Um, okay." I really hope the medication helps. The tingling drives me nuts. "So if I take the meds, it won't get worse?"

"Again Abby, I can't guarantee you anything. We have made tremendous strides with MS treatments, but it can be fickle. Stress, illness, and other environmental factors can affect your symptoms."

Elle squeezes my hand to get my attention. "Sounds to me like you need to get on the meds asap."

"I agree," Dr. Harris says. "There's a few things we need to discuss first."

"Okay..."

"What type of insurance do you have?"

"I'm on the marketplace."

"Is it a good plan?"

"Yes. Why?"

"This medication is very expensive."

Ugh. Great. "How expensive?"

"Ten thousand a month."

My jaw drops. "Ten thousand a month?"

Dr. Harris puts her hand up. "Before you freak out, the manufacturer offers a generous program to its users. You are only responsible for five thousand dollars of the costs per year. After that, they bill the insurance company for the covered portion, but not you."

28

I sigh with relief. Five thousand dollars is a lot of money, but much better than spending over a hundred thousand dollars a year.

"Also," Dr. Harris continues, "you need to be observed in our office for eight hours after you take the first dose."

"Eight hours?" Elle asks, eyes wide. "Why?"

"When they performed clinical trials of the medication, some of the patients experienced issues with their blood pressure. It only happened after the first dose."

Great. Something else for me to worry about.

I squeeze my eyes shut tight. I can't do this. Expensive medication. A lifelong concern about worsening symptoms. Side effects of the treatments. It's all too much.

"Abby, are you okay?"

I hear Elle's question, but I stare out Dr. Harris's window. Two children are playing hopscotch on the playground of the neighboring elementary school.

Kids these days still play hopscotch?

The silly thought during one of the worst moments of my life makes me giggle.

I turn to Elle. "I'm alive and breathing, aren't I?"

Dr. Harris smiles. "That's my girl."

***

"You sure you don't want me to stay?" Elle asks when she drops me off at my house. "Jackson is out of town at a conference. I can come in and hang out for a while."

"Another conference?"

She nods. "Yes. Fourth one this year, and he turned down two more."

"His new book must really be something."

"It's doing much better than he thought it would. He didn't think anyone would read it, but the tech guys are loving it. His boss made everyone in the office read it, and word spread from there."

"What's it about again?"

"Video game coding."

"Yeah, I got nothing on that."

"Me neither. I tried reading it, I did. But it's a foreign language to me. I know nothing about coding."

I chuckle. "Your boyfriend is too smart for us."

"Enough about boy genius. What do you want me to do? Shut up and leave you alone, or come in for a hard drink?"

A drink does sound good, but liquor won't solve my problems tonight. "I just want to be alone."

She frowns. "Okay."

"Don't take it personally."

"Promise me you'll call if you need anything."

"I will."

I walk into my house with a handful of brochures Dr. Harris gave me. I throw them on the coffee table, I can't deal with them right now. Oscar weaves through my feet, following me into the kitchen. His soft meows draw my attention to his empty food bowl.

"Ah, I see. You didn't miss me, you want dinner."

I take his food bag out of the pantry and bend over to pour some kibble into his red food bowl. Just as I'm tipping the bag, a tremor rolls through my hand. My fingers lose their grip and half the contents of the bag spills out onto the floor.

Fuck!

As I stare at the pile of fish-shaped pellets, an inexplicable rage rises within me. It fills every pore of my body until I explode. I unleash a sound that has never left my mouth before. A guttural, anguished scream that makes Oscar run and hide under the couch.

I scream until there is no air left in my lungs. Gasping, eyes watering, I step out my sliding glass door and onto my back porch. I need fresh air. I glance around my backyard, hoping my neighbors didn't hear my outburst. I'm still new here and I don't want them to think I'm nuts.

30

I stand outside, a gentle fall breeze blows through my hair. Tears swim in my eyes. I don't want this. I'm only twenty-eight. Why now? Why me?

A bright, red blur catches my eye. A cardinal lands on an old concrete birdbath left behind by the previous owners. The bird sits atop a dirty cherub, admiring his reflection in the water basin. After a moment, it cocks its head and looks back at me.

"Cardinals are messengers from our loved ones," my grandma told me once. "They are a sign that your ancestors are looking out for you."

"That's creepy," my eight-year-old self said.

She giggled and tousled one of my pigtails. "Not at all honey. It means they love you, and they are protecting you."

The bird flies past me, heading in the direction it came. I watch it with wonder. Sometimes the universe gives you exactly what you need.

***

"Are you sure telling them at a restaurant is the best way to go about it?"

Elle hands me a box knife and I cut through the old blue carpet in the lobby area of Judy's new office.

"Yes. Maybe they'll behave themselves in a public place."

"Need I remind you that your mother called your dad an 'ass-faced motherfucker' in front of our entire graduating class?"

I groan. How could I forget?

It was right after their divorce was final. They spent two bitter years in court fighting over nothing. To be fair to my dad, it was mostly driven by my mom's need to make him suffer. Despite their drawn out legal battle, my mom wasn't done. She let everyone know she was annoyed my dad brought my soon-to-be-stepmother with him to my college graduation.

Given that I was sitting with my fellow graduates, I missed the buildup. But everyone, I mean everyone, heard her when she stood up and yelled, "I'm not sitting next to you and your hussy, you ass-faced motherfucker."

I'd never heard my mother use the word "motherfucker" before, and I can't say I appreciated hearing it for the first time in such an embarrassing way. I slumped down so far in my chair I almost slipped out of it and onto the ground. Four years of hard work and a nearly perfect GPA lost in the midst of trying to keep my parents from killing one another.

I stand and tug on the corner of carpet I cut loose. "Pull."

Elle pulls back on the old carpet, dust flying into the air. Thank goodness I made us wear aspirators. The padding underneath is ancient and falls apart when I try to lift it.

"The only other option I have is inviting them over to my house, and that's not happening."

"Why can't you tell them individually?"

I shake my head. "No can do. Whoever I tell second will be pissed I didn't tell them first."

"How old are your parents again?"

We lug the old carpet out to the dumpster we rented for demolition. Our contractor and his team will do the bulk of the demo, but I like doing some of the hands-on work myself. Makes me feel more invested in the project.

I check my watch. "I gotta run. I need to shower and get ready for the dinner from Hell."

"Good luck. Take pictures when things go south."

"Ha ha."

***

"Abby, sit up straight. You're slouching."

Oy. Dinner is off to a great start. I've been sitting at the table for a total of five minutes with my mom and she's already told me I should drink more water, avoid carbs, and sit up straight.

"Where did you get this dress?" she asks me next. "It's interesting."

"Interesting" is Mom's code word for an outfit she wouldn't be caught dead in.

"Macy's."

32

"Hmmm," she says before taking a sip of water. "I didn't realize they sold dresses like that in Macy's."

I roll my eyes. "Mom, not tonight. Okay? I'm not in the mood."

She plays innocent. "What? I was asking about your dress. So sensitive."

Mom has her grey hair pulled up into a bun. Pearl earrings dot her ears and a matching pearl necklace lays nicely underneath the open collar of her white blouse. Her black pants are pressed perfectly. This was the outfit she wore nearly every day to the jewelry store she worked at for thirty years. The only difference is her black stilettos are now kitten heels. She continues to wear this outfit despite her retirement.

"A classic look never goes out of style," she explained when I asked why she doesn't branch out and try new things.

"Are you going to tell me why we're here tonight?" she asks after we've waited another five minutes for Dad to arrive.

"I will as soon as Dad gets here."

"Your father will be late to his own funeral," she grumbles. "Probably at the office."

"He's retired Mom."

Before she can sling another insult, I see Dad and my stepmom Samantha walk in. I wave my hand to catch their attention. Samantha sees me first and smiles.

Samantha is my mom's opposite. She is dressed in a black sweater with skinny jeans and red ballet flats. She keeps her hair dyed a honey brown and lets it hang loose. She has the sunny disposition my dad desperately needs in his life.

Dad glances our way after Samantha points to our table. Retirement treats my father well. He has a nice tan from their recent cruise to the Bahamas. His once-black hair is now a handsome silver. His green eyes match my own. He's wearing his trademark khaki dockers and a blue button-down shirt.

My mother groans beside me. "Of course he had to bring her. He can't go anywhere without her attached to his hip."

"I asked him to bring her," I whisper, then stand to greet Dad and Samantha. I give them both a hug. "Thank you for coming."

"Thanks for inviting us," Samantha says as we part.

There's an awkward moment when Dad and Samantha decide where to sit at the square top table. My mom despises my father, but hates Samantha even more. She narrows her eyes when Samantha attempts to take the seat to her right. Seeing my mother's glare, Samantha steps to the side and takes the seat next to me.

Once everyone is seated, we attempt small talk while we look over the menus.

"What do you recommend Abby?" Samantha asks.

"I've only been here once. I ordered the chicken cordon bleu and it was delicious."

Dad shuts his menu. "I'm getting the filet and a baked potato. Can't go wrong with that."

"Oh, that sounds good." Samantha closes her menu. "I'll get the same."

I glance over at Mom. Her hands are clasped on top of her menu. She is looking at everyone in the restaurant except for the people sitting at our table. "How about you Mom? What are you getting?"

"A salad," she says with no further explanation.

The waiter takes our order and brings a basket of fresh rolls. We all take one and I watch the butter slowly melt into the bread. Samantha asks me a few questions about the business and Mrs. Warner's house, but the conversation falls flat. This is not a group that assembles often, and everyone invited knows I have big news if I gathered them.

I clear my throat. "I have something important to tell you." I pause. When I practiced this at home, I came right out and said it. But now that I'm here in the moment, I feel like I should give more of a backstory.

"Whatever it is honey, we're here for you," Dad says with warm eyes.

I give him a small smile, appreciating his words, then continue. "Well, I started having these odd sensations in my hand. Sometimes it feels like my hand is falling asleep, but I can still move it and use it. Other times I have tremors and I'll drop whatever I'm holding."

Because he's sitting across from me, I see Dad's reaction first. His brow furrows. "Have you been to the doctor?"

"I have."

"Is it carpal tunnel?" Mom asks.

"No, it's not carpal tunnel."

"Sounds like carpal tunnel to me. Surgery can fix it."

I take a deep breath. "It's not carpal tunnel Mom."

Dad gives my mom the side eye before refocusing on me. "Go on honey. We're listening."

"I went to my family doctor and he referred me to a neurologist. She sent me to get an MRI last week. And, um, well... I have multiple sclerosis."

My mom gasps. My dad's eyes tear up. Samantha reaches out and takes my hand.

"I start the medication in two days. I have to sit at my neurologist's office when I take the first pill because some people have issues with their blood pressure after the first dose."

"Multiple sclerosis," Mom says as if she's delicately chewing on it. "Will you be able to have children?"

Of course this is her first question. "If I choose to, and if it's in the cards. Honestly, I haven't thought about it."

She turns to my dad. "She must have gotten this from your side of the family. No one in my family has it."

I sigh. "It's not necessarily a hereditary thing Mom."

"What does this mean for you long term?" Samantha asks, sympathy oozing off of her. "Will the medicine help with your symptoms?"

"It should."

She smiles a little. "Good. How are you doing with this news?"

"It's a lot to take in. I'm still processing it."

Dad rubs his chin. "Isn't multiple sclerosis what Annette Funicello had?"

"Yes, it was."

Mom sits up straight, suddenly rigid. "Annette Funicello? Wasn't she in a wheelchair?"

"She was," I confirm. "Some MS patients lose the ability to walk. It affects everyone differently."

"So you could end up in a wheelchair?" Alarm creeping into her voice.

"I could. Hopefully the medication halts the disease's progress, but it's not outside the realm of possibility."

"Oh my God. My daughter is going to be in a wheelchair." I recognize the expression on her face. Mom is about to go into full-on panic mode.

"Veronica, this isn't helping," Samantha says softly. "We need to be optimistic. No sense in worrying about something that may never happen."

Mom is not listening. "I have to call my doctor. I have to see if I have this too. I can't end up in a wheelchair."

Dad rolls his eyes. "For Christ's sake Veronica, this isn't about you."

She glares at him. "Well excuse me. I just found out my daughter may be paralyzed. So sorry I'm upset."

"Our daughter," Dad shoots back. "Not just your daughter, she's my daughter too. I'm upset for her. I'm certainly not worried about how her diagnosis affects me. Can you take your head out of your ass for five minutes and focus on someone other than yourself?"

Samantha and I exchange a glance.

"Mom, Dad, please calm down," I plead.

Dad turns his attention to me. "Sorry. Let's get back to the medication. How long has it been on the market?"

"A few years. It's been successful. Several people have seen a remission in their symptoms. There are even a few who saw improvements."

"Is it expensive?"

Mom tsks. "Always so worried about money."

I throw her a warning glance. She innocently takes a sip of water as if she didn't just make a jab.

"It is expensive, but my insurance coupled with the manufacturer's assistance program makes it affordable for me."

Dad nods. "That's good."

We sit in silence for a moment, I'm about to ask if they have any questions when my mom speaks up.

"What is your neurologist's name? I'd like to make an appointment."

Dad slams his hand on the table, making water spill from my glass. "Dammit Veronica! Enough!"

My parents start bickering again. Unreal. I push my chair back from the table, grab my purse, and make a beeline for the front door.

"Abby, wait," Samantha calls from behind me.

I keep walking, but she catches up with me. She gently grabs the back of my arm.

I turn to her, tears in my eyes. "I can't go back there."

She pulls me in for a hug. "I don't want you to go back there."

"You don't?"

"No." She steps back, her hands on my shoulders. "You don't need that craziness. You need peace and calm so you can make the right decisions. Call me any time, okay?"

I nod. "Okay."

She stands in the lobby and waves good-bye when I'm on the other side of the glass doors.

I send Elle a one-word text. "Disaster."

***

Half an hour after I get home, my doorbell rings. It's my dad.

He gives me a half smile when I open the door and holds out a styrofoam box. "Chicken cordon bleu?"

I swing the door open and let him inside. "Where's Samantha?"

"I dropped her off at the house. I'm giving her time to blow off some steam."

I raise an eyebrow. "Samantha needs to blow off steam?"

He shifts his weight. "Yeah. She wasn't too happy with how things went at the restaurant."

I walk toward my kitchen and Dad follows me down the hall. "Hiding at my house, huh?" I grab a fork from my silverware drawer and sit at my small kitchen table.

Dad takes a seat across from me. "No, I came to apologize."

"You don't have to do that."

"Yes I do. I'm not one of those people who believes you don't have to apologize to loved ones. You absolutely do. If anything, they deserve your apology the most."

"Mom was pushing your buttons. Trust me, I understand."

He sighs. "She always knew which buttons to push, but it's no excuse. I was upset about your news, and in a way, I thought I had to defend you. But Samantha made a good point on the way home – I should have focused my time and energy on you. Sinking down to your mom's level and bickering doesn't help you in the ways you need it."

"Dad, it's okay." I reach out and pat his hand. "You're here now. And you brought food."

He smiles, but his eyes dim after a moment. "How are you feeling about the diagnosis? You seem to be handling it well."

"I'm scared. Worried. On the other hand, hopeful. If the medication does what it's supposed to, I'll be fine. It's the not knowing that stinks."

38

He nods. "That is the hardest part, isn't it?"

"Yep. I've done a lot of research online, and of course the bulk of it is nerve-wracking and the worst case scenarios. Mom freaking out about me potentially being in a wheelchair is something I've thought about too."

"First of all, if you do end up in a wheelchair, you're going to be okay. Will life be different? Absolutely. One hundred percent. But you'll still live a fulfilling life."

"I know."

"And please, please, don't immediately jump to the dark clouds. Focus on the good outcomes."

I smile. "So don't be like Mom?"

"I hate to say it, but yes. Don't be like your mom."

I look out my patio doors, then back at Dad. "I knew she'd react that way." Annoyance rises within me. "Can't she think about me for one second? Did you see how she immediately started worrying about herself?"

Dad nods. "I did."

I continue my rant, needing to let it out. "She's so freaking negative. About everything. And here I am, with a serious life issue, and there is zero concern for me."

"That's not entirely true. Your mother loves you very much."

I cut open my cordon bleu, exposing the layers of chicken, ham and cheese. The cheese doesn't ooze out like it would when it's straight from the oven, but I'm too lazy to heat it up.

"Well, she has a terrible way of showing it. Critiques and put downs are not signs of affection."

"I agree." Dad rubs his chin. "She wasn't always like this. She used to be a happy person."

My jaw drops. "Mom? Happy?"

"Maybe happy is going a little too far, but she wasn't this bad when I met her."

"What changed?"

"She got angry with me when we didn't buy the jewelry store."

"Baumgartner's?"

"Yes."

This is news to me. I didn't know my parents could have owned the jewelry store Mom worked at all those years.

"Was it too expensive?"

"At the time it was. We were young. We just bought our first house. The white one on Mulberry."

I smile. "I remember that house. It was cute."

"It was, until we outgrew it."

"Why was she mad at you?"

"I could have asked Grandma for the money, but I didn't want to. My dad passed away two months prior to the store going on the market, and it didn't feel right to ask her for money at that time."

"Makes sense."

He sighs. "Not to your mom, it didn't. She couldn't go to anyone in her family for the money, so she expected me to run to Grandma and ask her for it. Mom would have given it to us, I know she would have. But taking money from a woman who is recently widowed?" Dad shakes his head. "I couldn't do it."

"That happened before I was born. She can't possibly still be mad about that."

He raises an eyebrow. "Oh yeah? Her attitude with me completely changed after the store was bought by the new owners. She started making comments under her breath. Then full-on insults and name calling. She was awful to live with."

I play with the au gratin potatoes in the box. "Why did you stay?"

"You. I stayed for you."

I look up at him. "You did?"

"Yes. Your mom never would have let me see you. This was back in the day when the courts gave women full custody of the

40

children no matter what. I didn't want to miss you growing up. And I wanted to protect you from her negativity, be a positive source of energy for you."

It's all coming together in my mind. Mom and Dad rarely spent time together when I was young unless it was a family vacation. Within days of me going off to college, Mom called in tears to tell me Dad moved out.

"You were Dad. You were a source of positive energy for me. Still are."

He squeezes my hand. "I want the best for you. It kills me to hear you have to deal with an illness. If I could take it from you, I would."

"I know." I force a smile. "I'm going to be okay Dad. I promise."

He smiles at me. "You'll be more than okay. You're going to live a fantastic life." After a moment, he stands. "Give me a hug kiddo. I better get home."

I push back my chair. "Thanks for stopping by Dad."

"Life throws curve balls," he whispers as we embrace. "Sometimes you dodge them, sometimes you take the hit."

"But you have to get up, don't lay in the shit," I finish for him, then giggle.

"Your Grandmother was something else, wasn't she?"

"She was, she really was."

"She'd be so proud of you."

I smile, tears threatening to spill. "I hope so."

"I know so."

I walk him to the front door. "You think Samantha cooled off yet?"

"Yes. She doesn't hold a grudge long."

"Good. Tell her 'thank you' for me."

I watch him drive off, grateful he stopped by. I don't like having a rift with my dad. I'm used to being upset with Mom

41

about something, but not Dad. A part of me is grateful he stuck it out with Mom to be with me. Most of the warm memories from my childhood include him in some way. On the other hand, it stinks to know he was miserable all those years.

It's hard for me to believe my mom is the way she is because they didn't buy the jewelry store. There has to be more to it than that, but I'll probably never know. She rarely speaks about her childhood and won't give direct answers to questions about her early years.

After a few cold bites, I give in and heat up my dinner. Oscar joins me on the couch to watch an episode of *The Crown*, not so subtly asking for a bite by pawing at my plate.

Another episode is about to start when my cellphone buzzes. "Hey Elle, what's up?"

"Have you seen Facebook?"

Her question surprises me. "No. I hardly ever go on Facebook."

"You might want to look."

"Oh no. What is it? Did Tommy Mitchell post another throwback picture of when you guys were dating?"

"No, worse."

"Worse than the time he posted a picture of you two making out at the pinning party?"

"Yes."

"Okay, give me a second." I open my laptop and log in to Facebook. "What exactly am I looking for?"

"You're tagged in the post. You'll know it when you see it."

She's right. I see the heinous post immediately.

The first thing I see on my Facebook page is my five-year-old self wearing a pink dress I could not stand. My mother made me wear it whenever we had guests. My hair is in my trademark pigtails and I'm forcing a smile on my face. I'm sure Mom threatened me with death to get that awkward smile.

"She didn't..."

"Oh, she did. Go ahead, read it. I'll give you a moment to take it all in."

Friends and loved ones, I'm sharing this post with a heavy heart. My precious daughter informed me this evening that she is afflicted with a disease known as multiple sclerosis. She is suffering and has a long road ahead. As a mother, I am doing all I can to stay strong for her and give her the support she needs. Please remember us in your prayers tonight.

My blood boils. "Are you kidding me?"

"I take it you didn't tell her it was okay to post this?"

"Hell no I didn't! I don't want people to know I have MS! How dare she? It wasn't her information to share!"

"Since when did your mother become the praying type? Didn't she get struck by lightning the last time she walked in a church?"

Elle's attempt at humor falls on deaf ears as I scroll through the comments on the post. Lots of sad face emojis and people sending my mom love and positive vibes. Mom's response to one of them makes me roll my eyes - "I'm doing my best as I fight through the tears."

"Unbelievable. As if she didn't make my night bad enough already." I give Elle a quick lowdown on dinner.

"Your dad is awesome."

"Yeah, he is."

"But your mom is a bitch."

"Elle!"

"Don't Abby, just don't. Do not defend her right now."

"Ugh, I guess I have to call her. Huh?"

"I suspect she'll be calling you in a few minutes."

"Why is that?"

"Hit the refresh button and look at the comments."

"What did you do?"

"What a best friend has to do."

Oh brother.

I hit the refresh button and gasp. "Elle! Delete it!"

"Nope. Not gonna happen. She'll have to take the post down if she doesn't want people to see it. And when she calls you, tell her I'll do it again if she posts another sob story on her page."

I start giggling, I can't help it. "She's going to shit."

Elle snickers. "I'd love to see the look on her face."

My mom will hit the roof. I'm sure she's checking her post to see how many likes and comments she gets. It's only a matter of time before she sees:

Wow Veronica! This sounds worse than your herpes outbreak last month, and that was terrible.

"Uh oh," Elle says, "she deleted the post. Which means you'll be getting a call in three…two…"

Elle doesn't make it to one before another call beeps in.

"She's calling me!"

"Don't answer it."

"She'll keep calling until I answer."

"Then turn your phone off when we hang up."

Despite how pissed I am, I don't like unresolved issues. I'd rather face the music than lay in bed later overthinking it.

"I gotta go. Thanks for the heads up, and for handling it for me." I chuckle again. "You want me to conference call her so you can hear her rant?"

"Tempting, but no. I'm video chatting with Jackson in fifteen minutes and I have to change into something sexy."

"For a phone call?"

"First of all, it's a video call. And second, when your man's been gone for a while, you have to show him what he's missing."

I laugh. "You're crazy."

"Later biotch."

44

"Later."

As soon as I end the call with Elle, my phone starts buzzing again. I can almost hear Mom yelling on the other end already.

I take a deep breath and harness my positivity. "Hi Mom, how was dinner?" Best to go on the offense first.

She clucks. "You know very well how dinner ended. You left me alone with your father and that bimbo he married."

So much for positivity. "Samantha is not a bimbo. You'd know that if you took the time to get to know her."

"Why in the world would I get to know my ex-husband's new wife?"

"Because you're forever connected by your darling daughter."

"I'm not in the mood for this Abigail."

"Funny, I'm not in a great mood either. Can't imagine why."

"Do you know what your nasty friend Elle just did to me?"

I smile. Elle loves that my mother refers to her as my "nasty friend." "No Mother, I do not. Please tell me what she's done."

"Enough with that voice."

I play stupid. "What voice Mother?"

"The one where you act like you're some hoity toity snob. And stop calling me 'Mother'."

As fun as it is to piss my mom off, I'm tired and over it. "You had no right to post about my diagnosis."

"I'm your mom. I'm allowed to post about you."

"Not my private business. And what's with this crap about sending prayers? Have you even opened the Bible?"

"I have," she insists.

"Oh yeah? When?"

She huffs. "That's completely irrelevant. Elle is slandering my name. Everyone will think I have an STD."

"There goes your love life…"

"Abigail! This is serious!"

45

"You know what else is serious Mom?" My inner bitch is about to unload. "A diagnosis for a long-term illness, something I will deal with every day for the rest of my life."

"Yes, I know, but…"

"But what? Your silly concern about your reputation is more important to you, isn't it?"

She backpedals. "I didn't say that."

"You didn't have to say it. Your actions did it for you. You wouldn't have called me tonight if it wasn't for Elle's comment. You would have gone to sleep knowing full well you made an ass of yourself at dinner and showed zero concern for my wellbeing. You would have slept like a baby with no sense of remorse for what you did. Probably with a big smile on your face knowing our family and friends are showering you with affection on social media. Giving you the attention you so desperately want."

I have no idea where my gumption is coming from. Maybe this was the straw that broke the camel's back. Her utter lack of concern for me never clearer than it is right now.

I wait for her response. Silence.

After a moment, her significantly weakened voice fills the line. "Abigail, I…"

"Stop. I don't want to hear it. I'm going to bed. Good night."

I end the call and turn off my phone. No more interruptions tonight.

Chapter Three

It's first dose day. The butterflies in my stomach are made of lead.

Dorothy, one of Dr. Harris's nurses, takes me to the back of the office. I smile when I see her Grumpy Cat scrubs. Her red hair is plaited in a French braid, and freckles run down her arms. She's older than Dr. Harris, and I suspect she knows as much about neurological disorders as the doctors do.

"We have a room back here for patients coming in for their first dose," she explains. "A regular exam room isn't fun when you have to sit for eight hours."

"How often do you have patients come in for their first dose?"

"You're the second patient this week, but we can go a week or two without any."

"Has anyone had a problem during their first dose?"

She shakes her head. "Not on my watch."

That makes me feel a little better.

We walk to the end of the hall, passing exam rooms along the way. Some empty, the rest with shut doors. Dr. Harris's practice has two other neurologists on staff. Judging by the people in the waiting room, they see patients all day long.

Dorothy unlocks the room at the end of the hall. Its door looks like the others, except it doesn't have a room number painted on it. Dorothy pushes the door open and flips on the light.

"Here's your hangout for today."

I smile when I see a comfy brown microsuede couch and matching armchair, a television, a small circular table with four chairs around it, a mini-fridge, and a basket with snacks. The room also has a kitchenette with cabinets and a sink.

"The Wi-fi code is brainwaves01, and there's a charging station on the counter next to the microwave." Dorothy rummages through a cabinet filled with medical supplies. "There's bottles of water in the fridge, and frozen meals in the freezer. Help yourself to whatever you like. I'm ordering Jimmy John's for lunch. If you want anything, let me know."

"Thank you." I set my laptop down on the table. "This is amazing."

Dorothy shuts the cabinet, a cardboard pill box in her hand. "This used to be our employee lounge."

"We took your lounge?"

"No, no, no. We got a new one. It's pretty snazzy."

I laugh. "Good for you."

I put down my bag filled with fabric samples and flooring catalogs. I plan to spend my day drafting plans for Judy's office. I considered bringing a book, but work will keep me distracted better than reading will.

"I'm going to take your blood pressure now, get a baseline number." She takes a blood pressure cuff out of the cabinet. "Have a seat."

I sit in one of the wooden chairs next to the table and roll up my sleeve. Dorothy stands by my side and wraps the cuff around my arm. She squeezes the bulb and the cuff slowly tightens.

"105 over 75," she tells me after a moment. The pressure from the cuff relaxes.

"I figured it would be sky high this morning."

She laughs. "It's okay to be nervous, but you'll be just fine."

"What happens if my blood pressure goes haywire?"

"I call the squad and they rush you to the hospital down the street," she says matter-of-factly.

I shouldn't have asked.

Dorothy opens the white box and takes out the packaging for my medication. There is only one pill in the box. She pulls back the silver lining and pops the pill into a Dixie cup. She walks over to the fridge and grabs a bottle of water.

"Did you eat breakfast this morning?" she asks.

I nod. "I did."

"Good." She hands me the cup and the bottle of water. "Bottoms up."

I look in the cup. The pill seems like any other pill. Nothing special about it.

"So this is it, huh? The magic pill?"

"Yes, ma'am. We'll send you home with a week's supply. If your box from the manufacturer doesn't arrive by then, give us a call. If you go more than a week without a dose, you'll be right back in here so we can observe you taking the first pill."

"Really?"

"Yes." She points to the cup. "Now or never girl."

I take a deep breath, then a sip of water. I tip the cup and feel the pill slip into my mouth. I take another swig of water to wash it down. The pill goes down smoothly, as if it's another dose of Tylenol and not my lifesaver.

I look down into the empty cup. There, I did it. I took my first dose.

Dorothy takes the cup and throws it in the trash. "Alright young lady, I'll be in every fifteen minutes to check on you." She hands me a device that looks like a pager. "If you start to feel faint or unwell, hit the button. I'll come running."

I smile. "Thanks Dorothy."

Dorothy shuts the door behind her and leaves me alone in the lounge. What to do now? I know myself well enough to recognize I need to occupy my brain quickly or anxiety will kick in. I'll overthink what's going on and give myself high blood pressure.

I turn on the television and cruise the channels until I find a morning news show. It keeps me occupied until they start talking about politics. Yuck. I don't need that kind of negativity in my life.

I sit at the table and take out the flooring sample catalogs. As I'm pondering what kind of flooring would be ideal for a chiropractor's office, Dorothy comes in for my first blood pressure check.

"You're good," she says with a smile.

Before she leaves, I ask, "Hey Dorothy, what kind of flooring do you have in the exam rooms? It looks like a laminate to me."

She nods. "It is. The doctors put down new flooring three or four years ago."

"How is it holding up?"

"Okay, I suppose." She glances down at my sample catalogs. "You getting new floors?"

"I'm an interior decorator. I just started working on a chiropractor's office."

"I see. Well, if it was up to me, I'd get that new waterproof vinyl flooring. It looks nice and it's easy to maintain. Patients can be messy sometimes."

I laugh. "I'll keep that in mind."

I'm three blood pressure checks in when Dorothy pokes her head in the door and announces, "You have a visitor."

"Huh?" I ask surprised. "A visitor?"

She pushes the door open.

My jaw drops when I see who my guest is. "Mom?"

Dorothy smiles. "I'll be back in ten minutes."

I want to beg Dorothy to stay, but she's gone before I can form words. Mom stands ten feet away, both of us staring at each other. She's in her usual outfit – black pants and a blouse. Today her blouse is light blue instead of white.

"What are you doing here?" I ask finally.

"You said you need to stay for eight hours. I thought you might want some company to help pass the time."

Mmm hmm. Right. I don't mince words. "You sure you're not here to grill my doctor and ask for a free examination?"

She sighs, her shoulders slumping. "No." She looks down at the ground, then back at me. "I am your mother. Whether you like it or not. I'm not the warm and cuddly mom. My mom wasn't either." She pauses, considering her words. "Neither was your grandmother for that matter. I come from a long line of ironclad, steel-hearted women. And while I will never be the mushy type, I like to think you're as strong as you are because I'm in your blood."

I am flabbergasted. My mom has never delivered a speech like this. I soften. I can't help it. She is the woman who held my hair back when I was throwing up from random illnesses as a child, the woman who was the safe place when I was scared at night, and now the woman who came to spend a long, boring eight hours with me at the doctor's office.

"Want to help me pick out flooring and wallpaper?" I ask.

Mom smiles. "Sure."

***

"Did they give you extra French dressing?"

Elle and I are camped out in what will be the employee lounge at Judy's office. Demolition is complete and we're in the rebuilding phase. The flooring arrived yesterday and will be installed tomorrow. After that, we'll put up the wallpaper in the lobby and start painting.

The bigger issue we need to discuss is two new potential projects. While both are amazing jobs, they have the same timeline.

I rummage through the bag of food we had delivered and find a plastic container of dressing. "Voilà!"

Elle pours the extra dressing on her salad. "We could take on both, but we'd have to split up."

I shrug. "We've split up before. We can do it again."

"I know, but we've never worked on a full restaurant before. That's a huge undertaking."

"True. The kitchen alone will be a massive project." I take a bite of my sandwich and contemplate the other project – a brand new condo in Dublin that is completely empty. "The condo project will be heavy lifting upfront, but whoever is working on that one will have time to help out at the restaurant."

"I wouldn't be so sure about that. The condo has to be perfect. It can lead to a lot of referrals. Pam Dobbs will be a big name around town."

Elle is right. Pam Dobbs is the new anchor of WGRN, the local news channel. She is moving to Columbus in two months and wants her condo ready for her arrival. We've only spoken to her via telephone, but she has high expectations.

"I want timeless. Sophisticated, expensive. I have a reputation to uphold," she told me during our telephone conversation. "I was given your number by Elizabeth Warner. I trust her judgment. Which is the only reason I'm willing to retain your office without meeting you in person."

"Pam could be a difficult client," I add with a frown. "She may expect one of us on hand every day."

Elle nods. "Yep."

"What do you want to do? I don't want to turn down either project. Both could be great opportunities for us."

"Agreed. On the one hand, Pam can get us referrals for residences, and on the other we can get in the door of restaurant renovations."

I tap my fingers on the table. "We need to do both."

"Which one do you want?"

"Doesn't matter to me."

"If you don't mind, I'll take the restaurant. It's close to my place and it will be a cool experience."

"You want the free food, don't you?" I ask with a smirk.

She blushes, cat out of the bag. "Well, that's a definite benefit."

I laugh. "That's fine. I'll take the Dobbs condo."

Elle picks at her bread. "I've been meaning to ask you – how are you feeling?"

Ugh. I hate this question. I've been getting it a lot lately. "Fine."

"Has the medicine helped?"

"A little, but it's only been three weeks."

I want her to change the subject, but she keeps going. "I researched MS online. Did you know a lot of MS patients suffer from depression?"

"Yes." I don't tell her that many of Dr. Kevorkian's patients suffered from MS.

"You'll tell me, right? If you're feeling sad?"

Elle means well, she does. But I don't need to be reminded of the mental health issues associated with my disease or the high suicide rates.

"Elle, I'm fine. I promise."

She hesitates but continues. "It's just that you've been here day and night."

"This is how I deal with things. What's the point in curling up in a ball and crying about it? I don't want MS to become who I am. I need to go on with my life."

"What life? You were a workaholic already, and now it's worse."

"I'll have you know I have a date tomorrow night, thank you very much."

Her eyes widen. "You do?"

"Yep. We're meeting at Bibbi Bistro for drinks and appetizers."

"Who's the guy?"

"His name is Chris. I met him on a dating app."

She gasps, then smiles. "A dating app? I didn't know you're on a dating app."

"I wasn't until two days ago," I admit. "What a nightmare."

She giggles. "Can't be too bad if you already have a date. What do you know about him?"

"He's six feet tall…"

She interrupts me. "No he's not. He's 5'10". But go on."

"Dark hair, brown eyes, an accountant. Likes comedies, hiking, and reading."

"Sounds normal."

I nod. "Exactly why I picked him."

"What are you going to wear?"

"No idea."

She glances at her watch. "We better go."

"Go where?" I ask confused.

"The mall closes in two hours and you need a new outfit."

***

I shift uncomfortably while I wait for my date. My new black dress reveals more cleavage than I'm used to.

"You look amazing. You have to buy this dress," Elle insisted when I tried it on.

"You don't think this is too much?" I asked, waving my hand in front of my chest.

"Nope."

"Are you sure? Because it feels like too much."

"That's because you're a prude."

"Gee, thanks."

"You're welcome," she said with a smile. "Go change. We need to find you some CFM shoes to match."

I don't need to ask her what CFM shoes are. It's a term we used in college for shoes that let a man know you're willing to spend the night with him.

I regret listening to Elle's shoe advice as I glance down at my four-inch heels. I'll be lucky if I don't snap my ankle by the end of the night.

"What can I get you?" the male bartender asks me from behind the bar.

I set up shop right in the center of the bar. "I'm waiting for someone." I look at my watch. "He should be here any minute."

"Gotcha. I'll check back when he's here."

I watch the early twenty-something bartender walk toward the end of the bar and resume talking to a group of girls around his age. He smiles warmly for them, whether for tips or for attention, his charm is working. The girls giggle and are smitten with him. If I was their age, I would be too.

As I'm admiring the bartender's dark hair and sparkly blue eyes, I feel a light tap on my shoulder. I turn to see my date.

"Abby?" he asks hesitantly.

I smile. "Yes. You must be Chris."

He shakes my hand and takes the seat to my right. "I think this is the first time my date actually looks like her profile picture."

I laugh. "Is that a good thing or a bad thing?"

He smiles. He either had braces as a teenager or was blessed with beautiful teeth. "A good thing. First, it lets me know you're honest. And second, I liked your picture."

I blush. "Thank you."

The bartender comes back and we order drinks – I get a White Russian and Chris orders a Jack and Coke.

"Nice to see a girl who orders something other than white wine."

"I can't do white wine. Gives me a headache. Red, I can do."

Chris gives me a onceover, pausing momentarily when he reaches my chest. I can't fault him for looking, they are out there for everyone to see. "You look nice."

"Thanks, so do you."

He glances down at his khakis and button-down shirt. "I pulled out the big guns."

I giggle. "So I see."

We engage in light banter until our drinks arrive. Typical date conversation – the changing weather, Ohio State football, and our jobs. I already knew Chris was an accountant, but he doesn't give off the bean-counter vibe.

"It's not exactly my dream job," he confesses. "But it pays the bills and I can afford to travel."

"Do you travel often?"

"As much as I can. Last summer I was in Brazil."

"Brazil? Is it safe there?"

"Safe as anywhere I suppose. I stayed away from any potentially dangerous areas."

"I'm not that brave," I admit. "If an area is on the 'do not travel list', I'm not going."

He takes a sip of his drink. "Understandable." He wiggles his eyebrows. "Not all of us can live on the edge."

After telling me about the sites he visited in Brazil, he asks about Interior Motives. He makes eye contact and asks questions, genuinely interested in what I'm saying.

"I'm jealous," he says.

"Why?"

"You're not shackled to a desk like me. You can come and go as you please."

"True, but I haven't taken a day off in a while. I'm trying so hard to get the business off the ground. Once things stabilize, I'll take more time for myself."

"You're young, you have plenty of time."

I smile. "My grandmother used to say believing you have plenty of time is the biggest myth of all."

He winces. "That got dark."

We both laugh. "Sorry, didn't mean to be a downer."

"If that's the case, then you better get your butt on an airplane and go somewhere new," he observes.

"I won't be travelling for a while." I cringe internally as soon as I say it. I don't want to go down this road, not on the first date.

"Why's that?"

56

I bite my bottom lip. I can easily say I'm busy with the new decorating jobs and won't be able to leave town anytime soon. But that's not what I meant. I decide to be honest.

"It's not a big deal, but I was recently diagnosed with MS. I want to stay close to home until I'm sure I won't have a reaction to the medication."

He is taken aback. "MS?"

I nod. "Yes."

"You don't look sick."

"It's not always obvious a person has it. My symptoms are relatively minor."

"What are your symptoms?" he asks concerned.

"Some hand tremors, occasional dizziness. Nothing major." I'm downplaying things so we can move on to another topic.

"But they could get worse, right?"

"They could, but the medication I'm on is supposed to stop any progression."

He shifts in his seat, his demeanor changing. "I'm sorry to hear that. It must have been difficult when you found out."

"Was it the best news? No. But my daily life hasn't changed." I shrug it off. "Anyway, what is your next big trip?"

He blinks a few times, a little lost, then snaps to it. "Aspen in December."

"Nice!"

"Me and a couple buddies from college go there every other year to ski."

"I've never been skiing, is it hard?"

"For beginners." He runs his finger down the condensation on his glass. "How does MS affect your physical abilities?"

Ugh. Back to this.

We spend the next fifteen minutes going over MS – what it is, how it could affect my body, and its treatments. I feel like I'm at a doctor's appointment instead of on a date.

When we finish our second drink, Chris walks me to my car.

"It was nice meeting you Abby." He leans in and gives me a kiss on the cheek. "Good luck with everything."

"Thanks. You too."

He walks off and I sulk as I get in my car. Wonderful. I blew it. I should have kept my big mouth shut.

***

"It was awful."

Elle hands me a bag of pretzels and a cold IPA. "You never know, he could call you."

I pull the blanket off the back of her couch, kick off my uncomfortable heels and tuck my legs underneath me. "He said 'good luck with everything'. I'm pretty sure that means he isn't calling me any time soon."

Elle takes a seat a few cushions down from me. I called her after my date to whine, and she invited me over. Jackson is out of town again and a late night watching a rom com on Netflix is in order.

"Why did you tell him?"

"I didn't intend to, but it came up. What was I supposed to do?"

"Wait a few dates, then tell him."

I take a sip of beer. "Is that fair?"

"Is what fair?"

"Not telling someone something about you that's important."

"Why is it important? It doesn't change who you are."

"Right, but it could affect my future."

"Way down the line."

I frown. "It might affect my ability to have children."

"You're getting way ahead of yourself Abby. It's a first date, not a proposal."

58

"True." I crunch a pretzel. "Should I put it on my dating profile?"

"What? No."

"If I do, whoever goes out with me will already know and I don't have to worry about it."

"No, don't put it on your profile. It's something incredibly personal and legally confidential. Wait until you find a guy you're really interested in, and then tell him. You're the one who keeps saying you don't want to be defined by your illness. So stop making it so important."

I consider this. "I see your point. But it would be a lot easier if I could just put it out there and not worry about the judgment. They need a dating app for people with chronic illnesses."

"What would you call it – Ill and Chill?"

I laugh. "Nah, nothing that naughty. Probably something cheesy like Lovesick."

"That's kinda cute actually." Elle steals a pretzel from the bag. "Lovesick. I like it."

"If only we knew how to make an app."

"I sure as hell don't, but my boyfriend does."

I laugh. "I doubt Jackson wants to use his mega brain to create a dating app."

"Yeah, probably not," she concedes before turning her attention back to the TV. "What do you feel like watching?"

"I need the big guns tonight."

Elle nods, no explanation needed. She scrolls through the choices until she finds *Overboard*. Nothing beats Goldie and Kurt.

Chapter Four

"This looks amazing." Judy walks around her nearly complete office, a smile on her face. "I love it."

This is the best part of the job for me. Seeing the client's expression when they walk into their new space is priceless.

"Phew, thank goodness! I'm so glad you like it."

She runs her hand across the granite counter of the receptionist's space. "I love this. I like the idea of not having the traditional glass wall and making the check-in experience akin to what you see at a spa. My patients will like it a lot."

"The glass walls are so sterile and cold. This is much more welcoming."

"I agree." Judy walks down the hallway toward the examination rooms. She smiles as she looks in each one. "This flooring is fantastic. It will be easy to clean and maintain. And I like how each room has its own distinct artwork scheme."

"The last space we need to finish is your office. I want to show you some wallpaper samples and you can let me know which is your favorite."

"Is it possible to do half paint, half wallpaper?"

"Sure. I don't see why not. It is your space."

She laughs. "True, but I'm no interior designer."

After spending half an hour with Judy, I shuffle out of her office and make haste to my car. My next appointment is in forty-five minutes and I have to be on time. I'm meeting with the infamous Pam Dobbs at her new condo.

I call my contact at Paint and Paper and order the white and gold wallpaper Judy chose for her office while I drive toward

Dublin. Pam's condo is the penthouse suite in the newest high rise built in the blossoming downtown Dublin area. What was once antique shops and quaint restaurants is becoming hip clothing stores and a popular spot for foodies.

I park my car on the street outside Pam's building and stop at the security desk to give my credentials. The elderly gentleman behind the desk mutes *The Price is Right* long enough to call Pam's penthouse.

"Sorry Miss," he tells me. "No answer."

I frown. "She must be running late."

"What does she look like?" he asks.

"It's Pam Dobbs."

He stares blankly back at me.

"The news anchor from L.A.," I explain, hoping that will ring some bells.

His eyes light up. "Pam Dobbs is moving into this building?"

"Yes."

"Well I'll be damned! This job just got a lot more interesting."

I laugh. "She isn't moving in yet. Her apartment needs to be decorated first."

"Is she coming here today? That's who you're meeting?"

"Yes. I'm walking through her condo with her for a consultation."

He flushes and tugs at his white-collared shirt. "I knew I should have shaved this morning."

I walk around the main floor of the building while I wait for Pam. It's an open space with a lot of windows and natural light. Black marble flooring with white paint, stainless steel elevators, and live plants scattered here and there. There isn't anything remarkable about the space, but it's clean and gives off an expensive vibe.

The sound of high heels clicking on the marble catches my attention. I turn to see Pam Dobbs in all her glory walking toward the security desk. She lifts her aviator sunglasses and rests them

62

in her perfect brown hair. Her makeup is flawless, highlighting her chestnut eyes and plump lips. An evergreen wrap dress is covered by a beautiful camel-colored peacoat. She walks effortlessly in her chocolate brown suede heels. I instantly envy her toned calves. She must put a lot of time and effort into her workouts. She is L.A. meets Midwest, and the security guard is left dumbfounded when she smiles at him.

"Hi. My name is Pam Dobbs. I'm a new resident. I'm supposed to meet someone here, but I'm terribly late."

I approach the security desk and catch her attention. "Hi Ms. Dobbs." I extend my hand. "Abigail Henry, it's nice to meet you."

She returns my handshake with a smile, her fingers dainty and delicate. "So sorry I'm late. My mom's doctor appointment took longer than expected."

"They always do."

The security guard mutters a good-bye as we walk away, still stupefied by Pam. Not that I blame him. She has a definite presence and I'm pleasantly surprised to find it's a warm one.

"This is the first time I'm seeing the condo in person," she tells me as we ride the elevator up to her floor.

"Really?"

She nods. "Yes. The builder sent me the floorplans and pictures of their previous projects. They also sent pictures as they were building it. Our contract has a contingency provision in it allowing me to back out if I don't like it."

"Good thinking."

Pam takes a deep breath. "It's been a whirlwind of a day."

"We can do this another time," I offer.

"No, no, no. That's not necessary. Plus, I'm leaving to go back to L.A. tomorrow morning."

"Oh, okay."

She smiles. "I flew in last night and leave tomorrow. My life is crazy."

The elevator stops on the 20th floor, but before the doors will open, Pam has to punch in a four-digit code. I look away to give her privacy. When the doors open, we are met by a canvas of white walls and windows.

"Wow," I say as I step out of the elevator, "this is gorgeous."

The autumn sun shines into the open space. Pam told me during one of our telephone conversations that the three-bedroom condo is 2,500 square feet. The main living area is completely open, including the kitchen which has no appliances or cabinets. All the outlets and necessary plug-ins are present, but nothing to go with them.

Pam smiles. "The pictures didn't do this place justice."

"Oh no?"

She shakes her head. "To be honest with you, I was a little nervous I wasn't going to like it. But now that I'm here, it feels right."

I know what she means. I've had many clients say they bought their homes because they liked the "feel" of the place.

"Do you want me to step outside so you can explore on your own?" I offer. "I can wait on the terrace."

She shakes her head. "No, that's okay." Pam does a 360 turn in her new living area. "I'm envisioning this as a formal living space that bleeds into the dining room and kitchen area."

I had the very same thought. "When you say 'formal living space', what does that mean to you?"

"An area where guests can mingle and relax when they come over. Comfortable, but classy seating."

"Most formal living rooms don't have televisions," I point out.

"Exactly. I don't want a television in this space."

"Do you want a media area at all?"

She considers my question. "Not really, but I realize when I have company they may want to watch television."

"There are several smart options for hiding a television. I'm sure we can come up with something you like."

"I don't want to walk into my home and have the TV be the focal point."

"No one wants to be reminded of work at home," I quip.

She smiles. "Very true. I think the magic of television is a bit lost on me seeing as I'm on it."

I examine the footprint I'm working with a little closer. "How about the back corner?"

Pam shakes her head. "I would like built-in bookshelves in that corner. I want to curl up on a comfy couch with a good book."

"Gotcha."

We walk through the area that will be the kitchen and dining room. Pam gives me a few ideas as she talks about her personal style. We glance out the tall glass doors on her eastern wall and look down at the City of Dublin. She has a beautiful cream stone terrace with a decorative metal handrail.

"What's going on down there?" she asks, pointing to a construction site.

"They're finishing the pedestrian bridge. It will connect the condo buildings with the new restaurants and shops downtown."

"Nice. The less driving, the better."

I laugh. "I'm sure L.A. traffic can be a bear."

"You have no idea. I won't miss it at all." She frowns. "I will miss the sunshine though."

"Yeah, winters in Ohio can be rough. But you probably know that if your mom lives here."

She nods. "I didn't grow up here, but I've visited often enough to know the winters aren't fun."

"Gives you an excuse to shop, right?" I ask with a smile. "You need a whole new winter wardrobe."

Pam chuckles. "Good point."

We move on to the bedrooms. Her master suite is as bare as the main living area.

"What kind of tub do you prefer?" I ask when I see her master bath doesn't have one.

"A jacuzzi tub would be amazing. I'm a candles and hot bath kind of woman."

We discuss stall showers, her preferred color palette, and the configuration of her huge walk-in closet.

"I definitely need a lot of space for shoes. They're my Achilles heel. No pun intended."

I laugh. "Shoes are my weakness too. Would you like a vanity in here?"

She surprises me when she says, "No. I don't wear makeup on my off days. I wear enough of it for the camera. I'm basically a slug on the weekends." She grins. "I'm all about leggings and hoodies when I'm home."

I take notes on my cellphone as we continue the tour, no way I'll remember all of this on my own. "How about your guest rooms?"

"One needs to be an office space, and the other a traditional guest bedroom."

I nod. "Okay."

She stops short when we walk past the empty guest bathroom. "I almost forgot, the guest bathroom must have a handicapped accessible tub."

I walk into the currently empty room. "That shouldn't be a problem, there's plenty of space in here for one."

I have no intention of asking why she needs an accessible tub, but she gives me one. "My mom may need to move in with me eventually. She has Parkinson's and macular degeneration."

"Oh wow, I'm so sorry to hear that."

Pam frowns. "That's why I moved here. She's doing well now, but she has a lot of doctor appointments and needs help. My father passed away and my siblings are back in Southern California where we grew up. When this job came open, it seemed like the universe was giving me a sign."

I wondered why a Southern California girl would give up the celebrity lifestyle and beaches she was accustomed to. Now I know. "I'm sure your mother appreciates you doing this for her."

"She does. She insisted I stay in L.A., but I couldn't leave her out here by herself. I thought about moving her back home to L.A., but she loves her ophthalmologist."

"Having a doctor you trust is incredibly important."

Pam nods. "Now if only I could find her a better neurologist. The one she has now made us wait two hours today, then saw her for less than five minutes."

"Ugh. Sitting in a waiting room is the worst."

"Agreed. I'll have to ask around. Maybe Elizabeth will know someone."

My mind races. I know a great neurologist, but I don't want to tell Pam about my MS. I don't want her to think I can't handle this job. I have to tell her about Dr. Harris though. I'll feel terrible if her mother continues to see a bad doctor.

"There's a great neurology practice in town. I'll email you their contact information."

Pam looks surprised. "You know a good neurologist?"

I nod. "Yes. Harris & Associates. They're wonderful. My, um, friend has MS. She raves about them."

"That would be great. Thank you."

"Sure, no problem."

We finish the tour of the condo a few minutes later. I have a good feel for Pam's style and her preferences. The trickiest part about the job will be configuring the main living space to fit everything she wants.

"Do you have any pets?"

"No, no pets."

"Anything you definitely do not want to see in here?"

"Toile. I don't like toile. And the modern farmhouse trend is not my thing."

I smile. "Duly noted. Anything else I should know?"

"Don't think so."

"Alright. I'll get started on my mockups. I usually put together two different floorplans so you have a few options. You can mix and match items, or you can tell me 'no' to both and I'll start from scratch."

"Sounds great." She pushes the down button for the elevator and we step inside. "One perk of the penthouse," she tells me, "a private elevator."

"That is definitely nice. You won't be standing downstairs holding groceries for ten minutes."

She laughs. "True." We stand quietly for a moment as the elevator begins its descent. She glances my way. "I'm sorry if I've been abrasive with you on the phone."

She has been, but I play it off. "Not at all, you've been great."

"With everything going on with my mom, and the move, the stress gets the best of me sometimes."

"I understand completely. No need to apologize."

"I'm hoping once I get moved and settled, things will slow down."

"I'm sure they will."

We say our good-byes a few minutes later and I walk down the sidewalk with a smile on my face. I can't wait to call Elle as soon as I'm in the car.

"Hey chickie! How did it go with Ms. L.A.?" she asks.

"Fantastic! She's wonderful."

"Seriously?"

"Yes. The condo is beautiful too. You should see her view."

"Man! I should have taken that job," she whines.

I laugh. "We don't have it yet."

"I have zero doubt in my mind you will put together a beautiful floorplan she cannot refuse."

"I hope so." I stop at a red light and watch pedestrians cross in front of me. "You ready for your consultation with the restaurant owner?"

"Yep. Meeting with him tomorrow morning."

"Awesome. You need help with anything?"

"No, I'm good."

"Alright. I'll head home and start working on floorplans."

I'm about to end our call, but Elle stops me. "Hey, wait a second. I have something else to tell you."

"Okay."

"I told Jackson about your dating app idea."

"My dating app idea?"

"Yeah, Ill and Chill."

I crack up. "You mean Lovesick."

"Whatever. Anyway, he likes the idea."

"He does?"

"Yes. He pitched it to his boss."

My jaw drops. "He did?"

"Uh huh. And get this – his boss wants to meet with you."

"He does?"

"Are you available tomorrow morning at 10 a.m.?"

"Tomorrow morning?" I am stupefied. "Elle, what am I going to talk to the guy about?"

"Your app."

"Since when do I have an app?"

"Since now."

"I was whining about my dating life. I wasn't serious."

"Well, you are now. Jackson already confirmed your meeting with him in the morning, so you have to go."

"What?! He set up the meeting without asking me?"

"Abby, this isn't the kind of guy with a wide-open schedule. When he offers an appointment time, you take it."

"Is Jackson going to be there?"

"No, he's leaving for Seattle tomorrow."

"He's going out of town again?" Since we started the project at Judy's, Jackson has gone out of town an additional three times.

Elle's optimism slips. "Yes. For a week this time."

"I'm sorry."

She sighs. "I'm sick of it Abby. I don't know how much more I can take. I'm trying to be a supportive girlfriend, but I'm not built for this kind of relationship. I like my man at home."

"It's temporary," I assure her.

"Yeah, maybe." She doesn't sound convinced.

"The man can't be on a book tour forever. He'll be old news eventually."

"Is that a good thing?"

I shrug. "He'll be home more."

"Anyway," she says cheering up, "enough about my relationship woes. Back to the important stuff. You should write a synopsis of your idea so you can leave it with Dean tomorrow."

"Dean?"

"Yes, Dean. Jackson's boss."

I shake my head, totally confused by all of this. "This is insane. I don't know a thing about creating an app."

"But Dean does. Give it a shot. What do you have to lose?"

"An hour of my time."

Elle tsks. "Tell you what - go to the meeting and I'll take you to dinner tomorrow night. Deal?"

"Condado?" I ask, referring to our favorite taco place.

"Condado."

I'll do damn near anything for tacos, but a meeting with a tech guy?

70

"So what do you think?" Elle prods. "Will you go?"

I chew at my bottom lip. I don't really want to go, but Jackson went to the trouble of getting me this appointment. Although I didn't ask him to do so, I don't want to put Jackson in an awkward position with his boss.

"Deal. Text me the info."

Instead of spending my evening preparing floorplans like I intended to, I find myself thinking about my meeting with Jackson's boss tomorrow morning. I am too OCD to walk into a meeting with a professional unprepared. I stare at my blank laptop screen.

What do you put in a synopsis for an app?

I call Jackson, desperate for his help.

He answers on the third ring. "Hey Abby, what's up?"

"Hi Jackson. I need help with a synopsis for tomorrow."

"A synopsis?"

"Yes. Elle told me I should bring one for my meeting with your boss."

"Oh, gotcha. It doesn't have to be anything complicated."

"So far I have the name of the app. Is that good enough?"

He laughs his deep belly laugh. "For Dean, it might be. I told him you're not in the tech industry, so he doesn't expect anything elaborate. Write a quick summary of what the purpose of your app is, who you think will benefit from it, and how it differs from anything else on the market."

"Okay. I can handle that. I think…"

"If you get stuck, email me what you have and I'll proofread it for you. It will be late though. I'm taking Elle out tonight so she isn't too upset with me for leaving town again in the morning."

My heart warms. "Aww, that's nice of you. She'll love it."

He yawns. "Excuse me. I'm so tired. This travelling is killing me. I can't wait to be a homebody again."

"Go get a nap so you can enjoy your night out."

71

"Sounds like a great idea. Good luck with your meeting tomorrow."

"Thanks."

"Oh, and Abby?"

"Yeah?"

"Don't worry about dressing up. Dean is a jeans and t-shirt kind of guy. No need to get fancy."

I'm so glad he warned me. I planned on showing up in a suit.

***

I doublecheck the address when I pull into the parking lot of a commercial complex. I expected to be downtown in the center of the hustle and bustle. Instead, I'm in an industrial area of town parked outside an old brick building. Yellow paint that once vibrantly read "Miners Coffee" is now faded and gives away the building's age. It's definitely a strange place for a tech company.

I grab my purse and my black leather portfolio with my synopsis tucked neatly inside. I laid in bed last night hoping I won't sound like an idiot when Dean reads it.

You shouldn't be worried about this, I scolded myself as I tossed and turned. This doesn't mean anything to you.

But somehow, it feels important. Like I should be paying it time and attention.

I catch a glimpse of my reflection in the glass door entrance. I followed Jackson's advice and kept it relatively casual. Dark wash skinny jeans tucked into brown leather knee-high boots, paired with a cream sweater. I went with my standard daily makeup, no need to go overboard. I kept my hair down, but added my signature waves for volume.

When I walk into the building, I am stunned. Did I step into a portal for another world? Instead of an old dusty warehouse, I walk into a massive and open office space. There are no cubicles or dividers, a trend amongst business owners under forty. Exposed brick remains uncovered by drywall and refinished wood floors run throughout.

A receptionist's desk made of tin roofing material and plywood sits in the middle of the floor. I can see several desks and workspaces scattered behind the desk. They are simple workspaces with computer setups that look like spaceships. None of the desk chairs match, and some only have yoga balls for seats.

I'm pleasantly surprised to see several live plants and trees scattered throughout the space. Natural light pours in from windows I can only assume were added after Dean bought the place. Vintage video game posters hang on the walls and I smile when I see a display of "antique" gaming equipment. A brand new Atari sits atop its mint condition box right next to a Nintendo with its original controllers.

"Can I help you?" the young man behind the reception desk asks. He's wearing a crisp, white polo shirt and it's possible he spent more time getting ready this morning than I did. His hair is perfectly coifed and his skin is flawless. He stands in stark contrast to the bulk of his coworkers who are wearing jeans and casual tops.

"Hi, I'm Abby. I have a 10 o'clock appointment with Dean."

The man searches a computer screen. "Ah, Abby Henry. Ill and Chill."

I cringe. "That's not its name."

He shrugs. "I kinda like it. I'll take you back to his office as soon as he gets off the phone."

"Okay, thanks."

"Would you like something to drink? We have water, coffee, espresso, green tea and an assortment of juices."

An assortment of juices? "No thank you, I'm good."

"Please have a seat," he points to a small lobby area in the corner. "Dean shouldn't be much longer. Feel free to try out our latest game – *Operation New World* – while you wait."

Before I can ask what the heck *Operation New World* is, the desk phone starts ringing and the receptionist does exactly what he's supposed to do and answers it.

73

I walk toward the waiting area, which consists of two black leather couches and a glass coffee table. Sitting on the table are six handheld gaming devices – three black and three hot pink. Out of pure curiosity, I pick up a pink game system and take a seat on the couch. A heavy bass drum makes me jump as the game comes to life.

An all too real looking male figure in a gas mask appears on the screen. "Comrade, glad you made it! We need your help." His voice sounds muffled and heavy as he breathes through the ventilator on his mask. "The original crew is down to only ten members. The rest have been killed by the local alien life or fallen victim to illnesses our civilization has never seen before. No matter what happens, do not take off your mask!"

Words flash on the screen, "Choose Your Avatar." I scroll through my choices and debate between a female character that closely resembles my own body frame, and a cute panda bear dressed in combat gear.

"Ms. Henry?"

I look up to see the receptionist standing next to his desk. "Yes?"

"Dean is ready to see you now."

"Oh, okay." I set the console down. "Seems like a pretty cool game."

He smiles. "The reviews are great so far. It beat our record for first day sales by a mile."

"That's wonderful. Good for you."

We walk through the office space, most of the employees are occupied by their computer screens and the music playing in their headphones.

"I had nothing to do with it personally, I just man the desk."

"You're still contributing. You can take some ownership in the company's success."

He blushes. "Thank you."

"What's your name?"

74

"Seth."

"Nice to meet you Seth."

"Likewise."

We walk through a narrow hallway that is brick on all sides. Skylights from above offer natural light. This must be a corridor between what was once the factory and its corporate offices. Neon colored spray paint covers the walls with cute versions of classic video game characters. I recognize all of them except for one.

"Which character is this?" I ask Seth.

He puts a finger to his lips. "Shhh. Don't let anyone hear you say you don't know who that is." He glances over his shoulder, then back at me. "That's Marina. She's the main character in our first video game release."

"Oh…my bad." How embarrassing.

He waves it off. "I didn't know who it was either until I started working here."

The hallway makes a right turn and opens up into another large, open space. Glass partitions divide several conference rooms, most of which are filled with large television screens and bean bag chairs. Arcade games line one of the walls, while a ping-pong table takes up space in the open floor area.

"Is it fun to work here?"

Seth shrugs. "Most days it is. The week before a release date can be pretty intense, but Dean throws a huge release party to make up for it."

"That's nice of him."

"He's a good guy. A bit eccentric, but most super smart people are."

We walk past the conference rooms and come to a stop in front of a large, metal door. It looks original to the building. The iron is rusted in the bottom corner and around a few of the rivets. Seth knocks on the door, then slides it open along the metal track its hanging from.

He leans his head in. "Dean, I have Abby Henry for your meeting."

"Sure, send her in," a deep voice says from the other side.

Seth pushes the door open further and steps out of the way. "You're up."

I smile. "Thank you."

I take a deep breath before stepping in. I have no idea what to expect from this meeting, but I'm not exactly a newbie at meeting new people and selling myself. It's the nature of the beast in the interior design business.

It's my designer's eye that takes in the office space before the man I'm meeting. He's sitting behind a massive metal desk that is painted to look like the face of a game controller. The back wall is all glass, the Columbus skyline in the distance. The refinished wood floors shine brighter in here, probably due to lower foot traffic.

The office itself is huge. A living room area with grey microsuede couches and a gorgeous white rug sits off to my right. A large screen TV is mounted to the wall with surround-sound speakers hanging on either side of it. The space is somehow cozy industrial.

"Jackson told me you're an interior designer, I should have cleaned up the place."

I turn my attention to the man of the hour for the first time. He's younger than I expected. Probably around my age, maybe a few years older. His brown hair is a bit shaggy, but cute. More likely the result of being busy as opposed to being stylish. His brown eyes are kind and his teeth are pearly white when he smiles.

He steps out from behind his desk and extends his hand to me. "Dean Porter."

Thank goodness I followed Jackson's advice and didn't wear a suit. Dean is dressed casually in a heather grey t-shirt, jeans, and all white tennis shoes. His sturdy stance and broad shoulders tell me he works out regularly.

76

I return his shake. "Abby Henry, and yes, I am an interior designer."

"Interior designer by day, app creator by night," he says, amusement in his eyes.

I laugh. "I wouldn't go that far."

"My grandfather used to say you can't trust a person with two first names."

Huh? "I'm not sure what you mean..."

"Abby Henry. A full name that could be two first names. He always said people with two first names are suspicious."

"Uh...okay."

He looks into my eyes, unnerving me for a moment. "Did you know green eyes, although the rarest of the eye colors, is a dominant gene?"

"I did not know that," I answer after a moment's pause, trying to catch up.

He smiles. "Sorry, I'm filled with useless knowledge, and it usually comes out in awkward ways." He walks toward his door. "I have a meeting in three minutes with my coding team. Walk with me."

Three minutes? I know he's squeezing me into his schedule, but three minutes?

He gestures for me to step out into the hallway. "What's the name of your interior design company?"

"Interior Motives."

"Interior Motives...I like it. Nice play on words."

"Thanks."

"Jackson told me about your app idea." He starts walking down the narrow hallway I was just in a moment ago. "I have a few concerns about it I'd like to discuss with you."

I reach into my portfolio. "I prepared a synopsis that I think..."

He puts his hand up. "Not necessary."

"Oh." Gee thanks for the unnecessary stress Jackson.

We walk out into the open office space. He stops in front of one of the glass conference rooms. I can't hear a thing coming from the other side of the glass, but I can see the group inside talking and laughing.

"My concern is the implication that people with long-term illnesses should not be active on other dating sites."

I'm shocked. "That's not what I'm saying at all."

"Isn't it though? In the sensitive society we live in, any type of segregation, even when done so with the best of intentions, is looked at as an insult."

"I would never, ever want people to think that."

He glances into the conference room, then back at me. "Of course not, and I know that isn't your motive. But I think you need to dig deeper."

"Dig deeper?"

"What can the app offer that goes above and beyond dating? What purpose will this app serve? What gap does it fill?"

"I, I haven't thought about it," I stammer. "This was something I came up with on a whim. I voiced a concern out loud, and the next thing I know, I'm here meeting you."

"I understand." He glances down at his watch. "I have to go. Can you come back tomorrow at the same time?"

"Tomorrow? Tomorrow is Saturday."

"Is that a problem?" he asks.

"Well, I suppose not. Let me check my schedule." I try to hide my frustration as I check my calendar. I spent the night worried about this meeting and I'm being brushed off. "Looks like I don't have any conflicting appointments."

He smiles. "Good. I'll see you then." He turns toward the conference room and swings the door open. "Who's ready to create *Operation New World 2 – the Galactic Frontier*?!"

Everyone in the room hoots and hollers. Their excitement is cut off when the door closes. Dean walks through the room giving the group high fives. They seem genuinely enthusiastic.

78

I don't share their excitement. What the hell just happened?

After the confusion washes out of my system, anger sets in. How dare he accuse me of being prejudicial! It isn't fair. I had a stray thought about how hard it is to date with my illness and all of the sudden I'm a shitty person? This isn't what I came here for. In fact, I didn't want to come here at all.

I'm so lost in my own mind, I storm past the reception desk without acknowledging Seth.

"Ms. Henry," he calls out before I can leave, "are you alright?"

The sincere look on his face cools my jets. Suddenly, tears spring to my eyes. "No," I answer honestly, "I'm not alright."

He jumps up from his chair and comes over to give me a hug. "What happened sweetie?"

I'm not usually one to cry in public, but for some reason I feel comforted by a stranger's hug. "I'm not an app developer. I shouldn't be here."

He pulls back to arm's length. "But that's what Dean looks for. Avant-garde, outside the box ideas. He wants the everyman's perspective, not a gamer's perspective."

I wipe a tear from my eye. "He accused me of being discriminatory."

"He did?" Seth asks with wide eyes.

"Yes. And it really hurt because I have a long-term illness and I would never, ever, try to hurt someone's feelings."

Seth steps away and hands me a tissue from the box on his desk. "I'm not making excuses for him, but Dean doesn't always come across well. The man is a genius, but he isn't delicate. I'm sure he didn't mean to accuse you of anything."

"Yeah, maybe," I say unconvinced.

Seth's computer pings and he glances at his screen. "He just calendared a meeting with you for tomorrow morning."

I nod. "I'm supposed to come back so we can talk more."

"You should. Talk this through with him."

Despite Seth's advice, I'm not sure I'll come back tomorrow. I don't need this. I have a business to run. I don't have time to deal with some techno-genius who makes me feel like crap. I have enough on my plate as it is.

I drive to my office, turning up the radio and trying to forget my meeting with Dean. I need to draw plans for Pam's condo and get them to her as soon as possible. I relax when I pull up to the two-story brick house in German Village that serves as our business's office space. We wanted something warm and inviting for our clients and this is certainly it. Red and yellow mums are still in full bloom along the cobblestone walkway. When we renovated the building, we tried to keep as much of the original architecture and character of the home as we could.

"You sure you don't want space downtown?" my dad asked the first time he saw the place.

"Yes. That's what everyone else is doing. We want our clients to have easy access and feel comfortable when they come to see us. Driving into downtown and fighting over a parking spot isn't the type of experience we want them to have."

As it turns out, our clients don't come here much. Most of the time we go to them and interact mostly through email or cellphone calls. But I absolutely love this place and I'm glad we made the choice we did. Its warm and cozy atmosphere puts me at ease. Plus, Schmidt's is within walking distance and I can't resist their world famous cream puffs.

I take the stairs to my office on the second floor and shut myself in. We don't have a full-time receptionist because it isn't necessary. The poor person would sit alone all day. Our contact information is posted outside if we have a potential walk-in client, but that happens so rarely these days. Most people find us online or are referrals from other clients.

I breathe a sigh of relief once inside my office. My core belief is that your space should make you feel happy and safe. I tell clients not to worry about trends and focus on the items that make them warm and fuzzy on the inside.

"Your office looks like an eight-year-old girl lives here," Elle teased when I designed my space.

"And yours looks like a sterile surgery could be performed in it," I shot back.

She giggled. "How are we best friends? Our offices couldn't be more different."

While Elle's office has bright white everything – furniture, paint, rugs, décor, and a large piece of glass resting on silver piping for a desk, mine is, as Elle suggested, very girly. My office also has a lot of white scattered throughout, but with a much cozier feel. An oversized grey couch with white and pink accent pillows is a comfy space to land when I don't want to sit behind my desk. The woodworking is a soft white and I've accented the walls with framed and matted quotes I painted myself in pretty pastel script.

The showstopper is my massive antique desk I found in a shop near Cincinnati. I worried the delivery guys would throw their backs out bringing it up the stairs. I sanded it down and exposed the light woodgrain underneath, then covered it in a thin coat of whitewash stain. Elle giggled when she saw the pale pink rug I put under the desk, but I absolutely love it. I added live plants that are easy to maintain in gorgeous pink, white, and gold pots made by a local artist as part of her "Yin Energy" collection.

No question it's a feminine space, but I love it. I've always been a bit of a girly girl and I have zero shame.

I fire up my laptop and turn on some music. I close my eyes and visualize Pam's condo. I start in the kitchen and mentally place different appliances, cabinetry, and countertops in the space. Pam told me she isn't much of a cook and isn't concerned with top of the line, restaurant quality appliances. I jot down notes as I consider the options.

Soon I am lost in the empty canvas that is my latest project and forget all about Dean Porter.

Chapter Five

"He did not say that!"

I sip my half-price margarita. "Yep, he sure did."

As promised, Elle met me at *Condado* for dinner on her. We've eaten an entire basket of nachos as we wait for our tacos.

"I can't believe it! Jackson said he is such a cool guy."

"He may have a point though."

"What?! No way."

"I think what he was trying to say is that if you create a dating app for people with long-term illnesses, you're cutting them off from the rest of the dating pool."

"Just because they're on your app doesn't mean they can't be on the other apps too."

"True, but maybe I should be considering an app for people with long-term illnesses that isn't focused on dating. I mean, we're not on this planet solely to meet partners. We have grander things we can accomplish than falling in love."

Elle snatches the last nacho from our basket and dips it in guacamole. "How very philosophical of you."

"You know what I mean. Yes, dating is a concern for me. But there are so many other issues to think about when you have an illness. Just the other day when I was talking to Pam, she mentioned struggling to find a new neurologist for her mom. That's a huge concern for people. Maybe the app could include something about doctors, and everyone's recommendations."

"That's a good idea!"

Her enthusiasm keeps me talking. "I want everything to have really cute names. I was thinking I could call that function Which Doctor. Like a play on the phrase Witch Doctor."

Elle smiles. "That's cute."

Our waiter drops off our tacos and I nearly salivate. They look delicious. Between bites of food, Elle and I talk about the other options an app could offer.

"Do you still want a dating component?" she asks.

I nod. "Yes. I want to keep that. It can be the Lovesick function."

"I still like Ill and Chill better."

I laugh. "Of course you do."

We are quiet a moment as we take huge bites of our tacos. Could this app idea really become a thing?

Elle wipes her mouth with a paper napkin. "When you told me about your diagnosis, I went online and read a ton of articles. What if you had a place with links to reputable sources? Information people know they can trust?"

"I love that! You're right, it's hard to tell when you're reading stuff online if it's trustworthy."

She smiles. "You could call it Sickopedia."

We kick around a few more ideas, including a function that would act as a virtual support group. "This way you can meet people who have the same illness as you," I explain.

By the end of dinner, I'm feeling much better about meeting with Dean again. His critique pissed me off at first, but I'm glad he said something. It forced me to think bigger and to really examine what I would like to see in an app.

"This is crazy," I tell Elle when she walks me to my car. "I shouldn't be spending energy on this. I have too much to do."

"Maybe this is happening for a reason. Just go with it. See what happens."

"I'm not a 'go with the flow' kind of girl."

Elle laughs. "Yes, I know."

***

I spend my normal amount of time getting ready the next morning. No sense in getting extra dolled up for Dean when he is Mr. Casual. I still check my reflection in the rearview mirror before getting out of my car. My makeup is on point and my hair has managed to maintain some volume.

I opted for a thin sweater with skinny jeans and my chocolate brown Uggs, my version of casual. I left my portfolio with the synopsis I created at home. I put a few notes in my cellphone in case I draw a complete blank, but I doubt I'll need them. Much to my surprise, I'm excited about this idea. It's an app I would use if it was available. And maybe Elle is right, I need to go with this. Create something people like me can use.

I pull on the door handle at the entrance to Dean's building and frown. It's locked. Crap. I don't even have his number.

I'm about to call Jackson when the door clicks and a voice comes out of a little black box built into the brick wall. "Abby, come in. I'm in my office."

I look up and see a camera pointing in my direction. "Okay," I say to the lens.

Yeesh. Thank goodness I didn't do anything embarrassing while I was standing here. I had no idea I was on camera.

There is a lot less hustle and bustle inside the building than there was yesterday. A single cannister light from above shines a beam of light onto Seth's desk. A few people are scattered throughout the workspace, but most of the computers are off. I walk down the narrow brick hallway and make my way to Dean's office. His office door is slid all the way open, but his desk chair is empty.

"Hello?" I call out.

"Come in," Dean's voice responds.

I walk in to find Dean standing in front of his television. He's watching the local news. Instead of jeans, he's wearing black track pants and a red OSU sweatshirt. He's ready for game day.

He turns off the TV, shaking his head. "I almost don't want to watch the news anymore."

"I know what you mean," I agree. "They rarely have anything good to share."

He steps behind his desk and motions to the two black leather chairs in front of it. "Please, have a seat."

"Oh, I get to sit down today?"

My comment was in jest, but his forehead crinkles. "It's been brought to my attention that I wasn't a very gracious host to you. I apologize. I was running around like a maniac yesterday, but my crazy schedule is no excuse."

I wonder who gave Dean the heads up. Seth? Elle via Jackson? But it doesn't really matter.

I take a seat. "No need to apologize. I know how it is when things get busy."

"I hope what I said yesterday didn't give you the wrong impression. I love your idea, which is why I wanted to meet with you. It wasn't my intention to insult you."

"It's okay. Admittedly, the delivery could have been better, but I appreciate your feedback."

"So you don't think I'm a dick?"

"I didn't say that," I respond with a straight face, then crack a smile.

He laughs out loud. "I like you Abby Henry." He leans forward in his chair. "Now, let's talk about your app."

"Okay."

"How did you come up with the idea?"

I shift in my seat. Talking about my MS makes me nervous. "I was recently diagnosed with multiple sclerosis."

"I'm so sorry to hear that," he says sincerely.

"Thank you, but there's no need to be sorry. I'm doing great."

"Good."

"Anyway, when I went on my first date after the diagnosis, I felt the urge to tell my date right away."

"Why?"

86

I shrug. "I don't know. I felt like it was something he deserved to know. But in retrospect, I'm not sure why."

"How did he respond?"

"Not well. Our date was going smoothly up to that point. He wished me good luck, and that was it."

"Good luck?" he says with disdain. "Yuck."

I giggle. "Exactly. When I got home and relayed the nightmare to Elle, I said I wish there was a dating app for people with illnesses so it's right out in the open."

Dean steeples his fingers. "I see." He's quiet as he leans his chair back and looks up at the ceiling. After a moment, he says, "I understand why you had the thought, and it's a good one. The point I did a sucky job of making yesterday is I'm worried about how it will be received by people with long-term illnesses or disabilities."

I nod. "I get it. I thought about it last night and I agree. If I want to help people like me, creating a dating app isn't necessarily the way to do it."

"Dating is an important aspect of our social lives, don't discount your idea completely."

"Oh, I'm not. I'm saying that my app could be something bigger. Something better. And a dating component can be included in it."

He smiles. "I like the way you're thinking. Go on."

I tell him about the ideas Elle and I came up with last night.

"Which Doctor, I like it," he says with a nod.

He laughs when I tell him about Sickopedia and agrees the dating function should be called Lovesick and not Ill and Chill.

"I would also like to set up a social networking component for people who are looking for a virtual support group."

He nods. "I like that too. What are you going to call it?"

I smile. "The best I've come up with so far is Friends with Health Benefits, but I'm open to suggestions."

He laughs. "You do love your wordplay."

87

"I want it to be lighthearted. Being sick is hard enough."

"True." He checks his watch. "It's almost 11:30 and we have a noon kickoff today."

"It's 11:30 already?" I ask surprised.

"Indeed, and I have tickets to today's game."

I jump up. "I'm sorry. I didn't mean to keep you. You should get going."

"No worries. I'll get there before the end of the first quarter."

As we walk out, he stops to talk to the people sitting at workstations.

"Go home," he tells each one of them. "Don't come back until Monday." When a young woman with dark hair and pretty blue eyes starts to argue, he won't hear it. "It can wait. Go."

"I'm guessing you're the Toyota," he says when we walk out into the autumn breeze. His eyes sparkle in the sunlight.

"Yep, that's me."

He smiles. "It was the only car I didn't recognize."

I'm about to say good-bye, but to my surprise, he escorts me to my car. Instead of farewell, I thank him for meeting with me.

"No, thank you for coming in on a Saturday." We stop next to my driver side door. "I think we should pursue this app idea."

"I agree, but I have no idea what the next steps are."

His grin widens. "Lucky for you, I do."

I laugh. "Okay tech genius, what are the next steps?"

"We present this idea to my think tank, and we see if they have any additional suggestions."

I raise an eyebrow. "Your think tank?"

"A group of my employees who represent a random sample of the general population," he explains.

"Okay. Sounds good."

We exchange cellphone numbers and agree Dean will text me with the date and time of the think tank.

"Any days or times that don't work for you next week?"

I check my calendar. "Tuesday at noon is out, and Wednesday at 3 p.m. is out too. Other than that, I'm open. For now anyway."

"Alright. I'll let you know once something is set up."

I get in my car and watch discreetly to see what type of vehicle he owns. What do tech millionaires drive? I'm not surprised at all when he walks toward a blacked-out Audi SUV with tinted windows. Classy, but not flashy.

As I drive away, I can't help but think first impressions may not be everything.

***

Monday morning, I am confident with the plans I drew for Pam's condo. I spent the remainder of Saturday and all day yesterday going room by room through the condo in my mind and creating what I believe are two viable options for her.

"Already?" she says when I call to tell her the news. "Wow, that was fast."

"Do you want me to email the plans to you?"

"I'll be back in town Wednesday evening. Can we meet on Thursday? I'd like to go over the plans with you in person. If that's okay."

"Sure, works for me."

"Great. I saw online that your office is located in German Village. Are you anywhere near the famous German restaurant?"

I grin. Cream puffs get them every time. "Yes, Schmidt's is a short walk from here."

"How about we meet at your office at eleven, and then have lunch at Schmidt's?"

"Sounds like a good plan."

"Great! See you then."

I hang up with a huge smile on my face. The fact that Pam wants to have lunch with me after our meeting is a good sign. A really good sign.

I send Dean a quick text:

Just wanted to let you know I am not available on Thursday.

Because my message sounds impersonal, I add:

Hope you had fun at the game.

I've forgotten all about my text when I receive a response an hour later.

Game was great. Lost my voice. Does Friday work for you? My team is available at 3 p.m.

It's hard for me to imagine Dean getting riled up and yelling at a football game, he seems too reserved for it. Then again, it is the Buckeyes and home games are wild.

Friday works for me. See you then.

My week is starting to fill up. I'm pondering what a think tank meeting will be like when my cellphone rings. It's my mom.

"Hey Mom."

"Hello Abigail."

Oy, the full name. She wants something.

"How was your doctor appointment?" I ask, knowing she met with her doctor this morning. I suspect she went to make sure she has no symptoms of MS, but she assured me last night she was going to have a spot on her arm checked out.

"He said the spot is nothing. Just an aging spot."

"That's good news."

"Getting old is good news?"

"Beats the alternative."

She sighs. "I suppose. How has your day been?"

"Really good. I have another appointment with Pam Dobbs on Thursday."

"Have you gotten the job yet?"

"Not yet, but it looks promising. I also have another meeting with Dean on Friday."

"Dean?"

"Yes, Dean. The video game guy…"

"I have no idea what you're talking about."

I roll my eyes. I told her all about it last night. She was probably too worried about her arm to listen. "He's helping me with my app."

"An app? What's an app?"

"For your cellphone. You know, cellphone apps."

"I don't have one of those computer phones."

I shake my head. "Never mind."

"What kind of app is it? Is it for interior design?"

"No. It's an app for people who have illnesses or disabilities. At first I wanted it to be a dating app, but he's helping me think bigger."

"A dating app? Are you dating?"

"Uh…yeah."

"Are you sure that's a good idea?"

"Excuse me? You're the one perpetually nagging me to date."

"That was before…"

I feel my temperature rising. Deep breaths Abby, deep breaths. "So because I have MS, I'm not allowed to date?"

"I didn't say that."

"What are you saying then?"

"Stop being difficult Abigail, you know what I mean."

I clench my jaw. I want to rip into her, but past experience has proven it's pointless. "What do you want Mom?"

"I want you to drop the attitude."

"Why did you call me?"

"Oh, yes. What are you doing for Thanksgiving?"

Is she kidding me right now? "Going to Dad's like I always do."

"I'm not working at the store this year."

I am in no mood to be kind to my mother. "Why don't you go to Aunt Jean's? She invites you every year."

Mom clucks. "She lives too far away."

"She lives in Sunbury. It's only half an hour."

"I'll see."

My mom's "I'll see" is equivalent to "no".

I know exactly what she's doing. She expects me to change my plans so she isn't alone on Thanksgiving. I'm not doing it. Especially after her comments about my personal life.

"I have to go Mom."

"Okay. Let me know about Thanksgiving." She hangs up before I can respond.

I avoid the temptation to throw my cellphone across the room like a discus. It's too expensive.

***

"Welcome to Gemma's Gym, how can I help you?"

"I'm not sure," I say to the well-built woman standing on the opposite side of the counter. On a whim, I stopped at the gym down the street from my house. I drive by it every day, telling myself I should join, but I haven't set foot in the place until today.

She extends her hand over the counter. "I'm Gemma, the owner. Tell me why you're here today."

"Nice to meet you Gemma. I'm Abby and I want to start working out."

Gemma smiles. "You came to the right place." She turns to the young woman standing next to her. "Will you cover the front while I give Abby a tour?"

"Absolutely!" her peppy assistant with a long, blonde ponytail says with a wide grin.

Gemma waves me over. "Come on. Let me show you around."

The gym itself is pretty much what I expected. It has free weights, a row of treadmills, elliptical machines, and every piece of equipment you'd see in any gym. But the atmosphere is completely different. There are a few women getting a workout in, but I don't see a single man.

"Is this a women's only gym?"

"Yes, it is. I've come to find women are more comfortable in a female only environment. I'm sure there are people who disagree with me, but it's my gym," she answers with a smile.

I'm certainly not going to argue with her. Her toned physique and no-nonsense aura tell me loud and clear she is a force to be reckoned with.

"What type of workout are you looking for?" she asks.

"I want to increase my strength and endurance."

"Are you training for an event?"

"No, not really. I mean, maybe."

She raises an eyebrow.

"I was diagnosed with MS and I want my body to be in the best shape possible in case something bad happens."

"Ah, gotcha. I've trained with women who have MS. I promise you, you can be in the best shape of your life, MS or not. Don't let it hold you back."

I nod. "I won't. Hopefully it doesn't progress and I'll never have to worry about it. But I want to be ready, just in case."

"That's incredibly smart of you. Being in shape will not only prepare you for something down the line, but it can help keep you healthy. Nutrition is important for you as well, but I'm sure you already know that."

"Yes. I've read more about nutrition in the last month than I ever thought I would need to know," I say with a laugh.

Gemma walks me through the machines and explains how each one of them works. Women occupying the machines demonstrate them for me. There are women of all shapes, sizes, and skill level here and I feel more comfortable than I thought I would.

"We also offer yoga and pilates classes. Have you tried yoga or pilates?"

I shake my head. "No, but I want to. I heard yoga is great for stress relief."

Gemma nods. "It is. It also helps with stretching and easing muscle soreness. Pilates focuses on strengthening the core and is great for your back. You should try them out if you decide to join us."

Gemma gives me the breakdown on the cost of the membership and I gladly hand over my debit card. I need to do this. I have to take care of my body. Based on the women I've met so far, I may even make some friends along the way.

***

"I'm so proud of you!" Elle gushes when she hears I joined a gym.

"Tell that to my aching arms," I whine.

We're sitting in my office, waiting for Pam to arrive for our appointment. I want Pam to meet Elle, even if Elle won't be working on the project.

"Once you get into a normal routine, the muscle soreness won't be so bad." Unlike me, Elle has been lifting since college. In fact, she and Jackson met at the gym.

"I sincerely hope so, because this sucks. I can't lift my arm above my shoulder."

Elle laughs. "It gets easier, I promise." She searches through her phone and shows me a picture of a professional grade oven with eight burners. "What do you think of this for the restaurant?"

"Ohh, I like it."

"I do too. The problem is - it's on backorder."

"I'm sure you can work some magic with Don."

Don is our appliance supplier and he has a huge crush on Elle. We got our hands on a refrigerator last month that isn't available

94

in retail stores yet because Elle batted her eyelashes and asked nicely.

"I'll see what I can do."

Our front door buzzes and I jump up. "Must be Pam."

Elle walks downstairs with me to greet Pam. Per her usual, Pam looks gorgeous. Her hair and makeup are flawless and her hunter green peacoat highlights her complexion perfectly. I would love to have her nude Louboutin pumps and Chanel handbag.

"Pam, so nice to see you again," I say as we shake hands.

"Nice to see you too Abby."

I turn to Elle. "This is my business partner and best friend Elle. I wanted you two to meet."

"Of course. Nice to meet you Elle."

The women shake hands and chat briefly about Pam's move.

"Well, I'll let you ladies get to it." Elle grabs her coat off the coat rack. "I have an oven to order."

"Good luck."

She winks. "I don't need luck."

Pam follows me upstairs. "This house is adorable."

"Thank you. We put a lot of love into it. It was in rough shape when we bought it."

"I bet the neighbors are thrilled."

I laugh. "The neighbor to our right brought over wine and a cheese basket. We increased his property value by twenty thousand dollars."

"Oh wow," Pam says when she walks in my office. "I love this space."

"You do?"

"Yes! Can you use it as inspiration for the office in my condo?"

"Sure."

She glances around my office again. "Except where you have grey, I want navy."

I imagine the color scheme in my mind. "Pink and navy go really well together. We can definitely do that for you."

"Great! I'm a true believer in pink being the ultimate boss bitch color."

I laugh out loud. "Will you tell that to Elle next time you see her?"

We talk through the design plans I put together and I'm encouraged when she "ohhs" and "ahhs" over my ideas.

"I love this kitchen configuration," she says. "The cabinet space is amazing and I never would have thought of putting in a pantry. I like the white cabinets, but what is your recommendation for the countertop?"

"Quartz is very popular, but granite is a good option as well. I usually take my clients to the vendor and let them walk around the showroom. If you go with granite, we'll pick the exact slab that will end up in your kitchen."

"Great. How about my living room situation?"

"I think I found an easy solution to your TV problem." I open my tablet and show her the sliding bookshelf I designed. "Anyone walking into your living room will see a bookshelf that extends the length of your wall. However, when you hit a button, this happens." I touch the screen and the animation shows the bookshelf sliding to the right and exposing a mounted television behind it. "Voilà! You have a TV."

"I love it! Can you really do that?"

"Yes. Our carpenter is fantastic. He's built hidden shelves for us in the past and he's already confirmed he can do this one."

We walk through her master suite, the guest room, her office space and the guest bathroom. She is appreciative of the handicapped accessible bathroom fixtures I found for her mother.

"Speaking of my mom," she says, "we have an appointment with the neurologist you suggested next week. She has a great reputation around town. We're both excited to meet her."

96

"Great! I'm glad I could help."

Pam stands and picks up her purse. "I love everything you showed me, and now I'm ready for lunch."

I laugh. "Me too."

Just as I'm wondering whether it's safe for me to assume we got the job, she says, "When can you start?"

***

"Oh. My. God. We got it?"

"Yes! We got it!"

I'm literally jumping up and down in my office. Pam and I had a wonderful lunch and I called Elle as soon as I got back.

"This is so freaking awesome! Good job Abby!"

"I can't believe it. We're decorating a celebrity's home!"

We both squeal again.

I flop down onto the couch. "Feels surreal, doesn't it?"

"It does. Our parents thought we were nuts when we started this business and look at us now."

Tears form in my eyes. I'm not usually a sentimental person, but the moment overwhelms me. "I'm so proud of us Elle."

"I am too. We're doing the damn thing."

I giggle. "Yes, we are."

"Oh, and guess who convinced Don to get his hands on a back-ordered oven by next week?"

"I knew you could do it. Never a doubt."

"I'll be putting in overtime at the restaurant next week because of the deliveries, but if you need me to sit in on any of the client meetings next week, let me know and I'll be there."

"Nah, I got it. Three of the meetings are for kitchens and the fourth is a master suite. Nothing too complicated."

"Okay. You're meeting with Dean tomorrow, right?"

"Yep. It's the think tank meeting."

"Jackson said Dean giving you time with the think tank means he wants to move forward."

I pause. "I'm not sure I want to go forward."

"What do you mean?"

"I already have enough going on. Pam's job will take a lot of time and energy. Plus, I'm working out now, and the holidays are coming up."

"Tell him that then. If you don't want to do it, don't do it."

"I know."

"I gotta go chica, Jackson is calling me, and I have to take what I can get."

I set my phone on my chest and stare at the ceiling. Despite what I told Elle, I'm not ready to give up on the app idea just yet. Something tells me I should pursue it, even if it's outside my wheelhouse.

I close my eyes and start to doze. I was up late last night planning my meeting with Pam for the hundredth time and a nap is sorely needed. Just when I'm about to nod off, my cellphone buzzes. It's a call from my mom.

Nope. I silence my phone and pass out.

Chapter Six

I play it casual again when I arrive at Dean's office. It's kind of nice to attend a meeting in jeans and Chuck Taylor's.

Seth greets me when I walk in. "Hi Abby. They're in the back conference room. You can go on in."

"Thanks Seth."

I walk past the sea of headphones and computer screens, nothing but a water bottle in my hand. I had no clue how to prepare for a think tank, I'm hoping Dean takes the lead. I find the group exactly where Seth said they would be. Six people sit at a long rectangular table and have their attention turned to Dean, who is standing in front of a giant monitor pointing to what appears to be a computerized volcano. He sees me on the other side of the glass and waves me in.

I'm only one foot in the door when he asks, "Abby, what do you think of this landscape?"

All eyes turn to me. "Um..." I analyze the screen, not sure what I'm supposed to say. "It looks like a volcano."

"What area of the world would you say it's in?"

I examine the screen again. The sun is high, reflecting off red sand. It reminds me of my dad's pictures of his backpacking trip through Arizona. He and a buddy spent two months hitchhiking across America after they graduated from high school.

"It looks like the desert in Arizona," I say sheepishly, not sure if I'm anywhere near correct.

Dean beams. "Exactly what we were going for. Nice job guys!" he tells the group.

"Are there volcanos in the desert?" I immediately regret letting my question slip. Dean's video games are none of my business.

"Actually, yes. There are three active volcanoes in the Mohave Desert, but most people don't associate volcanoes with the desert."

"Huh, I did not know that."

"Which is what we are banking on," one of the young women in the group tells me. "We're trying to create alien environments that really aren't that different from what we have here on Earth."

"You guys created this?" I ask, looking at the screen again. The image looks so life-like, almost like a photograph.

"Indeed." Dean turns off the television. "Alright guys, let's talk about the real reason we're here. I sent you all an email yesterday with the talking points. First things first, what is your gut impression of the app?"

I breathe a sigh of relief. From the sound of things, Dean already did most of the heavy lifting. He takes a seat at the head of the table and motions for me to sit in the chair next to him. I glance around the table and smile when I see everyone is wearing name tags on my behalf. Sasha, Tony, Richard, Melissa, Jim, and Brian.

Sasha, the woman who explained the volcano to me, speaks up first. "I like the idea. I researched the medical apps currently available on the major platforms and none of them offer the social components proposed in this app."

"Same here," Brian chimes in. "Most of the apps are informative as opposed to interactive."

Dean nods. "Good to know. We want to fill a gap. No point in adding to an area that is already saturated. What were your initial reactions before doing any research?"

"I think it's a great idea," Melissa says. "My brother is deaf and constantly complains about the dating scene and how hard it is for him. I told him about this, and he asked if we are including individuals with disabilities and not just illnesses."

"Absolutely," I answer. "If we decide to go forward with this, we have to make sure the app is easy to use for people with disabilities."

"One hundred percent," Dean agrees. "What else?"

"I like the names of the functions," Jim notes, "but what are you calling the app itself?"

"I haven't decided yet," I admit.

"I thought it was Ill and Chill?" Dean teases, knowing full well I don't like that name.

Everyone giggles.

"Ill and Chill was the silly name my friend came up with when this was just a dating app," I explain to the group. "I think it's too casual. I want the app to be taken seriously."

"What about 'Illing It'," Dean suggests.

"Illing It?"

"Yeah, you know, Killing It, but without the K. Another play on words like the names for the functions."

The group really likes the name, but I'm not so sure. "I'll have to think about it."

"Fair enough. What else guys?"

"One thing I think should be added," Tony says, "is a charity component."

"Such as?" Dean asks.

"Our company emphasizes philanthropic efforts. You give us time off to help build homes with Habitats for Humanity, or to volunteer at food pantries. We should extend that into the app somehow."

I glance over at Dean. It's clear his employees respect and adore him based on the way they interact with him. The fact that he supports charities makes me like him even more.

"I like the charity idea," Richard chimes in. "I was also thinking about an events tab where people can post about 5ks or charity events raising funds for medical research."

"Do Good, Feel Good," I mutter under my breath.

"What was that?" Dean asks.

"Do Good, Feel Good," I repeat louder.

He smiles. "I like it."

I listen as the group discusses the various functions of the app, some of it gets too technical for me at times, but from what I gather, they all like the idea.

Dean surprises me when he asks, "Do you think there's enough meat here to support a full website?"

Everyone agrees they think there is.

Dean checks his watch. "Alright, it's 5:30. Time to head home. Thank you for your feedback."

It's 5:30? Did I enter a time warp when I walked in?

When I start to stand, Dean touches my shoulder lightly. It sends a warm, tingling sensation down my arm. "Do you mind hanging back for a little while? I'll order food if you're hungry."

I'm surprised by his invitation, but welcome it. "Food sounds great, I'm starving."

"I'll grab a couple menus. Be right back."

I check my cellphone for messages and answer an email from the contractor who will be working on Pam's condo. He's pushing back the start date by two days, but promises to finish on time. I politely tell him, "you better" in my response. I want Pam's renovations to go as smoothly as possible.

Dean walks back in the conference room. "Our choices are Chinese, Mexican, pizza and sushi. Any of those sound good to you?"

I love Mexican food, but it's not a good idea to try a new Mexican place when I'm this far from home. My stomach isn't always happy with spicy food. "Have you ordered from the Chinese restaurant before?"

"I have, it's good."

"Chinese it is then."

I scan the menu and decide on chicken with broccoli and a cup of wonton noodle soup.

"That went well," I say after Dean orders our food.

"It did. I suspected it would. What do you think of their suggestions?"

"I like them. Adding a charity and event tab makes a lot of sense, and I love the idea of the app helping to raise funds for research in some way."

"Agreed. I'm not sure why I didn't think of it sooner."

I laugh. "You seem pretty busy. I'm sure this app isn't on the forefront of your mind."

"To the contrary, I've thought about it a lot. I want it to be successful."

I don't tell him I haven't spent much time thinking about it because of how busy I've been with work. "What happens next?"

"We build the app."

"Build it?"

"Yes, we code it and get it ready for trial use."

"How do we do that?"

He shrugs. "My team will handle it."

"Aren't you creating a new video game?"

"We are, but we can work on the app on the side."

I shake my head. "You don't have to do that."

"No I don't. But I want to."

I ask the question I've wanted to ask from the very beginning of all of this. "Why? Why are you interested in this?"

He smiles. "Do I need a reason?"

"I suppose not. It just seems light years away from what your company does."

He shakes his head and chuckles softly.

"What?" I ask confused. Did I say something funny?

"I just realized I have a much bigger ego than I thought."

"How so?"

"My dumbass assumed you Googled me before we met or read my bio on Wikipedia."

"You have a Wikipedia page?"

"Yep. Half of it isn't true, but it makes me sound more interesting."

I laugh. "Sorry to disappoint you, but I didn't research you before we met. Sounds like I should have."

"Here, this may explain it." Dean takes off his hooded sweatshirt and pulls down the collar of his Black Crows t-shirt.

My jaw drops. "A port scar."

"You know what it is?" he asks surprised.

"Yes. My grandmother had breast cancer. I sat with her a few times during her chemo treatments."

He puts his sweatshirt back on. "I was diagnosed with leukemia when I was nine."

I'm stunned. Dean is the picture of health. "Oh my gosh. I'm so sorry."

"Don't be. It made me who I am today."

"Still though, nine? That must have been so hard."

"It was harder for my parents than it was for me. The treatment sucked, but my poor mom lost thirty pounds during the ordeal."

"I can't even imagine..." my voice trails off. It was so hard watching my grandmother suffer the side effects of chemo. It's no wonder Dean's mom lost weight. It must have been excruciating to watch her child go through it.

"I was lucky in the sense that I had the most common type – acute lymphoblastic leukemia – and my body was responsive to chemotherapy. But it took its toll on my overall health for a while."

"I'm sure it did. You look healthy as a horse now."

Dean nods. "I am, but I go for regular screenings and bloodwork to be on the safe side."

We fall silent for a moment. I'm shocked by his revelation, but it all makes sense now. He understands what it's like to deal with an illness and how it impacts your life.

"That's how I got into video games," he continues, leaning back in his chair.

"It is?"

"Yep. I had my Gameboy during treatments, and my mom insisted I stay indoors to avoid germs. So it was me and my video games for months. I don't know what I would have done without them."

"Ah, I see."

He nods. "Some people decide to be doctors or nurses to help people through illnesses they themselves had. I decided to create a pastime for kids who are sick like I was. Something to keep their minds off the hell they're going through. Especially nowadays when everything is online and cooperative. Sick kids can communicate and have fun with their classmates by playing interactive video games with them."

"I've never thought of it that way."

"Most people don't. If I didn't live through the experience myself, I probably never would have either. It's the reason I work so hard and try to make amazing video games. I can't help but picture me as a little boy finding so much joy in the escape those games provided."

Listening to him explain his life mission with a gleam in his eyes, I realize Dean may be one of the most amazing people I've ever met. Smart. Caring. Empathetic.

Before I can tell him so, a bell chimes on Dean's cellphone. "Food's here. I'll go grab it."

As I wait for him to come back, I try to imagine a nine-year-old going through chemotherapy. My grandmother was violently ill after her treatments. I've heard chemo has changed drastically since then, and I hope that's true. I wouldn't wish it upon my worst enemy.

"It will all be worth it," my grandmother would say when she saw the concern on my face. "A year from now, I won't even remember being sick."

My memories are interrupted when Dean walks back in the conference room. The heavenly aroma of our dinner fills the air.

"That smells amazing!"

He sets the bag down and grabs two bottles from a mini-fridge I didn't notice sitting in the corner. "Water okay?"

"Perfect."

"You sure? We have a Coke machine in the lounge."

"No, water's great. I'm cutting back on sugary drinks."

He takes a seat and hands me my water. "I'm trying to, but sometimes the craving for an ice cold soda hits and I can't help myself."

"Soda, huh? I guess you're not an Ohio native."

He laughs. "You caught me. I lived in Florida until I graduated from college. Some kids called it soda, others called it coke. My house was a soda house."

"I'm a pop girl myself. Midwest through and through."

"Have you ever lived outside of Ohio?"

I shake my head. "Nope. Grew up in Westerville and went to OSU. Elle and I started our business right after college." I laugh. "We shared a tiny studio apartment for two years."

"You must be doing something right. You have a nice office in German Village now." He blushes when I raise an eyebrow. "I Googled you."

I laugh out loud. "I should have expected a tech guy to internet stalk me."

"Whoa, whoa, whoa," he protests. "Just because you don't look someone up online like everyone else in America doesn't mean I'm a stalker. I haven't even trolled your Instagram account yet."

"Don't have one. Well, our business has one, but I don't have a personal account."

"You don't?"

"Nope. I don't have time for it. Do you have one?"

106

"I do, but I rarely post. Same reason, too busy."

"My life isn't interesting anyway. It mostly consists of working, sleeping, and eating. Although I have thrown working out into the mix."

"Nice! I work out almost every day."

"Every day?" I ask shocked. "How do you have time for that?"

"We have a gym here, and I have a smaller one at home. Whenever I'm having trouble focusing or stressing about something, I can go in there and get in a workout. They're not always long sessions, but they're a good reset."

He opens the bag of Chinese food and hands me my order. The chicken and broccoli looks amazing, but I dig into my wonton soup first.

"What type of stuff do you do? Are you a cardio guy?"

"A little of everything. I prefer lifting, but I throw the treadmill in every now and then." He opens his chicken lo mein and spins noodles on his fork. "I want to be in shape in case the cancer comes back."

I frown for a second. It sucks he will worry about cancer for the rest of his life. "I understand. That's why I started working out – in case something happens with my MS."

"Do you mind me asking what your prognosis is?"

"Not at all. It's good. I'm taking meds and they seem to be helping. If all goes well, the disease will stop progressing and maybe even improve. But there's no guarantees. It's unpredictable. It's a different animal for everyone who has it."

"For what it's worth, you're handling it like a champ."

I smile. "Thanks."

He shifts gears. "Enough heavy stuff, tell me what you do when you're not sleeping, eating, working or hanging out at the gym."

Our conversation flows easily as we eat our food straight out of the containers. I tell him my one and only creative hobby is the occasional attempt at wall art for my interior design projects.

"Most of them come out terrible, but I have one or two original pieces hanging on former clients' walls."

I'm not surprised when he tells me he's an avid reader. "I love graphic novels, which of course only adds to my dorkiness."

I giggle. "You're not a dork."

"I'm a coder who loves graphic novels and the occasional game of backgammon. I'm an absolute dork."

"I have no idea how to play backgammon," I admit as I finish my dinner.

"Maybe I can teach you sometime," he says softly.

I look into his eyes and my stomach flutters. Did he just ask me out?

Before I can respond, he stands and starts cleaning our mess. "How was your food?"

"Delicious. I ate way too much."

"I'm glad you liked it." He puts my leftovers in the bag and walks with me to the lobby.

"You heading home?" I ask.

"Not yet. I have a little more to do."

"I thought you said it was quitting time?" I tease.

He smiles. "It's never quitting time for the owner."

"Ugh. I can relate." We reach the front door and I stop before stepping out. "Thanks again for doing this. I know you're super busy."

"Un unh, I'm walking you to your car."

"You don't have to do that," I insist. "I'll be fine."

"It's dark out. No way I'm letting you walk to your car alone."

I check my watch. Holy cow! It's 7:30. How long were we in there?

Dean lets me step out first, then walks beside me. "This is incredibly awkward, but I think we should draw up a contract."

I raise an eyebrow. "A contract?"

108

"Yes. This is your idea, and you're welcome to shop it elsewhere…"

"Shop it elsewhere? Why would I want to do that?"

He meets my eyes. "In case you prefer to work with someone else."

"No way. You're putting up resources, and spending time on this. I would never go to someone else."

"Okay," he says relieved. "I only brought it up because my legal team thinks we should put something in writing."

"That's fine with me." I lighten the mood. "My dad's a retired lawyer. He'll tell me if you're trying to screw me over."

Dean laughs. "Fair enough."

We stop by my car. "Thanks again for everything. The think tank. Dinner. Walking me to my car to make sure I don't get abducted by aliens."

"Hey, you're a precious commodity now. I can't have my app designer disappearing on me," he jokes.

"App designer? Can I add that to my resume?"

"Of course. It won't help you get any jobs, but it will look cool."

We pause a moment, both a little unsure how to end our meeting. Finally, I stick out my hand and he smiles as he returns my shake.

"I'll send you the contract in the next few days." His hand drops to his side. "No rush. I'll keep you posted on the app's progress."

"Sounds good." I open my car door and take a seat. "Until next time Mr. Porter."

He smiles. "I look forward to it Ms. Henry."

***

"Ohhh, he likes you," Elle teases as she helps me sort through the unpacked boxes in my house.

"No he doesn't."

109

"Then why the backgammon invite? I mean, what's sexier than backgammon?"

I laugh. "What is backgammon anyway?"

She shrugs. "No clue."

"He's just being nice."

"Uh huh." She breaks down a cardboard box. "Where do you want these extra towels?"

"In the laundry room. They've been in a box for months, I should probably wash them."

Later, as we're binge watching *You*, Elle checks out Dean for herself.

"Wow Abby, he's cute."

"Let me see." She shows me a picture she found online of Dean at a gaming convention. He's dressed up in a suit and tie. Underneath his picture it says, "Keynote Speaker." I have to admit, he cleans up nicely.

"You should ask him out," Elle suggests.

"What? I can't."

"Why not?"

"We're in the middle of a business thing. We're going to sign a contract for crying out loud."

"You know who else signs contracts? People who are about to get married."

"This is hardly a prenuptial agreement."

"Maybe it could be a 'pre-getting it on' agreement."

I roll my eyes. "You're ridiculous."

When Dean texts me the link for the contract a few days later, I smile thinking of Elle's comments. She'd be disappointed to read the not-at-all-steamy legal mumbo jumbo in the five-page document.

"This looks fair," Dad says after reviewing the contract for me.

"I thought so too, but I wanted a professional opinion."

Samantha sets down a cup of coffee for each of us and takes a seat at their dining room table. "An app, how exciting."

"It's unexpected," I say with a smile, "but it's fun."

Dad is perusing the contract again. "The terms are basically that you agree to let him use your idea in exchange for his services at no charge and you will split any proceeds made from the app fifty-fifty."

Wait...what? "Proceeds? The app isn't designed to make money."

"Maybe not right now, but something could change down the road."

"I don't want to make any money from this," I scoff. "That's not my intent."

Dad looks over the top of his reading glasses. "You better make sure it's not his intent."

The provision about proceeds nags me for the rest of the day. I can't imagine Dean trying to make a quick buck, but why have it in the contract? When I can't focus on my plans for a new kitchen remodel Elle secured for us yesterday, I decide to bite the bullet and call Dean.

"Great minds must think alike," Dean says when he answers the phone.

"How so?"

"I was just about to send you a text about the app."

"Oh, is something going on?"

"Nothing major. You first. What's up?"

Hmmm, how to approach this? "My dad reviewed the contract you sent over. I have a question about one of the provisions."

"Okay. I may or may not be able to answer it. I know little to nothing about legalese."

I laugh. "Same. Anyways, there's a paragraph in there about us splitting the proceeds evenly."

"I have that section highlighted as well."

"You do?"

"Yes. Tell me your issue with it."

"I don't want the app to make money," I say pointblank.

"Good. Neither do I."

"You don't?"

"No."

I breathe a sigh of relief. "Thank goodness. Why is the language in there then?"

"My legal team drafts contracts like this for other technology companies all the time and it's a common provision for apps created to generate funds."

"Pardon my ignorance here, but how do apps make money?"

"Advertisers mostly. But some also have in-app purchase capabilities."

"My concern with advertisers on our app is we will look biased toward those companies."

"Exactly," Dean agrees. "I don't like the idea of it either."

"Aside from potentially collecting donations for our charitable events, I don't want to charge people anything or have a membership fee."

"No, no, no. Me neither. I'll talk to the attorneys and tell them to change this. I'll have them send the revisions your way."

"Thank you, that's awesome. I'm glad we're on the same page about it. What did you want to text me about?"

"Oh, right. The team started coding the app and they asked about the logo. We haven't talked about a logo at all. Do you have an image or picture in mind? It would also serve as the icon people see on their phones when they want to click on the app."

I pause for a moment before saying, "I did think of something, but it may be too silly."

"Spill it. Let's hear it."

"A stethoscope, but with the piece that touches your body in the shape of a heart."

"Photo realistic, or hand drawn?"

"Hand drawn, but not cartoonish."

"Okay. What color?"

"Um, pink."

"Hmmm. I like all of it but the pink."

I laugh. "Pink is too girly, isn't it?"

"Stereotypically speaking, yes."

"How about a black stethoscope with silver touches?" I suggest.

"I like it. I'll have the team use a few different background colors to see what works best."

"Do you have someone who can draw the stethoscope?"

"I'll do it," he says without hesitation.

"You will?" I ask surprised.

"Yes. In addition to honing my gaming skills, I drew a lot as a kid. Mostly comic book characters."

"Wow. Is there anything you can't do?"

Dean laughs. "How much time you got? I'll give the logo a shot and send it your way."

I smile. "Sounds good."

A few days later, I receive a text from Dean with a photograph of his drawing. It looks exactly how I pictured it in my mind. How did he nail it?

Perfect! I love it.

Are you just saying that, or do you really like it?

I giggle.

Yes, I really like it.

He isn't satisfied with my response.

I can have someone else draw another version for comparison.

Men.

Quit being ridiculous. It looks great. Use it.

I'm smiling when he sends me another response.

> *You talked me into it. I'll have my team spruce it up a bit and send it to you for approval.*

I check my watch.

> *It's 7:30 p.m., why are you still working?*

> *Why do I have the sneaky suspicion the pot is calling the kettle black? Besides, I'm drawing, not working.*

He caught me red-handed.

> *Construction starts on my new project tomorrow. Just making sure everything is in order.*

> *I knew it! Ever the worker bee.*

Yeah, I'm lame like that.

There's a longer pause between texts this time, and I think he's ended the conversation, but then another message comes through.

> *I admire your work ethic and passion for what you do. Plus, if I acknowledge your lameness, I'd be pointing the finger at myself too.*

LOL. Oh, I see. Preserving your own coolness, I get it. ;)

Oh God! Did I just send him a winking face? What am I doing? I can't get flirty with him. This is Dean! The guy creating my app. He'll think I'm completely unprofessional!

My stomach sinks when I get his response.

> *Hate to run, but I have to go. Good luck tomorrow.*

Ugh…

Chapter Seven

"There's nothing offensive about a winky face emoji," Elle assures me the next morning as we walk Pam's empty condo. "No way he was put off by that."

"I don't know...he ghosted as soon as I sent it."

"Total coincidence."

"You sure?"

She raises an eyebrow. "Why are you so worried about what Dean Porter thinks?"

I shift my weight. "Because we work together. I want to keep it on the up and up."

"Says the girl who sent the winky face emoji," Elle smirks.

"It wasn't really an emoji. It was an emoticon."

"Argue the semantics all you want. Whatever you sent, it was winking." She lets me off the hook and focuses her attention on Pam's condo. "This place is stunning. I want to live here."

"Isn't it great? It's going to be amazing when it's done."

"Definitely. When is Derrick and his crew starting?"

"Today. They'll be here any minute to put the first coat of paint in the kitchen. They can hang cabinets next week."

"The cabinets are already in?" Elle asks surprised. She looks around at the empty room. "Where are they?"

"Derrick has a connection who works with the supplier, and they sent the cabinets right away. He's bringing them with his crew today."

"Nice!"

I nod. "I know. He's getting us the vanities and materials for the bathrooms by next week as well."

"Damn. That's awesome."

"Agreed. He's even going to work next Friday."

"He's coming in the Friday after Thanksgiving? Wow."

"He's happy we're using him again, especially for this job. He wants to make as good an impression as we do."

"References, references, references."

"Exactly."

We walk through the rest of the condo and end the tour in front of the glass wall overlooking Dublin.

Elle admires the view. "I don't know how much Pam paid for it, but this condo is worth every penny."

"Agreed."

We stand quietly for a moment, soaking in the peace and quiet. Or at least I am. Elle surprises me with a question.

"Would you tell me the truth even if you thought it would hurt my feelings?"

"Of course."

She glances at me, the sparkle in her eyes gone. "Do you think Jackson is having an affair?"

My mouth drops. "Jackson?" I shake my head. "No way."

She sighs. "He's not going to be home for Thanksgiving."

"Why not?"

"He'll be in Phoenix Tuesday for a conference, then has another presentation on Friday in Tucson. He doesn't want to fly back and forth. Or so he claims."

"Why don't you go with him?"

She snorts. "And incur the wrath of my mother for skipping Thanksgiving at my grandma's? No thanks."

"We're adults now. We can do what we want on the holidays."

She's quiet for a moment. "I just don't understand it. I'm proud of him for his accomplishments, but it seems like he wants to be away. And to miss a holiday?"

Elle rarely, if ever, shows her weak side. Even to me.

As delicately as possible I ask, "Have you talked to him about it?"

She nods. "I have. He says he has to strike while the iron is hot. Do as many of these speaking engagements as he can now because it will fizzle soon. And I get that."

Jackson's logic does make sense. Who knows how long he'll be able to book the speaking engagements.

"This is temporary Elle," I assure her.

"I hope so." She sighs. "I feel like a terrible, bitchy, clingy girlfriend."

I pull her in for a hug. "You're not any of those things. You're worried, that's all. Anyone would be in your situation."

Our girl talk is interrupted by the binging of the elevator. The doors open and our contractor and two of his helpers step out.

"Morning ladies. You ready to fuck this place up?"

Elle and I exchange a glance. The man may be crude, but he does a fantastic job.

Elle grins. "Let's do this shit."

***

"How are the medications working for you?"

Dr. Harris shines a light in my eye. I try not to blink.

"Good. The numbness and tremors in my hand have faded significantly."

"When was the last time you had the numbness?"

I rack my brain, when was the last time? "Had to be at least two weeks ago."

"You used to get the numbness daily, right?"

"Yes."

"Excellent." She scribbles notes in my file. "What about side effects? Exhaustion? Nausea? Dizziness?"

I shake my head. "No. Nothing that I've noticed."

117

She swivels her chair toward me. "Stand up and walk to the door and back for me."

She has me do this every visit, along with the classic, "close your eyes and touch the tip of your nose" routine. After a few more exercises, she tells me to take a seat.

"Everything looks great Abby. My recommendation is to stay on this course of medication and have an MRI in three months. See if there are any changes."

"Sounds good."

She jots down a few more notes, then makes small talk with me as we walk out to the lobby area. "Any plans for tomorrow?"

"Staying in town. I always go to my dad's for Thanksgiving. How about you?"

She groans. "It's my turn to host. I'll have twenty-five people at my house tomorrow."

"Yeesh. You better leave now and get started."

"One more patient and I'm out of here."

I shake her hand. "Thank you so much Dr. Harris."

"You're welcome. Call if anything comes up, and have a nice Thanksgiving."

"I will. You too."

A woman in the waiting area catches my eye on the way out. She's younger than me by a few years, fresh faced and smiling. Her auburn hair has beachy waves and her blue eyes shine next to her alabaster skin. I'm admiring her tan suede booties when the nurse calls out, "Nancy!"

When she stands, I'm surprised to see her grab a cane and lean on it as she walks. Her cane is a beautiful rosewood with honeybees and flowers carved into it. Her positive energy is apparent despite any of the trials and tribulations she may be going through.

Abby, I think to myself, that is the way to be.

***

"I did it bitch!" Elle yells into the phone when I pick it up at 7:30 a.m. the next morning.

"Did what?" I mumble into the phone, still curled up under my down comforter.

"I booked a flight! I'm on my way to Tucson."

"What?!"

"Yep, I followed your advice."

I yawn. "There's a first time for everything."

"Ha ha."

"How expensive was that?" A flight at the last minute, on Thanksgiving none the less, must have cost an arm and a leg.

"Money, schmoney. We only live once, right?"

"So they say." I rub the sleep from my eyes. "Good for you! I bet Jackson is thrilled."

"That's the best part – I haven't told him yet. It will be a total surprise."

"Nice. He'll be so happy to see you."

"I gotta run. I have twenty minutes to pack and get out the door."

"Alright chica. Have a good time!"

I hang up wishing I could go with her. The late lunch at my dad's will be fine, but then I have to stop over at Mom's for dessert. All I really want to do is lay in bed and catch up on sleep. It's been a hectic few weeks.

I turn on the parade as I get ready. Watching the floats reminds me of my grandmother. Every Thanksgiving morning she would come over to our house and make apple pies with me while we watched the parade.

"You're going to be a Rockette one day," she told me while I tried my hardest to emulate the beautiful women on TV.

"You think so Grandma?" I asked with a wide smile.

"I know one thing for sure young lady, you're going to be whatever you decide you want to be."

119

My dream job changed over time, one year a Rockette, the next an astronaut, but Grandma steadfastly believed I could be any of the people I threw out there.

I finish putting on my makeup and find a comfy pair of skinny jeans to wear, the pair with elastic in the waistband. Samantha is an excellent cook and I'll eat way more than I should.

"I'll bring you back some turkey," I promise Oscar.

He rubs against my legs as I walk through the kitchen. He's been home alone a lot lately, but he doesn't seem to mind. He always welcomes me with a soft meow and cuddles when I get home.

Just as I'm grabbing my car keys, my phone buzzes inside my purse. I decide to check it in case it's Samantha asking me to pick something up on my way over. Last year I saved the day with sticks of butter for the mashed potatoes.

To my surprise, the message is from Dean. I giggle when I open it. A dancing turkey crosses my screen doing all the popular dance moves from the '80s to the tune of "You Can't Touch This."

Before I can respond, another text comes through.

> *Happy Thanksgiving! Sorry I cut it short the other night. I hope you have an amazing holiday with your family.*

His text makes me feel much better about "winky gate" as Elle dubbed it.

> *LMAO. That turkey has better moves than I do. No worries about the other night. I hope you have a great Thanksgiving.*

I wait a moment before putting my phone back in my purse to see if he responds. I'm a tad disappointed when he doesn't, but relieved I didn't upset him the other night. I walk out the door humming M.C. Hammer.

***

"This looks fantastic," I gush when I see Samantha's dining room table.

She's taken her autumn theme up a notch this year. An ornate cornucopia serves as the centerpiece, fresh rolls and biscuits spilling out of it onto her garnet tablecloth. Frosted orange plates with gold rims sit under burgundy cloth napkins wrapped in gold rings. Her silverware shines under the light of the chandelier and there isn't a single water spot on her wine glasses.

"Really? You like it?" Samantha asks as she sets trivets on the table to hold her hot dishes.

"Yes. It's stunning."

She smiles. "That's high praise coming from an interior decorator."

"What can I help with?"

"Almost everything is ready. Just waiting for Austin and Kelly to get here."

Austin is my stepbrother. Admittedly, I don't know him well. We met for the first time as adults and only see each other on holidays. His temperament is similar to Samantha's and his wife is a sweetheart. They had a baby, Rosie, six months ago and she is the cutest thing in the world.

"We should go to them on Christmas," I suggest. "It can't be easy to make the two-hour drive with a baby."

Samantha nods. "I agree. They've come here the last five years, we can go to them this year."

Austin, Kelly, and their cutie pie arrive fifteen minutes later. We all "ooh" and "aah" over the baby before taking our seats at the dinner table.

"Rosie has your beautiful blue eyes Kelly," I tell her from across the table.

"Aw, thank you. I think she's starting to look more like her daddy though."

"Poor thing," Austin jokes.

Austin and Kelly are both attractive people, so Rosie can't go wrong with whichever parent she favors. Kelly's light blonde hair and blue eyes stand in contrast to Austin's dark hair and brown eyes, but they are both tall with lean frames.

Dad carries in the turkey, which looks like it came straight out of a cooking magazine. The spread is amazing: mashed potatoes, green bean casserole, cranberry sauce, stuffing, macaroni and cheese, sweet potatoes with melted marshmallows, and roasted carrots. All of it homemade.

"You've outdone yourself once again Samantha," Kelly says with a smile.

Samantha blushes. "Thank you."

Dad reaches out his hand and places it on hers. "You know how to make the day special."

I can't help but smile. I have a newfound appreciation for Dad's happiness after the heart to heart we had about his relationship with my mom.

Everything is delicious, and as predicted, I eat way too much. We're all sitting at the table, letting the food settle, when Austin asks me how the business is doing.

"It's going great. We're really busy."

"She's being modest," Dad interjects. "She just landed Pam Dobb's condo."

Kelly's jaw drops. "No way! I love her! What's she like?"

"Super nice. An easy client to work with."

"I follow her on Instagram. She has the best style. I want her wardrobe."

I laugh. "Me too."

"Abby is also working on an app," Samantha tells her son and daughter-in-law.

This catches Austin's attention. He runs the IT Department of a financial corporation in Cincinnati. "Now we're talking my language. What kind of app?"

"It's an app for people with long-term illnesses. A place to socialize, find a reliable doctor, learn more about their illness if they were recently diagnosed, and organize charity events."

"Sounds amazing!" Kelly is holding little Rosie while she feeds her. "What are you calling it?"

"Well, Dean wants to call it Illing It, but I'm not sold on that name yet."

"Dean?" Kelly tips her head to the side. "Who's Dean?"

"Dean Porter. His team is designing the app."

Austin nearly spits out his drink. "Dean Porter? You're working with Dean Porter?"

"Yes. Elle's boyfriend works for him."

"Holy shit!"

"Austin!" Samantha exclaims. "Language!"

"Sorry Mom, but Dean Porter is a big deal. A really big deal. He's created the greatest and most successful video games of our generation. The guy is a genius."

Kelly's smile is wide. "You've impressed both of us Abby. Me with Pam Dobbs, and Austin with his gamer crush."

I laugh. "I'm moving up in the world."

"What's he working on now?" Austin asks. "There's rumors they're making a sequel to *Operation New World*. Is it true?"

Apparently, I am privy to top secret information. I know for a fact they are making a sequel to *Operation New World*, but I can't let the cat out of the bag.

"Dean and I only work on the app together. I have nothing to do with the games."

Austin frowns. "That stinks."

"How did you come up with this idea Abby?" Kelly props Rosie against her chest and burps her softly.

I give her my speech about going on a date and how hard it was to decide whether to tell the guy or not, and how my whining to Elle led to my first meeting with Dean.

"You've never told me why he's so interested in this," Dad says. "Why does a video game guy have an interest in an app for health and wellness?"

123

Before I can answer, Austin pipes up. "He's a cancer survivor."

"Wow. That would definitely explain it."

"Ten percent of the proceeds earned from *Operation New World* went to pediatric cancer research groups," Austin continues.

Now it's my turn to be impressed. "Ten percent? Really?"

Austin nods. "Yep. He did it undercover too. Or at least tried to. One of the hospitals let it slip by painting a mural on their wall of a scene from the game."

"He sounds like a wonderful man," Samantha notes before pushing her chair back. "Anyone ready for dessert?"

I wince. "Oh, I forgot to tell you, I have to leave a little earlier than normal to stop by my mom's. I told her I would have dessert with her tonight."

Samantha smiles. "That's nice. I'm glad you get to spend some time with her this year. Let me make a plate of leftovers for you to bring over."

I sometimes wonder if Samantha is real. Her kindness seemed too good to be true when I met her. I kept waiting for a crack in her positive façade, but she is a genuinely gracious person. Every now and then I'll see annoyance flash across her face, and she won't hide it when she's upset, but she will find the kindest way to tell you her thoughts.

One time when we were shopping together, instead of telling me I looked bad in an outfit, she said, "You are such a beautiful girl, and that dress doesn't do you justice."

Kelly stands. "I better check Rosie's diaper before we dig into dessert."

I push my own chair back. "I hate to leave, but I should head to Mom's before she sends out a search party."

Kelly walks with me toward the guest bedroom where I laid my coat and purse. "Will your app have anything for celiacs?"

"We aren't limiting it to any particular illnesses. I want it to be an open forum where people can chat generally, but I'm sure there will be smaller sections for people to talk about their specific illness."

"I wish there was something like that when I was first diagnosed. It was so hard to find any information on celiac disease."

"You have celiac disease?" I ask surprised. "How did I not know this?"

She laughs. "I don't talk about it much. Samantha knows and she makes special things for me that are gluten free, but I guess it's never come up in conversation."

Now that I think about it, Kelly was the only one who didn't take something out of Samantha's bread cornucopia. "Is it hard going out to eat?"

She lays Rosie down on her portable diaper pad. "Not anymore. I know what I can and can't eat. But at first it was daunting. Almost depressing in a way. I loved eating breads and cereals, and then all the sudden I couldn't."

"How did you figure out you have celiac?"

"I was getting really sick after eating foods with gluten in them. I didn't make the connection at first, but my family doctor had me keep a food journal to track everything I ate. I was vomiting and doing other unpleasant digestive things. They did lots of tests and eventually came up with a diagnosis."

"Wow, that sounds awful."

She nods. "I didn't believe it at first. How could gluten be doing this? I'd eaten it my entire life. But I couldn't deny how much better I felt after going gluten free for a few weeks. I had more energy, my digestive issues stopped, and I lost five pounds because I wasn't bloated all the time."

I shake my head. "Kind of scary to think something you're eating could do that to you."

"Agreed. I just hope Rosie doesn't have to deal with it." She gives Rosie a kiss on the cheek after fastening the new diaper.

"Although there's so many gluten free products available now, it isn't as bad as it used to be."

"I tried gluten free bread once." I crinkle my nose. "It wasn't great."

Kelly laughs. "It's gotten a lot better. One nice thing about the gluten free diet fads is there are so many more options, and they taste good. I don't miss the pasta I used to eat at all. I like the stuff I eat now better."

"What about restaurants? Do they have more gluten free options now? I've seen memes where waiters get pissy because people ask for gluten free food."

"Yeah," she sighs, "that's the downside to the fad. People think I want gluten free food to lose weight, when I'm really trying to stay healthy."

"Sounds like you're doing well though."

She smiles. "Absolutely. It was scary and overwhelming at first, but you figure it out. Then it's the new norm. I hardly think about it anymore."

I ponder Kelly's story as I drive to Mom's, a huge plate of leftovers in tow. Anyone newly diagnosed with celiac would feel much better about their diagnosis if they spent time with Kelly. Maybe I should reach out to people who have MS. Hear their stories and learn from their experiences.

I pull into Mom's driveway and gather all the patience I have. She'll make comments about my going to Dad's for dinner, it's a given. Hard telling what else she'll throw my way.

Walking up to her front door is always a trip down memory lane. She lives in the house she bought with Dad when I was in junior high. She converted my bedroom into a sewing room when it became obvious I wasn't moving back in, but most of the house remains the same.

"I'm too old to move," she told me when I asked why she doesn't sell the two-story, three bedroom home.

"Too old? You're sixty-five. You have a lot of life left."

"Both of my parents were dead by this age," was her response.

126

"Yeah, but you're not," I pointed out.

I ring the doorbell, then use my key to open the door. "Mom?" I call out.

She comes down the steps wearing her red pajama pants with a matching shirt, her navy blue robe, and grey slippers. "I was wondering if you were going to make it."

I check my watch. "It's 6:30 p.m. on the dot. I'm not late."

"Hmph. I thought we said six." She walks past me toward the kitchen. "The pie is in the fridge. Did you bring Cool Whip?"

"No, you didn't tell me to."

"Yes I did."

I sigh. "No you didn't."

As suspected, this is going to be a miserable evening.

Lucky me.

Mom walks into her kitchen, the same oak cabinets and cream laminate countertop we had when I was in my teens greet me. I offered to redo Mom's kitchen for her, but she refused. Something about not wanting to waste money on frivolous things.

Mom grabs the pie from the fridge and sets it on the small table in the breakfast nook. "I have vanilla ice cream, that will have to do."

"Pie ala mode is better than whipped cream any day." I hold out the plate of food Samantha made for her.

"What's this?" she asks without taking it.

"Leftovers."

She looks at me like I'm holding a plate of steaming poo. "Leftovers? From your dad's?

"Yes."

"I don't want that."

"Why? It's delicious."

"You take it home then," she snaps.

"Fine. Your loss."

I grab two plates from the cabinet, and find a knife and a pair of forks in the drawer next to the sink. I pause when I cut into the pie. "Cherry? You made cherry pie?"

She shrugs. "It's my favorite."

"I don't eat cherries."

"Oh, you don't?"

I set the knife down. She knows damn well I don't eat cherries. She ate the cherry off my ice cream sundaes my entire childhood. This is my punishment for not having dinner with her.

"Why would you make cherry pie on Thanksgiving? Can't you make pumpkin or apple like a normal person?" My anger is rising, despite my intention to get through the evening without drama.

She crosses her arms. "What do I know about Thanksgiving? I don't get to celebrate it."

"That's it. I'm out." I turn on my heels and head for her front door.

She follows behind me. "Oh, so you are leaving me all alone tonight too?"

I spin and face her, deciding to let her have it. "Your happiness is not my responsibility. You are a grown ass woman who decided to sit by herself today and make herself miserable. I had absolutely nothing to do with that. With the way you treat me, you're lucky I stopped over here in the first place."

"Excuse me. I didn't realize I'm a burden."

"Well you are! You're a gigantic pain in my ass who makes me feel like shit. You tried to gaslight me over Cool Whip! Cool Whip Mom!"

She stares at me, speechless.

I soften my tone. "I understand, to an extent, why you are the way you are. But that doesn't mean I have to tolerate it. I have plenty of people in my life who love me without judgment and don't make me feel like I'm a piece of dirt when I spend time with them. Figure your shit out. When you decide to be a pleasant person to be around, call me."

I walk out the door feeling a hundred pounds lighter. I'm done playing nice with her just because she's my mom. I'm no longer tolerating her bullshit.

I don't feel any guilt over my tirade when I get in bed. I swung back by Dad's and ate a piece of pumpkin pie with him and Samantha. If you don't have pumpkin pie on Thanksgiving, is it even Thanksgiving? They didn't ask any questions when I told them Mom wasn't feeling well, but their side glances gave away their suspicions.

I'm not sure where my newfound moxie is coming from. Is it because I'm older and have less patience for it? Is it because I've seen what a healthy household looks like thanks to Dad and Samantha? Or has my MS and all this talk of illness made me realize life is too short to accept anything less than what you deserve?

I yawn and turn off my bedside lamp. My stomach is heavy, loaded with ten pounds of food. I definitely need to hit the gym tomorrow.

Chapter Eight

The gym is nearly empty the next day. Everyone is either Black Friday shopping or recovering from all the food they ate.

I'm able to use every machine when I'm ready for it, which is nice. I slept like a rock last night and feel rejuvenated and refreshed. I get in extra reps for almost all of my shoulder exercises and I bust out five more bent knee push-ups. I'm super pumped about my progress and write it in my workout journal as soon as I get home.

"You should track your workouts," Gemma told me after my first session at the gym. "Seeing your progress will give you the motivation to keep going on those days when you're not feeling up to it."

She's one hundred percent right. It's a great feeling when I write down my accomplishments and see how much progress I'm making.

Before I hop in the shower, I check my cellphone and smile when I see a message from Dean. It's a picture of the stethoscope he drew with several background choices. Blue, green, purple, yellow, orange, and hot pink, which I'm sure he threw in there for my benefit. I scroll through them again, unable to decide which color I like best.

It's funny he reached out to me today. I got a great idea while working out and planned to call him Monday. It is a holiday weekend after all. But he's clearly working if he sent me the drawing. It's okay to call him, right?

I mull it over in the shower and decide to give him a ring. If he doesn't want to talk shop, he doesn't have to answer the phone. I throw on a pair of black leggings and a long sweater, my nerve waning. Maybe I'll wait until Monday...

Stop being a wuss, I chastise myself. You're calling him about the app, nothing more.

My heart beats in my ears as the phone rings. What the hell is wrong with me? Get it together girl!

He answers on the third ring. "Abby, hey! Did you get my text?"

"I did. I kinda like all of them."

"Really? The pink one doesn't stand out amongst the others?"

I giggle. "Why can't people pick the color they want? Why do we decide what shows up on their cellphone?"

"Wow…I've never thought of that before. You're absolutely right. It should match their individual color schemes. Hold on a second, I gotta write that down."

"Look at me, revolutionizing cellphone apps."

Dean laughs. "This is why I like an outsider's perspective. Your designer's eye considers aesthetics while my mind focuses solely on function."

"We make a good team." As soon as I say it, my face warms.

"Yes, we do. We should collaborate more often."

"I'm not sure how many more app ideas I have in me." I continue talking before he can respond. "There is one other thing I want to run by you."

"I'm all ears."

"My sister-in-law was telling me last night about her experience with celiac disease."

"Celiac can be rough."

"For sure, but her story is uplifting. She is doing wonderfully, and she mentioned something about wishing she had a place to turn to early on where she could hear stories of people with the disease and how they dealt with it."

"Okay."

"Can we add a feature allowing people to share their stories? It may help others see the light at the end of the diagnosis tunnel."

132

"I like it," he says after a moment's pause. "I like it a lot."

"You ready for the name?"

"Of course."

I smile. "Sick and Inspired."

"Ohhh, I see what you did there. I dig it."

"I thought you would."

"I'll forward this on to the team, have them add it in."

"Thank you."

"No, thank you."

I'm not ready for the conversation to end. "What are you doing working today?"

"I could ask you the same question."

"I'm not at the office. I'm at home."

"Same."

"Oh." My tone softens. "I didn't mean to bother you at home."

"You're not bothering me at all. No Black Friday shopping for you?"

"Nope. I slept in, then went to the gym."

"Nice." He pauses. "This is probably the dorkiest question ever, but I'm seeing the new *Star Wars* movie today. Do you want to go with me?"

And my heart is pounding again. Is he asking me out on a date?

"It's okay if you don't want to," he quickly adds. "I know *Star Wars* isn't for everyone."

"I'd love to go."

"You would?" He sounds genuinely surprised.

"Yes. I love *Star Wars*."

"You do?" he asks, even more shocked.

"Yes. I want to see the new movie, and I don't have any plans. Let's do it. What time?"

"There's a showing at 1:30 p.m. and another at 2:15 p.m. Either of those work for you?"

I check my watch. It's only 11:30 a.m. "I can do either one. Which theater do you go to?"

"I like the theater in Dublin. The one off Sawmill and Bethel."

I smile. "That's where I usually go too. Cheap tickets and reclining seats."

"Exactly."

"I'll meet you there about 1:15 p.m. Sound good?"

"You sure? I can come get you."

"Is it out of the way for you?"

He laughs. "I don't know. I don't know where you live."

"You didn't find my address during one of your stalking sessions?" I tease. "Here, hold on a second." I text him my address. "Am I on your way to the theater?"

"No, but I'm still coming to pick you up."

"You don't have to do that."

"Yes, I insist. Chivalry is not dead you know."

"Are you sure? I can…" I'm cut off by a loud chime.

"Was that your doorbell?" Dean asks.

"Yes." I walk over to my bedroom window and look down at my driveway. "That's weird, Elle's car is here. She's supposed to be in Tucson with Jackson. Hold on one second."

I trot down my stairs and swing my front door open. "Elle, what are you…"

She charges past me. Furious and stomping. Oscar dashes back up the stairs. He wants nothing to do with this.

"That asshole was with another woman!" she declares while throwing her scarf and hat on the back of my couch.

Her eyes are bloodshot. Her hair is pulled back in a sloppy bun, stray strands hanging loose. Her wool coat looks like she slept in it, wrinkled in awkward places.

"Who are you talking to?" she asks, pointing to my phone.

"Oh, uh…" I put the phone back to my ear. "Dean, I gotta go."

"So I hear. I hope everything is okay. Raincheck on the movie?"

I'd love to go to the movie, but there's no way I can bail on Elle. "Yeah, I'm so sorry."

"No, no, no. Go take care of Elle."

"Thank you. I'll catch up with you later."

"Sure."

I end our call and put my phone on silent. Elle is pacing across the pale blue rug in front of my couch. Her coat is unbuttoned and swirling around her. She's in a dress, which is very unlike her, paired with her favorite tan Uggs. My best guess is she dressed up for Jackson, then ditched the heels when she made her escape.

"Do you want a drink?" I ask her.

"No."

"Are you sure?"

She stops pacing. "Whatcha got?"

Assuming she doesn't want tea, I offer bourbon.

"Hook me up with that. And a granola bar if you have one."

"Take off your coat," I call out as I walk toward my kitchen. "Sit down and catch your breath."

I find the bottle of bourbon my dad gave me as a housewarming gift in the back of my pantry. Now seems like the appropriate time to open it.

I'm dumbfounded. Jackson? A cheater? He doesn't seem the type. And Elle is fantastic. Yes, she's my best friend and I'm biased, but she's gorgeous. She's in great shape, makes good money, is hilarious, and has a kind heart. Why would he cheat?

I fill two tumblers with ice, put a shot of alcohol in each glass, and stir in Coke. I take a sip of one and recoil. It's way too early for booze.

Elle is laid out on my couch when I get back with our drinks and granola bars. I hand her the glass and she leans up long enough to take a swig, then flops back down. I set her drink on the side table and take a seat in my recliner.

"Okay, tell me."

She looks up at the ceiling. "I already did. He was with another woman."

"Details, please."

"She was pretty."

"So are you."

"She was shorter than me. Probably fifteen pounds heavier. A blonde. Trashy eyeliner. Bright red lipstick. It was smeared on his shirt."

I wince. "I'm sorry." I take another drink and crinkle my nose. "What happened? How did you find them?"

"I rented a car at the airport and drove to his hotel. He told me his room number yesterday - 919. He thought it was funny because that's my birthday."

September nineteenth, exactly two months after mine.

"I didn't have a room key. The hotel wouldn't give me one. I think they were expecting room service, because when I knocked, she pulled the door open and said, 'About time!' all snotty."

"Sounds like a peach."

Elle glances over at me. "You should have seen the look on Jackson's face."

"I bet."

"He turned pale. Both of us too stunned to say anything. We just stood there staring at each other."

"Did the woman say anything?"

"She asked who I am. I told her 'I'm the woman he lives with.'" Elle sits up, fury creeping onto her face again. "And do you know what she said?"

I shake my head. "What did she say?"

136

"She said, 'Elle? You're Elle?'"

My jaw drops. "She knew about you?"

Elle takes another sip of her drink. "Yep. Knew about me the whole time."

"Wow…"

"Bitch," she mutters.

"What did Jackson say?"

"He's leaving me for her."

"No way!"

"Yep. They met in Dallas during one of the conventions. Had an instant connection, blah, blah, blah. She's been to every one of his events since then." Elle shakes her head. "It's been going on for months."

"What does she do for a living? How can she afford to follow him around?"

"She quit her job as a bank manager."

"Quit her job?"

"Yep. She's going to travel with him during his book tour, then they're going to settle down in Dallas."

I put up my hand. "Whoa. Dallas? What about his job here with Dean?"

"He's putting in his notice. He doesn't plan to ever come back to Columbus."

"What about his stuff?"

"He asked if I'd send it. Sure I will. Straight to Goodwill."

I snort. "He had the balls to ask you to send his stuff? Good luck with that."

We sit quietly for a few minutes, sipping our drinks. I'm not sure what to say. Jackson and Elle have been together for so long, I assumed marriage was in their near future. To hear how quickly he moved on with this other woman is shocking, to say the least.

"Will you help me throw out his stuff?" Elle whispers, less fury in her voice.

"Of course. I can handle it. Make an appointment at a spa, pamper yourself. When you come home, it will be gone."

She shakes her head. "No, I need to do it. I can't pretend it's not happening."

"True, but you don't need to suffer through it either."

She's quiet for a moment. "Yeah, maybe you're right."

"Do you want to stay here for a while?"

"I have to go home. I only packed this dress and lingerie. I can't show up on the jobsite in a teddy."

"Well, you could." I smirk. "The contractors would really like it."

She grins, but then her smile falls. Tears form in her eyes. "What am I going to do Abby?" For the first time since she walked in the door, sadness takes over. She sits up and starts sobbing in her hands.

I jump up and sit beside her, pulling her into a tight hug. "You're going to be just fine Elle. It's better to find out now before you married the guy. Or worse, had kids with him."

"I know," she snivels. "But it still hurts. Bad. I gave him so much of myself. And for what? For what? To be treated like crap."

I squeeze her. "It sucks. He sucks."

"It's all because of that stupid book. He thinks he's so important now. Do you know how many times I did the chores around the house, or cooked for him, or ran errands so he could write? And this is how he repays me? By running off with some cheap slut?" The sobs kick in again. Her body shaking as she lets it all out.

I don't say soothing words because they won't work. All I can do is sit beside her and comfort her while she's raw and wounded. When she's all cried out, she lays down on the couch and closes her eyes.

"Have you gotten any sleep?" I ask.

"No. I was too angry."

138

"I have a really comfy bed in my guest room with your name on it."

"Is it okay if I lay here for a little while?"

"Of course. I'll grab a blanket." I run upstairs and pull the comforter off my guest room bed. By the time I cover her with it, Elle is asleep.

I take our glasses into the kitchen and rinse them out. I'm not sure what to do with myself. I'm not tired enough to take a nap too, and I don't want to do anything that's noisy. Elle needs all the rest she can get.

I decide to finish unpacking the boxes in my bedroom closet and bathroom. I make a throw-away pile of makeup that is more than six months old. I have a terrible habit of opening a product, using it for three days, then getting distracted by a shiny new product I want to try. Ulta gets way too much of my money.

Next up, I go through my closet for anything I will never wear again. This is easier said than done. What if a month from now I need that emerald green cardigan I haven't worn in two years? Or those boots with a cracked heel that are really cute otherwise? I fill a trash bag with summer dresses and tops I didn't wear at least once last summer. No point in keeping them if they never saw the light of day.

I move on to the guest room closet, filled with old sheets, towels, and blankets. Linens are another of my obsessions. I love crisp bedsheets fresh from the dryer. It's also a quick way to refresh my bedroom. As often as I buy new linens, I am hesitant to let go of my old ones. What if I don't do laundry and something spills on my sheets? I need the extras. I talk myself into getting rid of three sets, but keep four. Just in case.

My stomach rumbles. A granola bar was not enough. I tiptoe downstairs and peek into the living room. Elle is still fast asleep. I slink into the kitchen and peer into my pantry. Slim pickings. I'll order food once Elle wakes up. I pour myself a bowl of Lucky Charms and take it back to my room. I turn on the TV with the volume at the lowest level I can hear it over the crunch of my cereal. Oscar joins me on the bed and snuggles in close. His gentle purrs vibrating softly against my leg.

After my long workout, the Elle drama, and my cleaning spree, I feel a nap coming on. I turn off the TV and crawl under the covers. I drift off to sleep within minutes.

I'm dreaming about choosing lip gloss in an endless aisle of lipsticks similar to the golden bricks of Oz when a loud noise wakes me.

Was that my doorbell, again?

I throw back my blanket and sit up. It takes a second for my head to stop spinning from the quick motion. Once I've got my bearings, I make a beeline for the front door hoping to get to it before the bell rings again. I don't want to wake Elle.

Too late. Elle is standing at the front door taking food bags from a delivery guy when I make it downstairs.

"Hold on a sec, let me grab my wallet," she tells him.

The delivery guy smiles. "No need. He put an awesome tip on his credit card already."

"Oh, okay," she says confused.

Elle shuts the door, then turns to me. "Did you order food?"

I shake my head, as stupefied as she is. "No. Is there a name on it anywhere?"

Elle scans the receipt stapled to one of the bags, then smiles. "Dean Porter."

"Dean?" I take the bag from her.

Sure enough, Dean's name is listed as the customer. "How did he…" I stop short. I just gave him my address for the movie. "Wow. That was so nice of him."

Elle walks past me toward the kitchen. "Must be all those winks you send him."

We open the three bags of food to find an array of choices from the Chinese restaurant up the street, including chicken and broccoli and wonton noodle soup. He remembered what I ordered the night of the think tank.

140

"This guy is really into you Abby." Elle takes out container after container of food. "He sent enough food for an army. Look at all of this."

"He's just being nice. He heard how upset you were."

"He did? How?"

"I was talking to him when you got here."

"You were? About what?"

I blush. "Going to see a movie."

"I knew it! He's into you."

"We were going to see the new *Star Wars* movie. It's not like we were going to see a romance or anything."

Elle rolls her eyes. "Whatever. Deny it all you want. I'm starving."

While Elle scavenges through my kitchen for silverware and napkins, I find my cellphone. I have a missed call from my mom, which I have no intention of returning, and a calendar reminder about a delivery to Pam's condo on Monday.

I type out a quick message to Dean.

> *Thank you so much for the food. It was an amazing surprise. You're a lifesaver!*

While I have my phone, I check my email in case the contractor at Pam's has any questions or issues. I'm happy to find I have no correspondence from him. The less I hear from him, the better. I don't want any bumps in the road.

Dean must have had his phone handy because he sends me a response before I set my phone down.

> *I figured you could use some sustenance. Make sure you have at least one Chinese doughnut. They're delicious.*

I giggle.

> *Will do. No way I'm passing up a doughnut! Sorry I had to cancel our plans.*

He makes me laugh again with his response.

141

Friends are more important than the fate of the galaxy.

Another message comes through before I can respond.

For real, I hope everything is okay. You may already know this, but Jackson just emailed me his notice of resignation. Stunned.

I sigh. Jackson already put his new future in motion. Quitting his job seals the deal. Not that I would encourage Elle to get back with him, but I just can't believe Jackson's upending his entire life like this.

So am I. Unreal. Can't believe he emailed you his resignation. Douche.

His response is quick.

LOL Email is the preferred method of communication for us IT guys. I am sorry for Elle though. How is she?

I glance into the kitchen and see my best friend sitting on a bar stool at the kitchen island. A fork in her hand, but no food on it. She's staring at the food, lost in thought.

Not good. This one will hurt for a while.

Do I tell her Jackson quit? Or should I wait to tell her? I'm terrible at keeping secrets.

Let me know if you need anything.

I smile at Dean's message. He is so nice. I ask him if I should tell Elle that Jackson quit.

Is she a rip the Band-Aid person, or a little bit at a time person?

I consider his question. Elle is definitely a rip the Band-Aid person. Plus, she'll be upset if she finds out I knew and didn't tell her.

Alright, I'm going to break the news. Thanks again for dinner. It was so thoughtful of you. I'm buying next time.

Instead of pondering whether sending an open-ended dinner invitation was a good idea, I head back to the kitchen to dig into some food.

"How is it?" I ask Elle.

She shrugs. "Don't know yet."

"You haven't eaten any?"

"Food sounds good in theory, but the thought of eating makes me want to throw up."

I frown. I've never seen Elle like this. "Elle, you have to eat something. Even if it's just a few bites."

"I know, I know." She swirls lo mein noodles onto her fork. "How do people stress eat? I can hardly stomach the smell of food right now."

"I'm the same way. I'll lose five pounds from stress faster than dieting."

I survey the options and land on sweet and sour chicken. I spear a piece of chicken with my fork and dip it into the yummy sauce. "Did you get a good nap?"

She nods. "I did. How about you?"

"Definitely. I cleaned my bathroom and closet too."

"Look at you, all ambitious and such."

"Only took me two months to do it." I pause before saying, "I just spoke with Dean. Well, texted him."

"Did you tell him 'thank you' for me?"

"Yes. He told me we have to try the doughnuts."

"Okay."

"He told me something else. Something about Jackson."

She peers over at me. "What did he say?"

"Jackson quit."

"Already?" she asks, eyes wide.

I nod. "Yep. Sent him an email."

"Holy shit." Elle sets her fork down. "This is real."

143

"It appears so." I wait for her reaction.

She shakes her head. "I'm such an idiot."

"No you're not!"

"I knew it Abby. I knew it. I knew he was cheating. My gut told me all along, and I ignored it. Hoping it wasn't true. Maybe I got on that plane to catch him, not because I wanted to see him. But because I knew, deep down, something wasn't right."

I let her stew in silence for a moment. I'm never sure how to act in these situations. Do I continue the conversation? Or remain quiet?

"Men are jerks," I say finally.

She sighs. "You got that right."

"I wonder how long he would have played this out if you hadn't caught him."

"I asked him the same thing, why didn't he tell me sooner? He said he didn't want to ruin my Christmas."

I snort. "Are you serious?"

"Yep."

"At least you won't have to buy him Christmas gifts this year," I try to joke.

She smiles. "True. He is a pain in the ass to shop for."

We fall silent again. I switch from the sweet and sour chicken to the egg foo yung. Might as well taste a little bit of everything.

"I can safely say this was the worst Thanksgiving ever," Elle observes.

I groan. "Agreed."

"Why? I mean, besides this? Did something happen?"

"My dad was great. My mom was awful." I tell her about my blowup with Mom.

"Your mom is such a bitch."

"She is, isn't she?"

"I don't get it. You bend over backwards for her and she treats you like crap."

"I know, and I'm not sure how to handle it. She called me today. She probably wants to act like nothing happened, like we always do. But at what point do you cut off a toxic person?" I stand and clean our dinner mess. "I shouldn't be talking about this, not with everything you're dealing with."

"No," Elle insists, "I want to talk about anything but Jackson. Even your awful mother."

"You know what's crazy?" I put our dishes in the dishwasher and dry my hands on the hand towel hanging on my oven handle. "I have more in common with Samantha than I do with her."

"Samantha treats you better too."

"She does. She treats me like I'm her own daughter."

"That's the type of person you need more of in your life. Not someone who insists on bringing you down all the time."

I sigh. "She's my mom though, Elle. I can't ignore her forever."

"Sure you can. Don't take her calls or go see her."

"What if she shows up again like she did at the doctor's office?"

"Don't be your usual nice self. Tell her to go away."

I doubt Mom will let me off the hook that easy, but I'm done talking about her. "We'll see. Anyways, are you staying here tonight?"

"I can't. I don't have clothes."

"You can borrow mine for the night, or I can drive over to your place and get you a change of clothes. I can also grab enough outfits for you to wear until I have Jackson's stuff out."

"I don't know Abby. Getting rid of his stuff may take a while and your schedule is full."

"I can do it tomorrow if you want," I offer.

She brightens. "For real?"

"Sure. I have this weekend blocked off from work, so I'm free."

Elle sits quietly, pondering what she wants to do. "If you don't mind, I'll stay here tonight. We'll figure out what to do beyond that tomorrow morning."

"Sounds good." I open a white paper bag and pull out a sugar coated doughnut. It looks delicious. I take a huge bite and savor the sweetness. "I'll tell you one thing about Dean, the man knows his doughnuts."

Chapter Nine

The next two weeks fly by in a blur. I managed to get all of Jackson's stuff out of Elle's place the weekend after Thanksgiving. I paid extra to have two college-age boys come and haul it out.

"What do you want us to do with it?" the freckle-faced redhead asked.

"I don't care."

"Is it okay if I keep these shoes?" the other boy asked, holding up a pair of basketball sneakers.

I cringed at the thought of wearing used shoes, but I told him to go for it. He acted like I'd given him a hundred dollar bill. For all I know, I gave away a collector's edition basketball shoe, but I don't care. The deed was done.

Progress is steady at Pam's condo. I check in every day and do some of the handiwork myself. I'm pretty good at setting tile and trim painting. We're on schedule and everything is going as well as I could have hoped for.

I'm also stopping by the restaurant to make sure the finishing touches are perfect. Elle is an empty shell of herself. She's going through the motions, and doing the best she can, but I find myself picking up her slack.

Jackson called her once to smooth things over. His guilt wanting her to accept his apology. She told him to fuck off and never call again. He hasn't.

Several new clients contacted us for projects. Despite telling them we're booked until spring, they are scheduling consultations. Don't get me wrong, I'll never turn down a new job and I love the increase we're seeing. But it's happening at a terrible time. Elle is a space cadet and I'm overwhelmed.

On top of that, Mrs. Warner called me this morning to ask a favor. "If you have the availability, can you stop by my house and give me your opinion on my Christmas décor? I switched things up a bit this year and I'm not one hundred percent confident in the way it looks."

It's already December 10th and her party is on the 23rd, less than two weeks away.

"Do you have the decorations up already?"

"I do, but I'm not loving it. I'd like your thoughts and suggestions."

I don't really have the time, but I can't turn down Mrs. Warner. Not after everything she's done for me. "I'll stop by tomorrow night. Does that work?"

"Yes! Oh thank you Abby! I'm so excited. Stop by anytime, I'll be home."

I sigh when we hang up. Add that to my growing and seemingly endless to-do list. I console myself by remembering this is for Mrs. Warner. Not a pain in the ass client I don't like. Plus, it's Christmas decorations, how bad can it be?

I put Mrs. Warner on the backburner and focus on the task at hand – shopping for artwork. Pam sent me pictures of artwork she likes and wants me to find similar pieces created by local Ohio artists. Thankfully, I know just the person to see.

"Juliana! The gallery looks wonderful!" I beam when I walk into my former college roommate's gallery.

Juliana was an art major who ignored everyone's jokes about her future unemployment. She parlayed her love for art into a business venture with local artists. She is now one of the premier local art dealers in Columbus. I've come to her gallery in the Arena District several times over the years when I had clients with room in the budget for original artwork.

She jumps up from her desk. "Abby! What a nice surprise!"

Juliana looks wonderful. Her silky brown hair is styled perfectly on its side part, her brown eyes dazzling under the gallery lights. She is wearing a form fitting white dress with thin

148

black piping along the seams. She's my stylish friend, the girl I went to in college when I needed help with makeup.

Juliana gives me a big hug. "It's so good to see you."

"You too!"

"What brings you into the gallery?"

"I'm looking for artwork for a client who is moving here from L.A. She found pieces she likes out there, but she prefers to have work done by local artists. I figure you're the best person to ask for suggestions."

"Of course! What does she have in mind?"

I show Juliana the pictures Pam sent me and she takes a moment to analyze each one. She's looking at a beautiful watercolor peacock when she glances up at me.

"You got a message." She hands me my phone. "I tried not to read it, I swear."

I laugh. "No worries. I'm not dealing in foreign trade secrets, so I'm sure it's nothing worth reading."

I smile when I see it's a text from Dean. He and I catch up every now and then. He hasn't asked me out again since the infamous Black Friday incident with Elle, which is a little disappointing, but we've both been busy with work obligations.

> *Hey! The team has mockups of the app done. Can you meet tomorrow to go over them with me?*

I turn to Juliana. "Sorry, I need to respond real quick."

She waves me off. "Take your time. I have some ideas. Come find me in my office when you're done."

> *Tomorrow is fine. I have an appointment in the morning, but I can be there by 2, at the latest. If it runs late, I'll let you know.*

Tomorrow morning will be insanity for me – two consultations and a stop at Pam's condo, but I don't want to miss a meeting with Dean. The way our schedules have been, it could be after the new year before we both have time to work on the app.

> *I'm here all day tomorrow. Come when you can.*

I put my cellphone in my purse, a smile on my face. Dean's messages have the tendency to do that.

***

"My concern about stainless steel appliances is all the fingerprints. We have a five-year-old and a toddler. They'll look awful."

I glance at the clock. It's already noon and I still have to swing by Pam's before I can head toward Dean. Of course my 10:30 a.m. appointment is an OCD soccer mom with a million and one questions. I'm being totally unfair, she's great. It's just that I'm in a hurry and want to get out of here.

"They have stainless steel appliances now that won't show smudges and fingerprints. They're amazing. You get the look without the upkeep."

My new client's eyes widen. "Really?"

"Yep. I've used them several times and my clients love them. The only concern with the newer models is the ice makers. They can't seem to figure that out. My recommendation is to pay a little extra upfront for the extended warranty. It will be worth it down the road if there's an issue."

After I've successfully convinced her to go with the new smudge-less option, I jump in my car and head to Pam's. Surprisingly, things are ahead of schedule. The contractor is working overtime to get this one done. I've kept a close eye on the quality of the work given how quickly it's being done, but it looks amazing.

"When is your carpenter coming to put together your fancy built-in?" Derrick, my contractor asks.

"Next Tuesday."

"How long will it take?"

"It will only take a day to install. He does the bulk of the work at his shop. All he has to do when he gets here is put it together."

"Good. We'll paint it and start the flooring when he's done."

We walk through the condo and I mentally check things off the to-do list. I frown when we walk in the guest bathroom. One of the most important items is still missing. "When is the handicapped accessible tub coming?"

Derrick frowns. "My guy told me it would be here yesterday, and as you can see, it's not. I called him this morning and left a message."

"Should I order from someone else?"

"Nah. He'll get it to me."

"Okay, but let me know if it's going to be an issue sooner rather than later. It's very important to her."

"Are we doing subfloor heating in this bathroom? I have it on the worklist for the master, but not in here."

"Yes. Sorry about that. She wants it in here as well." Crap. How did I miss that?

I leave Pam's with mixed emotions. I'm thrilled at the progress, but I'm nervous I've forgotten something else important in the work orders. I am meticulous with my instructions and missing the heated flooring in the guest bath irks me. I'll go through everything later to make sure all bases are covered.

The drive to Dean's office is a peaceful one. I put on relaxing music and let go of the stress from this morning. I'm in constant motion, but I want to slow my roll before I see Dean.

Seth greets me with a smile when I walk in. "Go on back, he's not on the phone."

The hustle and bustle of the programmers is in full swing. Two of the conference rooms are occupied, a heated discussion being had in one. I smile when one of the guys dramatically falls backwards onto a beanbag chair. Everyone in the room laughs, his pratfall a break in the tension.

I knock softly on Dean's closed door.

"Come in!"

I slide the door open and poke my head inside. "Is now a good time?"

He smiles. "For you, it's always a good time."

"Uh huh. I bet you say that to all the girls." I push the door the rest of the way open. "Are we meeting with the group today?"

"Nope, just us." He steps out from behind his desk and walks over to a table pushed against the wall. He turns on the overhead light and lays out six sheets of paper. "This is where I look at game stills. I like laying them out in a sequence."

Something about him seems different today. He's more laid back, and not just his outfit. He looks good in his black basketball pants, blue sweatshirt, and white Air Jordans. His demeanor is more relaxed than the first time we met.

I stand beside him and examine the sheets he laid out.

"This," he says pointing to the sheet furthest to our left, "is the main screen of the app."

I give it a onceover. The stethoscope Dean drew floats in the middle of a pink background, surrounded by the names of the different tabs. I like the font they used for the functions. I can read "Lovesick" and "Which Doctor" plain as day.

"I thought you were worried about pink," I tease.

"This is one of the color options. When a user downloads the app, they pick the color setting they want to use." He slides his finger to the bottom of the page. "These are the other color choices."

I smile. He followed my advice about letting users pick the color they want. "Gotcha."

He shifts his attention to the next sheet. "This is the screen a user sees when they select Lovesick. When they open it for the first time, they'll be asked basic questions. After that, the screen will look aesthetically the same, but show their matches."

"Wait a second," I ask confused, "what are we asking them?"

"The typical dating app questions. Name, age, sexual preference, hobbies, what they're looking for in a partner, and the ability to upload a picture."

Oh yeah. Duh. "Do we ask them to disclose their illness or disability upfront?"

152

He shakes his head. "No."

"Okay, good."

"If it's information they want to disclose in their bio, fine. But we don't outright ask."

"I wasn't even thinking about what to ask people when they sign up for the dating function. You are so much more on top of this than me."

"I would love to take credit for it, but it was my team who put this together. To be honest, I've never used a dating app."

"You haven't?"

"Nope."

"You probably don't need to," I say before turning my attention to the next sheet.

"Why do you say that?"

I glance up at him. "You're cute, you're funny, and you're loaded. I'd say you're a chick magnet."

He laughs. "I wish."

"You don't date?"

"I try to."

"You try to? What does that mean?"

He examines the next sheet with me. "I work a lot. I don't get out much. And when I do go out, people have preconceived notions about me." He meets my eyes, then looks down at the table. "I hate to disappoint them."

My mouth drops open. "Disappoint them? Are you crazy?"

"They expect some millionaire playboy, and I'm just a dork who would rather be home playing video games."

"Hey," I place my hand on top of his, "you are a great guy. To hell with expectations. You don't want those kinds of friends anyway."

He meets my eyes again. "Thank you."

153

"You're welcome," I say softly, a warming sensation filling my chest. After staring back at him a moment, I stand tall. "Okay, back to business."

We go through the remaining pages and discuss a few more items. Overall, it looks fantastic.

"I have an odd question," he says when we're done.

"Okay."

"Does this skew too young?"

I tilt my head to the side. "How so?"

"I was reading in *AARP Magazine*..."

"Whoa, whoa, whoa," I stop him. "You read *AARP Magazine*?"

"Yes. It's a great publication."

"Why do you read *AARP Magazine*? Unless you're a lot older than you look, you're not their target audience."

He shrugs. "I will be some day. Well, hopefully anyway."

I smirk. "You are an interesting person."

"People are so afraid of aging. Reading that magazine has shown me there is plenty of good life to live after retirement." He pauses. "Where was I going with this?"

I giggle. "I'm not sure."

He rubs his chin, then his eyes light up. "Oh yes, the app. Do you think older people would enjoy an app like this as well?"

"Huh, I've never thought about it."

"The post-retirement population has to deal with an onslaught of health issues – cholesterol, osteoporosis, hearing loss."

I raise an eyebrow. "You're losing points on the 'looking forward to aging' thing."

He smiles. "What I'm trying to say, very poorly, is that maybe we should make a version of the app for older folks. People who aren't millennials, but could benefit from a community like this."

I consider his point. "It's not a bad idea. I definitely don't want to exclude anyone."

"Plus, the older generation may have valuable lessons and experiences to share within the Sick and Inspired portion of the app. Things they've learned along the way."

"Makes sense. Sounds good to me."

He takes his cellphone out and starts typing furiously. "Hold on one second, I just got an idea about producing video games for seniors. It may help to sustain or improve their cognitive function as they age."

I walk over and sit down in a chair by his desk. My feet are aching from being in heels all day. "How do you think of these things? You see a wider view of the world than most people."

"I don't know about that. I'm just a weirdo."

I stare back at him. "You don't even see it, do you?"

"See what?"

"How amazing you are." Did I say that out loud?

He blushes, then plays it off. "I am pretty damn cool, aren't I?"

I giggle. "The coolest." I divert us away from my shameless flirting. "I like the idea. The graphics may need to be a little different to appeal to an older audience, but everything else could stay the same."

Dean gathers the mockups and puts them in a file on his desk. For the first time, I notice his sweatshirt has a Florida Gators mascot on it.

I crinkle my nose. "What are you doing wearing that? I thought you were a Buckeyes fan?"

He glances down, then back up at me. "I haven't done laundry in a while."

I shake my head. "Inexcusable."

"If it bothers you that much..." He pulls the sweatshirt over his head, his t-shirt rising up with it, allowing me to catch a glimpse of his beltline.

Holy Mary mother of God...he has hip flexors. My suspicion that Dean has a killer body is confirmed.

"Better?" he asks, waving his hand in front of his Deadpool shirt.

I put my eyes back in their sockets. "Yes. Much."

"The guys gave me shit today for it too. Last time I wear a Gators shirt in Columbus."

"Probably wise." I cover my mouth as I yawn. "Excuse me."

"I know it's rude to say this, but you look tired." Dean sits in his desk chair.

"I'm exhausted. I'm running around like a maniac covering for Elle."

"How is she?"

"Eh, she's alright. As good as can be expected under the circumstances."

"Jackson's stuff is still in his office. I reached out to see what he wants me to do with it, but he never responded. Does Elle want it?"

I shake my head. "Nope. I donated all of his stuff to a pair of moving guys. Do whatever you want with it."

"Will do."

We talk about the next steps with the app. His team is busy working on the new video game, and probably won't finish the coding for the app until after the new year. Which is fine with me. Tabling the app for a while will give me time to get through the Elle madness and the onslaught of work.

When our app talk is over, I'm not quite ready to leave. I like hanging out with Dean. He makes me feel comfortable and like my world isn't spinning. Something about him relaxes me. We are opposites in a lot of ways, but our core values are the same. Plus, he makes me laugh.

Before I know it, I've kicked off my heels and we're laughing about our favorite scenes from *Goonies*. Don't ask me how we got there because I don't know. Too soon, we're interrupted by the buzzing of Dean's desk phone.

Seth's voice comes over the speakerphone. "Dean? Carl Frame is on line two for you. He wants to discuss the media campaign for the new game. Do you want me to send him to voicemail?"

Dean clears his throat, his boss face on. "Tell Carl I'll call him back in five minutes."

I'm disappointed it's time to go, but put on my heels and stand. "I'll get out of your hair."

"What are you doing tonight? My call won't take long. We can grab dinner if you want," Dean offers.

I check my watch. How the hell is it 5:30 p.m.?!

I sigh, disappointed I have to turn him down. "I'd love to, but I can't. I have to go to a client's house."

"Tonight?"

"Yes. She wants my help with Christmas decorations. I told her I would stop by tonight."

He frowns. "Oh, okay."

"That was before I knew I was meeting with you," I add, wanting to make it clear I didn't purposely give myself an out.

"Duty calls for the both of us then."

I nod. "It appears so."

We both fall silent. I don't want to end on a sour note, but I don't know what to say. I'm so bad at these things.

"So, um," Dean breaks the silence. "I know you're really busy with work right now and life is crazy for me too. But I would like to spend some time with you. Outside the office. Maybe after the holidays I can cash in the raincheck you owe me for a movie."

Poor guy is as awkward as I am. He's so sweet. And hot on top of it.

I smile. "That sounds wonderful."

Dean's phone buzzes again. "He insisted on holding," Seth huffs into the phone. "He's on line five."

Dean shakes his head. "I'm sorry Abby, I have to take this."

157

"I understand." I glance over my shoulder before I go. "Later Gator."

***

"Is it too cliché to wear red to a Christmas party?"

I step out of the fitting room and show Elle my latest look.

"Ohh," she gushes. "I like that one. It fits you perfectly."

I walk down to the three-way mirror and give myself a look. The dress is different from anything I have at home. It's sleeveless with a high neckline, form fitting through the waist, then flows out from the hip. The hemline is kissing the floor at the moment, but it will be the perfect length with a pair of heels.

"I don't own a red dress."

"Then you should get it. Step outside the box."

I turn to Elle. She is slumped in a chair in the corner of the fitting room. "Why aren't you trying on your dresses?"

"I don't feel like it."

"Get up lazy ass." I pull her onto her feet. "Mrs. Warner's party is in two days. We have to get dresses tonight."

"But I don't want to…" she whines, sounding like a five-year-old being forced to eat broccoli.

"You love trying on clothes. Get your butt in there. The black lace dress is calling your name."

She trudges into a fitting room and closes the door. "I don't want to go to this party anyway," she pouts, her muffled voice coming through the louvered door.

"It's the biggest party of the year."

"Exactly! I'm not feeling biggest party of the year-ish right now."

I laugh. "It will be fun. Plus, I spent all that time decorating the damn place. The least you can do is come and see it."

I've spent a few hours every night at Mrs. Warner's. She failed to mention during our call that she decorates her entire house for Christmas. Not only have I set up ten different Christmas

158

trees, I also helped coordinate the outside decorations. It's been fun, for the most part. But I'm drained.

Elle swings her door open. "Will this work?"

The black lace dress I picked out for her while she was too busy moping to shop looks fantastic. It's long sleeve with a beautiful shell lace effect across the shoulders and neckline. It hugs her curves and stops a few inches above the knee.

"You're a knockout in that dress!"

She walks down to the three-way mirror and turns side to side. "It does fit well."

I join her at the mirror. "You look awesome."

She stands tall, seems happy for a second, then slumps again. "My mojo is gone Abby."

I smile at her in the mirror. "It will come back. I promise."

"When?" she asks our reflection.

"You don't even realize it's happening. You wake up one day, and you think – wow, I feel really good."

She walks over to the chair and sits down. "I know Jackson cheating isn't about me, it's about him. But I can't help thinking about it. Did I do something wrong? Could I have done something differently?" She picks at the hem of her dress. "I don't want him back. I don't want the last six months of the relationship back. But I miss what it was when it was good."

"You'll find it again. You'll find it with someone better. Someone who puts you first, and doesn't take you for granted."

"I know. It's just hard being alone. We were together for so long. My place feels empty now."

I nod. "I understand. I promise it gets easier though. You figure out how you want to spend your time. What you want out of life, without the opinions or influence of someone else. Then, hopefully, the right guy comes along and he fits seamlessly into the life you've built for yourself."

"Abby, Abby, Abby. Ever the romantic." She grins, then stands. "I'm getting this one."

159

I narrow my eyes. "Are you getting it because you're too lazy to try on anything else?"

She feigns shock. "Of course not."

"Mm hmm."

Before closing the fitting room door, she turns to me. "Abby, thanks for the pep talk. I really needed it."

***

"Are you sure about the white poinsettias?" Mrs. Warner asks for the hundredth time.

"Oy, again with the poinsettias," June mumbles under her breath.

Mrs. Warner gives June a playful shoulder bump. "I know I'm a pain. I want everything to go perfectly this evening."

A sea of white poinsettias waits to welcome the two hundred guests who will begin arriving any minute. We also draped strands of white poinsettias across the top of every door frame and the bannister. The result is a classy holiday look that home décor magazines would put on their covers.

"Everything looks beautiful Mrs. Warner. The white poinsettias scream holiday, but with a unique flare. Besides, it's too late to change anything."

She smiles. "You're right. What's done, is done. It's time to enjoy the party."

Wait staff shuffle by with trays of appetizers and drinks. They are dressed in red satin shirts with white ties. Some are wearing the complimentary Santa hats Mrs. Warner offered, while others go without.

Mrs. Warner opted for a crisp, white suit with bright red Louboutin pumps. A ruby and diamond Santa hat brooch adorns her lapel. Her nails are painted a festive red and every strand of her hair is in place.

"She always freaks out before a party," June tells me when Mrs. Warner chases after a waiter to make sure he has both vegan and non-vegan options on his tray.

160

"I bet." I smile. "You look fantastic by the way. I love your dress."

June glances down at her navy blue floor-length gown. "Thanks. I buy a new dress for this party every year, and it never sees the light of day again."

I laugh. "I'm sure that will happen with my dress too."

I walk through the house one last time to make sure nothing is askew or out of place. The twinkling lights and decorations make Mrs. Warner's home look like a winter wonderland. Her main living room has a Santa's workshop theme for her grandchildren to use on Christmas day, while the formal sitting room's theme is cozy Christmas. There are plates of Christmas cookies and small dessert bites on almost every flat surface. I'll gain ten pounds tonight if I'm not careful.

Mrs. Warner personally greets each guest as they arrive. I stand by just in case she needs help with anything. She introduces me as people come through, telling everyone that I did all the renovations.

"You should be handing out business cards," she whispers between introductions.

"That's a little tacky, don't you think?"

She shrugs. "Look at my house. Since when have I been afraid of tacky?"

I am pleasantly surprised when Pam Dobbs walks through the front door. She is stunning in a gold floor-length dress and white shawl. A diamond choker adorns her neck and a diamond tennis bracelet shines against her satin white gloves. She is old Hollywood come to life.

"Pam!" Mrs. Warner pulls her in for a hug. "You're gorgeous as always."

"Thank you, Elizabeth. I love the decorations." Pam turns to me. "And you look amazing in that dress."

I smile. "I can say the same for you."

Pam waves off my compliment. "This old thing?"

161

Elle makes her appearance a few minutes later and Mrs. Warner gives her a big hug as well. "I've been telling your business partner here she needs to do a better job of hustling up more work."

"No worries Mrs. Warner, I'm on it."

"That's my girl!"

I'm about to give Elle a tour when the gentleman crossing the threshold catches my eye. He's tall, dressed in a nicely tailored black suit and white dress shirt. He skipped the tie, and chose to leave his top button undone. His black dress shoes look expensive, yet laid back at the same time. His hair is perfectly gelled and combed. He could easily pass for a GQ model.

I pick my jaw up off the ground. "Dean?"

He glances my way and smiles. "Hey Abby! I didn't know you would be here."

"You know Mrs. Warner?"

"Doesn't everyone?"

I laugh. "I suppose so. Makes sense you know her given you both own tech companies."

"Actually, I met her through Children's Hospital. We're on the board together."

"I see." Before I can explain how I know Mrs. Warner, Elle elbows me. "Oh, uh, Dean Porter, this is my best friend and business partner, Elle."

"The infamous Elle." He extends his hand. "Nice to meet you."

"Whatever bad things Jackson said about me, they're probably true," Elle says with a smirk.

"I've heard nothing but good things."

"Yeah, right." She glances at me. "Where would a girl get a drink in this place?"

"The bar is in the dining room."

"Excellent. You guys want anything?"

I shake my head. "No thanks, I'm good."

She turns to Dean. "How about you Dean? Are you ready to imbibe?"

"I'll get something in a few minutes, thanks for the offer though."

"Suit yourselves."

"So how do you know Mrs. Warner?" Dean asks when Elle saunters off.

"Elle and I did the renovations."

"You did?"

"Yes. And I helped her put up the Christmas decorations."

"Is this the client you had to help after you left my office a couple weeks ago?"

"Yes, it was."

He glances around and whistles. "No wonder you had to leave. This must have taken forever."

"I was here every night for the last two weeks. God bless her, Mrs. Warner fed me dinner every night."

"Of course she did. She didn't want you to leave."

I chuckle. "What's funny is I set up ten Christmas trees for her, but none at my own house."

"You don't have a Christmas tree?" he asks surprised.

"Nope."

"Dean!" Mrs. Warner calls out. "You made it!" She comes over and gives him a hug.

He smiles. "I can't miss the social event of the year."

She puts her hand on my shoulder. "Didn't Abby do a fantastic job?"

"I was just telling her that Elizabeth. The house looks amazing."

"Come here, let me show you what this wonderful girl has done."

163

Dean glances over his shoulder and smiles back at me as Mrs. Warner pulls him away for a tour. I give him a small wave and head off to look for my wayward business partner. I find Elle in the living room lounging on a leather sofa listening to the piano player Mrs. Warner hired. He's playing *White Christmas*. Mrs. Warner told me he's a senior at the local arts college. His fingers fly across the keys effortlessly.

I take a seat beside her. "I always wanted to learn how to play the piano."

"Why don't you?"

"I'm a little too old for piano lessons, don't you think?"

"Last I checked you aren't dead yet, so no."

He transitions to a familiar, yet unexpected tune. "Is he really playing George Michael right now?"

"It's actually Wham!" Elle corrects me.

Before I can stop her, Elle jumps up and starts belting out the lyrics to *Last Christmas*. I shush her, but it only eggs her on. She uses her champagne flute as a microphone and sways to the beat. My horror turns to shock when the other guests in the room join her. Next thing I know, we have a full-on sing-along.

I'm laughing when Dean walks up behind me. "How many glasses has she had?"

"Only one."

We watch her move through the crowd, the living room her stage. Everyone captivated by her charm and energy.

"It's so good to see her like this," I whisper to Dean. "She hasn't been herself lately."

He stops my heart when he asks, "Is she ready to date? Or is it too soon?"

I'm blindsided by his question. I can't form words.

I glance over at my friend, smiling and dancing and winning the love of everyone in the room. Including Dean.

"I, uh, don't know," I say finally.

"Let me know when she is. I have a friend who is perfect for her. He went through a bad breakup earlier this year, but he's back on the market."

Relief floods through me. A weight lifts off my chest and I can breathe again.

"You okay?" Dean asks, his brow furrowing.

I smile. "Yes, I'm great. I don't know if Elle wants to date another tech guy. No offense."

He smirks. "None taken. Besides, Tom is my accountant."

"I didn't realize you're a matchmaker," I tease.

"I'm usually not, but she reminds me a lot of him. Tom would be up there singing and dancing with her."

When the song is over, Elle leans on me, winded by her efforts. "I need some water."

"You did great," Dean tells her. "Very impressive."

"If this whole interior design thing didn't work out, I was going to be a lounge singer."

I snicker. "You were?"

She nods. "That or a stripper. Tough call." She walks away without further explanation.

We watch her steal a canape off a waiter's tray. "Yep, she's perfect for Tom."

"He must be..." I stop short when I hear the piano player start singing one of my favorite songs acapella.

I turn toward him, instantly mesmerized. His voice is soft and melodic, hitting all the notes perfectly. I am entranced. It's one of those songs that stops me in my tracks whenever I hear it. I'm not sure why, but it hits the very core of me.

"Beautiful song," Dean whispers in my ear.

I smile up at him. "I love this song."

"What is it?"

"*Hallelujah*. Pentatonix has a popular version they released a few years ago."

Dean scans my face for a moment, then turns his attention back to the piano. He places his hand on my shoulder, his touch warm on my bare skin. I close my eyes and listen to the last verse of the song, peacefulness filling my veins for the first time in a while.

When the song is over, Dean's hand falls from my shoulder. I turn to him. "I'm sorry, I spaced out for a second."

His eyes meet mine, deep and intense. "I haven't had the chance to tell you how beautiful you look tonight."

I blush. "Thank you. You don't clean up so bad yourself."

"Abby, I…"

"Abby!" Mrs. Warner's voice interrupts us. She is heading our way with Pam Dobbs in tow. "Pam was just telling me about the work you're doing in her condo."

I gather my wits, disappointed my moment with Dean was cut short. "Yes, it's a fun project."

"She told me about the disappearing TV bookshelf."

"I hope you don't mind, I snuck in the condo today to check the progress," Pam confesses. "The shelf looks amazing."

I smile. "I'm so glad you like it. You'll like it even more when it's painted."

"I want one," Mrs. Warner says abruptly. "I hardly ever watch television, but I need one for when my grandchildren are here."

Dean rubs his chin. "Sounds like I need one of these handy bookshelves too."

I glance his way and smirk. "Gotta do what the cool kids are doing, huh?"

He smiles. "I'm nothing if not trendy."

Mrs. Warner glances between the two of us. "How do you two know each other?"

"We're working on an app together," I explain.

"An app?" Pam asks. "What kind of app?"

Before I can respond, Dean launches into the details. "Abby came up with a wonderful idea for a dating app for people with long-term illnesses and health issues. We're expanding it to become an informational tool, as well as a social community."

"An informational tool?" Mrs. Warner asks.

"Yes," I chime in. "A place for people to learn more about their illnesses and know it's a reliable source of information. There is so much bad info out there on the internet."

Pam raises an eyebrow. "Sounds interesting. I'll be on the lookout for it. What is it called?"

Dean and I exchange a glance. "We're not sure yet. Dean likes 'Illing It.'"

"Illing It?" Mrs. Warner looks confused. "I don't get it." Then her eyes light up. "Oh…like killing it without the 'k'."

"Yes, exactly," I confirm with a smile.

"It's still a work in progress," Dean continues, "but I anticipate it will be ready in the next month or two."

I turn to Pam. "We're developing a version of the app for seniors too. It will have the ability to read content to people with vision impairments, so your Mom will be able to use it if she wants."

"My mom will love it. She's looking for people with Parkinson's to meet with."

"Well, I think it's a wonderful idea." Mrs. Warner pats Dean's shoulder. "I'm sure your experience as a child and your work with the Children's Hospital was very informative."

"Actually," Dean says, "it was Abby's experience with her diagnosis that was the most informative."

Uh oh. I give Dean a panicked look. I haven't told Mrs. Warner about my diagnosis.

Mrs. Warner stares at me. "Your diagnosis?"

My skin clams up. "I, uh…"

Crap.

"Abby, is everything okay?" Pam asks concerned.

"Yes, I'm fine."

167

"What is Dean talking about Abby?" Mrs. Warner presses. "You told me you're feeling better."

"I am feeling better. I'm fine," I repeat, then glare at Dean.

He shifts his weight and clears his throat. "This is awkward. I'm so sorry Abby."

Mrs. Warner turns to Dean. "What diagnosis?"

I take Mrs. Warner's hand. "I was diagnosed with MS a couple months ago."

"Oh wow, Abby. I'm sorry to hear that," Pam says softly.

Mrs. Warner's eyes tear up. "How awful."

"It's not awful, I'm just fine. I'm great."

"If you'd told me, I wouldn't have made you stay here every night helping me," she says with regret and sympathy.

I sigh. "Which is exactly why I didn't tell you. I don't want you to worry about me. I'm fine."

How many times have I said, "I'm fine"? Three, four, one hundred?

A waiter walks over and whispers something in Mrs. Warner's ear. She squeezes my hand. "I have to go. We'll discuss this later." She walks off toward the kitchen to handle whatever calamity the waiter brought to her attention. Hopefully nothing more than a dropped tray of crab cakes.

I shoot daggers at Dean. He pulls at the collar of his shirt, evading my glare by glancing around the room.

Pam clears her throat. "I see you two have some talking to do. I'll give you privacy."

When Pam steps away, Dean finally meets my eyes. "Abby, I'm so sorry. I didn't mean to..."

I cut him off. "Did you see that? Did you see the way they looked at me? Thanks a lot."

I push past him, but he follows me. "I didn't know you weren't telling anyone."

168

"Why would I tell people?" I weave through the crowd, wanting to get outside for fresh air.

"Why wouldn't you tell people? It's nothing to be ashamed of," he insists as I reach the front door.

I step out into the night, a sigh of relief when the chilly air hits my hot skin. I close my eyes and breathe it in. I am furious with him, trying desperately to control my anger. Warm tears fill my eyes.

I stare out at Mrs. Warner's grand fountain in the middle of her circular driveway, refusing to look at him. A cupid monument is pulling back his bow, about to shoot a love arrow into the back of the unsuspecting woman who sits on the fountain's edge.

I wrap my arms around myself. "I don't want people to see my disease when they look at me."

"You should be proud of yourself. You are the perfect example of a person accomplishing great things despite your health."

I spin on my heels. "I don't want to be an example. I don't want to be the face of MS. I just want to be me. And you took that from me. They will never look at me the same."

"That's not true," he says softly, his eyes pleading for forgiveness.

"Yes it is. They already feel bad for me. They think I can't handle my job."

"No they don't." He extends his hand to touch my shoulder, but I pull away.

"Oh yeah? Then why did they both apologize to me? Why was sympathy in their eyes?"

He looks down at the ground, then back at me. "I'm sorry Abby. I don't know what else to say. It was a mistake. I wish I could take it back, but I can't."

"No, you can't." I hug my arms tighter, a tear sliding down my cheek. "Is that why you're so nice to me? Because you feel bad for me?"

169

Dean's brow furrows. "What do you mean?"

"It is, isn't it?" I press. "You feel bad for me because I have MS."

He clenches his jaw and inhales deeply through his nose. "I think I better go."

I deflate. "I think so too."

"There you are!" Elle calls out from the front door. "I leave to get a drink and you go AWOL on me." She heads down the steps toward us, but stops when she sees the expression on my face. "What's going on?"

"Nothing," Dean responds. "I'm leaving."

"Oh," Elle says surprised. "Already?"

"I have a long day tomorrow."

"On Christmas Eve?"

"Elle, let him go," I whisper.

Dean gives me one last look, anger underlying his usually calm demeanor. "Good night."

He turns and walks down the remaining steps. I head the opposite direction toward the house, not turning to watch him go.

Elle trails behind me. "What the hell was that about?"

"Nothing."

"Sure didn't look like nothing."

I cross the threshold into the house and pull Elle toward the corner of the front entrance. "He outed me to Mrs. Warner and Pam."

"Outed you?" she asks confused. "Are you gay now?"

I roll my eyes. "No. He told them I have MS."

"So?"

"I didn't want them to know."

"You didn't tell Mrs. Warner?"

"No. I didn't want her to know. I don't want anyone to know," I say, my voice cracking.

"Why?"

"Because I..." I sigh. "Never mind."

I spend the rest of the party in a daze. I don't want to be here anymore, but I promised to help Mrs. Warner with the cleanup efforts. Elle mingles and answers questions about the work we did in Mrs. Warner's house. I have a feeling we'll be getting several calls next week.

I should be ecstatic about the potential uptick in our business, but I can't shake the look on Dean's face when I accused him of being nice because of my MS. He was disgusted with me. It wasn't fair of me to say that to him. I'm the classic hothead who instantly regrets the nasty things I say once I cool down.

Pam finds me before she leaves. "I hope everything is okay with Dean. I noticed he left after our conversation."

"He didn't know I was keeping my MS on the DL."

She nods. "I figured as much. Men accuse women of being gossips, but I call them first when I need a break in a story."

I laugh. "So true."

"I want you to know, it doesn't change a thing between us. I'm sorry if my reaction wasn't a good one. I was just so shocked that someone as young and vivacious as you is dealing with something like MS."

"It's okay. I didn't tell you because I don't want people to feel bad for me."

"I don't feel bad for you. I'm proud of you. Keep it up girl." She squeezes my shoulder. "I'll see you after the new year. I'm sure you're ready to spend some of my money at the furniture store."

I laugh again. "Definitely."

I cleared the air with Pam, now it's time to do the same with Mrs. Warner. I find her in the kitchen thanking the wait staff and giving them white envelopes as they leave. One of the waiters peeks inside as he walks by me, beaming when he sees the contents.

171

After the last person is gone, I offer to help Mrs. Warner pack the leftovers.

"That would be wonderful. I have a stack of new Tupperware containers in the pantry."

Mrs. Warner's pantry could stock a small convenience store. I find the Tupperware containers next to a year's worth of paper towels. I wash my hands before transferring the food from the trays to the plastic containers.

"Mrs. Warner, you have enough food to feed an army."

"I hope so. The local shelter will be here in an hour to get it."

"Really?"

She nods. "I always order way more than I need, then they come and pick it up for their Christmas Eve meal tomorrow night."

"That is so incredibly kind of you."

"I am a blessed woman, but I don't forget my roots. I spent a week in a shelter once. The scariest week of my life."

My jaw drops. "You did?"

"Yes. My dad lost his job and we were evicted from our home. He was too proud to tell anyone in our family, so we stayed at the shelter until my grandfather drove by one night and saw us walking in. We stayed with my grandparents until my dad found work. His new job ultimately led to his love for computers, and mine as well."

"I had no idea. That must have been so hard for you."

She nods. "I was only five. I was terrified. My older brother stayed up and made sure no one bothered me. Most of the people in shelters are you and me, just in worse circumstances."

"I forget how lucky I am. If my finances went awry, my parents would help me in a second. I take that for granted."

"But you have your own crosses to bear, don't you?"

I glance over at her. "I'm fine Mrs. Warner."

"I know that. I know you're more than fine. I'm not sure why you didn't tell me about your diagnosis. You promised you'd tell me what the doctors said."

172

I cringe. "I didn't actually promise..."

"No, you didn't say the words, 'I promise', but friends don't keep secrets."

"I'm sorry. I'm still processing it. But you're right, I should have told you."

She nods. "It's okay. I understand."

We get back to work, Mrs. Warner humming a Christmas tune. We have the food packed and ready to go when a young woman from the shelter arrives to pick it up.

"This is amazing!" she exclaims. "There is more than enough here for our holiday meal."

We help her carry the food to the van she drove and Mrs. Warner insists she take ten of the poinsettias with her when she mentions how beautiful they are. I watch her drive away with a smile on my face.

"Will you help me put out the gifts for my grandchildren?" Mrs. Warner asks as we walk inside.

"Of course."

We trek up to one of her guest rooms and I marvel at the stack of gifts on the bed.

"Holy cow! Your grandkids are going to flip."

She laughs. "I can't help myself. It's too fun shopping for them. I think it's more for me than it is for them. The joy I get watching them tear through the paper is addicting."

We set the gifts under her fifteen foot tree in the living room and stand back to admire our work. Mrs. Warner beams. Tonight was about friends and former colleagues. Tomorrow will be about family.

I touch one of the beautiful hand-blown glass ornaments on her tree. The scene is two children dressed in their winter gear and building a snowman together. The inscription on the bottom reads "Columbus Children's Hospital". I immediately think of Dean and wonder if he has the same ornament on his tree given that he and Mrs. Warner are on the board together.

173

I turn to Mrs. Warner. "Can I make another confession?"

"Certainly."

"I think I lost a friend tonight."

"Let me guess – Dean?"

I nod. "Yes. I said something not very nice to him. After he told you and Pam."

"Dean is a great guy. He'll forgive you."

"I'm not so sure." Tears threaten again. Thank God for waterproof mascara or I'd be a mess.

Mrs. Warner puts her hand on my shoulder. "Here's the thing about friends, Abby. Real friends, the ones worth keeping, see you at your absolute worst, but love you anyway."

I smile. "Thanks."

She lets go of my shoulder. "Now get your butt home and get some rest. Some crazy lady has been working you like a dog these last two weeks."

"She was pretty demanding," I joke.

"Here." She tries to hand me an envelope, but I won't take it.

"No, no, no. I helped you as a friend."

"Oh, I know. I'm giving you a Christmas card as a friend. Open it."

I open the envelope and find two tickets to a Blue Jackets game. Except they're not just any tickets, they're tickets to an all-inclusive VIP suite.

"Mrs. Warner, I can't accept these."

"Of course you can. You mentioned that you enjoy hockey and it stuck with me because you seem like more of a lipstick than hockey stick kind of girl."

I laugh and give her a hug. "Thank you."

"Maybe you can bring Dean with you," she suggests when we step apart.

"He's from Florida. What does he know about hockey?"

"Hockey schmockey. I go for the beer and nachos."

I drive home thinking of the best way to reach out to Dean and apologize. Maybe I can use an invite to the hockey game as an olive branch.

I replay the events in my mind. While it's true Dean shouldn't have assumed everyone knows about my MS, I shouldn't have flipped out on him the way I did. I was upset and went too far.

I'm exhausted and need a good night's sleep. I kick off my heels as soon as I get home and flop down on my couch. Oscar jumps on me, wanting attention and pets. I'm so tired, I don't even care that he's getting fur all over my dress. I fall asleep five minutes later to an episode of *Holiday Baking Championship*.

Chapter Ten

I wake up at 7 a.m. with a kink in my neck. I've officially reached the age when I cannot sleep more than a couple hours on the couch. Oscar stretches and yawns as I start to move, then curls into a ball on the armrest of the couch and falls back to sleep.

I trudge up the stairs and slip out of my dress. I consider taking a shower, but I think a workout is in order. I clean last night's makeup off my face, praying I don't break out after committing a huge skincare no-no.

I grab a protein bar and my cellphone before heading out. It's nearly dead from not getting charged last night, but it will get a little juice on my car charger. The radio is playing Christmas music when I get in. I can't help but ruminate on the fact that for the first time in my life I didn't put up a Christmas tree. I was too busy.

The gym is practically empty. Everyone is at home with their families. I don't have to be at Dad's until 1:30 p.m., so I have plenty of time to get a good workout. I put in my earbuds and listen to my gym playlist while I lift.

I go through my usual reps and sets, trying not to think about Dean. I need to clear the air with him. Secret spiller or not, my question about his motives was unfair. I'm worried I not only ruined our business relationship, but much worse, our friendship.

Unfortunately, it's Christmas Eve and I don't want to bug him. Plus, Dean may need more time to cool off. He was pretty pissed last night.

I wish Gemma "Merry Christmas" on the way out, and she reminds me that I'm about to get some new gym buddies.

"The New Year always brings a big crowd," she warns. "For the first few weeks anyway."

177

"When is the best time to come?"

"Mornings are best. Evenings between five and eight are the busiest."

Great. Looks like I'll be getting up even earlier than normal.

On the drive home, I rundown my to-do list before I leave for Dad's. I have to wrap the gifts I bought for baby Rosie. I found her the cutest outfits and a stuffed bunny I just could not put back. I have to make the onion dip, and can't forget to grab the chips. Oh, and I have to…

Wait a second. Who's parked in my driveway?

The SUV is a familiar one. My heart skips a beat when I realize it's Dean.

Oh my God. It's Dean. What is he doing at my house? I try to suppress the excitement building inside me. Maybe he feels as bad about last night as I do.

Dean gives me a tentative smile when I pull in next to him. I shut off my car and take a deep breath. I glance in the rearview mirror to check my makeup, then remember I don't have any on. My sloppy gym bun isn't doing me any favors either.

Good grief. Of course he shows up when I look my absolute worst. I want to slide down my seat, but it's too late to hide.

I steady my nerves and open my car door. When I step out, Dean does the same. We walk toward each other and meet in the middle.

"Hey," I say, trapping a stray strand of hair behind my ear.

"Hey." He puts his hands in the pockets of his black puffer jacket. He's back to wearing his usual attire – jeans and basketball shoes.

"How long have you been waiting here?"

"About half an hour."

"Half an hour?" I ask surprised. The poor guy has been here a while. "I'm so sorry. I was at the gym."

He glances down at my yoga pants, then back at me. "So I see."

I blush. "I wasn't expecting company. I don't usually wear yoga pants in public."

"Me neither."

I smile at his joke, then get serious. "About last night..."

He cuts me off. "That's why I'm here. I feel terrible Abby. I couldn't leave town without apologizing to you."

"Leave town?"

"Yes. I'm going to Florida for the holidays. In fact, I have to leave for the airport soon."

"Oh. Well, I hope you have a good time. I'm jealous you'll be in the sunshine." I look down at my pink gym shoes, then back up at him. "I'm really sorry for what I said last night. On the steps. I was upset, but that's no excuse."

"It's okay. I would have been upset too. I don't talk about my childhood cancer much because I know the look you're talking about. The sad, sympathetic look people give you when they find out you're sick. I don't like that look either."

I nod. "I was more afraid they would think I'm weak, but I talked to Mrs. Warner and Pam last night. They were great about it. You were right – they don't see me any differently. It was all in my head."

"All the same, it's your life. It's your business, and it wasn't mine to share. I got to talking about the app, and you, and it came out. It won't happen again." His warm eyes say it all – he's being genuine.

"I'm not worried about that. I just don't want you to be mad at me." I glance down at the ground again, playing with a stray rock on my driveway with my shoe. "Our friendship means a lot to me."

He takes a step closer. "It means a lot to me too."

I meet his eyes. "I know you're not nice to me just because of my MS. I hit below the belt last night, and I'm sorry."

"Stop apologizing. Please. I understand. Trust me, I understand." He opens his car door, leans in, and takes something out of the passenger seat. "As if my showing up unannounced at your house isn't creepy enough, I got you this." He hands me a box from Cheryl's Cookies.

"What is this? You didn't have to get me anything."

"Just open it."

I giggle when I open the box. It's a large sugar cookie shaped like a Christmas tree. The green icing has silver sprinkles for tinsel, red candy Christmas bulbs, and a yellow candy star at the top.

"It's the best I could do on such short notice," Dean explains. "Everyone should have a Christmas tree."

"I love it!" Before I know what I'm doing, I lean up on my toes and kiss his cheek. His aftershave fills my senses, masculine and tempting. Then it hits me.

Holy crap! I kissed him!

I step back quickly, hoping I didn't commit a huge faux pas.

Dean is the opposite of upset, he's blushing. I'm not sure which one of us is redder.

"I'm glad you like it," Dean says when he's recovered. "I hate to run, but I need to go before I miss my flight."

"Of course!" I step out of his way. "Have fun. And Merry Christmas."

"Merry Christmas Abby." He climbs into his SUV and flashes me a smile before closing the door.

I give him a small wave before turning toward my house. I blink a few times, a goofy grin on my face. My Christmas just got a heck of a lot better.

***

"What do you mean you haven't talked to your mom since Thanksgiving?"

"Uh, just what I said. I haven't talked to Mom since Thanksgiving."

180

My dad frowns. He and Samantha are sitting in the front seats of their Honda SUV. Dad is at the helm driving us to Austin and Kelly's house for our gift exchange.

Samantha turns to look at me. "I had a feeling something went wrong when you came back for pumpkin pie."

I nod. "It wasn't fun."

"Do you want to talk about it?"

I tell her and Dad the pie story. It doesn't take long.

"So you're mad because of cherry pie?" Dad asks.

"No, it's not because of the cherry pie. It's about everything with her. She makes me feel like crap and talks down to me. Then expects me to bend over backwards for her."

"She did come to your doctor's appointment," he points out.

"She did, but I think she does things like that sometimes because she knows it's what a good parent would do. Then she gets to tell everyone she did it. Like, look at me! I'm such a great mom. I sat with my daughter for eight hours at the doctor's office."

Dad sighs. "She's your mom, Abby. You can't cut her off."

"Why?" I shoot back. "You did."

He doesn't have a response to that.

"Listen," I continue, "I know she's my mom and I shouldn't write her off, but at what point do you end a toxic relationship? Yes, she's my mom. But she's not Grandma. She's not supportive, or loving. In fact, she's the opposite. She puts me down, she causes drama, and she isn't nice to me. She pushes and pushes until I reach a breaking point. And then the cycle starts over."

"I understand," Dad relents. "It's just a shame. I was hoping she wouldn't be like that with you."

"I don't have the best relationship with my father," Samantha says as she looks out her window. "I only talk to him on holidays. I'll call him tomorrow, and maybe again on New Year's Day. After that, I won't talk to him again until his birthday in May."

"I'm sorry Samantha. That must be hard."

181

"It is and it isn't. I'm used to it now. I used to hope for something better, but it led to disappointment. I've come to terms with the nature of our relationship, and that's it. I don't try anymore. I can't let him drain my energy."

It's hard for me to imagine Samantha's parents being anything other than incredibly kind like she is. "I may call Mom tomorrow, but I'm not holding out any hope."

"Has she reached out to you?" Dad asks.

"She called me twice, but didn't leave messages."

"Don't do anything out of guilt," Samantha advises. "I played that game too. If you reach out to her, do it for you. Because it's something you need. Not because you feel obligated to call her."

"I can't imagine not having a relationship with my daughter," Dad muses. "It pains me to even think about it."

"That won't happen with us Dad," I assure him. "We get along great. And even when we have an issue, we talk it out like adults. Mom's a different animal."

"She is a unique person," Dad agrees.

I chuckle. "Unique isn't how I would describe it."

The subject drops and we move on to lighter topics. As I watch the scenery along I-71 South pass by, I debate whether I should call Mom. I can't say I've missed her. Which is a sad realization. Then again, I've been so busy. It's possible my workload distracted me from our fight.

Despite our tussle, I bought Mom a gift in case we do end up reconciling. A dainty necklace with a sapphire, her birthstone. Does that mean I subconsciously want to mend fences with her?

I decide to table the issue until later when we pull into Austin and Kelly's driveway. I want to have a fun day with my family. Besides, Mom and I don't usually get together until Christmas Day anyway. I can deal with this tomorrow.

As if she knows my innermost thoughts, Mom calls me half an hour into dinner. I decline the call. I'm not stopping the food train for a chat with her. After eating way more than I need to, and adding a piece of the gluten-free chocolate cake Kelly made on top of it, I step into the guest bedroom to call Mom back.

"Hello?" she answers on the third ring.

"Hey Mom. I saw I missed your call."

"Did you not see the other ten times I called you?"

I sigh. "You called me twice."

"So you did see my calls?"

"Yes."

"Why didn't you call me back?"

"Because I was mad at you."

"Does calling me back now mean you're not mad at me anymore?"

"It's Christmas Eve. I planned on calling you tomorrow. But when I saw your call, I decided to call back."

"I was calling to see if you're going to Aunt Jean's tonight."

"No. I spend Christmas Eve with Dad, and usually see you on Christmas Day. I've never gone to Aunt Jean's."

She huffs. "Of course you're with your father."

"That's my usual Mom. Nothing new here."

"I was hoping you'd drive me to her place. It's snowing and you know I hate driving in snow."

"It's not supposed to get bad until later tonight. You have plenty of time to get to Aunt Jean's and back."

"Why can't you take me?"

I grit my teeth. "I already told you. I'm not going to Aunt Jean's. Besides, I'm not in Columbus."

"Where are you?"

"I'm at Austin's house in Wilmington."

"Austin? Who's Austin?"

Oy. "Samantha's son. My step-brother."

"Can't you leave there and come home? I really need a ride."

"No Mom! I can't."

"Some daughter you are," she tsks.

My blood boils. "See? This is the root of our problem."

"What is?"

"You think because I'm your daughter, I have to take your shit. I don't."

"Well, Merry Christmas to you too."

"Merry Christmas Mom. I'll talk to you on your birthday." I end the call and sit on the edge of the guest room bed. I need a moment to gather myself before I join the group.

I don't know why I thought Mom would be any different because of the holidays. My mom is who she is. She isn't going to miraculously change overnight and become the mom I always wished she was.

It's moments like these that I miss my grandmother the most. She was the mother I needed in my life when I was younger. She's the mother I need in my life now.

There's a soft knock on the door. Samantha pokes her head in. "Everything okay?"

I nod. "Yeah, it's okay."

"Are you sure?" she walks over and sits beside me.

"I called Mom."

"How did it go?"

"As bad as expected."

Samantha gives me a side hug. "You tried. You can be at peace with it now."

I lean my head on her shoulder. "All my friends have great relationships with their moms. They go shopping together, hang out, and give great advice. Why can't my mom be like that?" I choke up a little. "Why doesn't she love me?"

"Oh sweetheart," Samantha squeezes me tighter. "I'm sorry you feel that way. I don't know your mom well, I don't know her heart. I only know what your dad told me about her. It sounds like

184

she comes from a cold-hearted background, and that's how she chose to be too. You're not a cold-hearted person though, and that's why it hurts."

"Is that how your dad is?"

"Yes. I think in his own way he loves me, but doesn't know how to show or express it. He is a taker, and I'm a giver. It was a bad combination for a long time. I tried so hard to get his approval. Then one day I finally realized I could be the best daughter in the world, and it wouldn't be enough."

"That's how I feel too. I'll never make her proud."

"Let me tell you something, okay?"

I look up at her.

"Your father and I are so incredibly proud of you. You are an amazing young woman. Never, ever doubt how much your dad and I love you. You mean the world to us."

My heart warms. "Thank you."

"You're so very welcome." She pats my knee. "I'll give you a few minutes to yourself."

As I watch Samantha slowly close the bedroom door behind her, I finally realize the mother I've always wanted has been with me all along.

***

The nice thing about not putting up a Christmas tree? Not having to take it down when the holiday is over.

I send Dean a picture of the Christmas tree he gave me sans its star.

Sorry, I couldn't help it. I ate it.

This led to an hour long conversation via text. He bragged about all the fun things he's doing in the sun, and I rubbed it in that he missed the first big snow of the season. We talked about our Christmases and the gifts we got. His new drone doesn't seem nearly as exciting as my new purse.

I'm right back to work the day after Christmas. As expected, we have an onslaught of calls from new clients who attended Mrs.

Warner's party. I push the bulk of them off until after the new year, but a few want to meet before then. They'll be the pushy clients. Hopefully they don't want anything too extensive.

I shuffle back and forth between Pam's and the office. Elle is back in the saddle again, so to speak. She's helping with the new client consultations, but I do all of the design layouts. I stay up way later than I should working on design plans. By the 29th, I'm worn to a frazzle.

"How's it going Derrick?" I ask my contractor when I walk out of the elevator and into Pam's condo.

I stop in my tracks. There is a huge crack in the marble tile flooring we installed in the entrance yesterday.

"What is that?"

Derrick grimaces. "One of my guys dropped his toolbox this morning. I'll fix it, I promise."

Annoyance fills me. I don't have time for this. I suppress my anger and move on. "Okay. How is everything else?"

"I have more bad news."

Deep breaths Abby, deep breaths. "Okay…"

"It's about the tub in the guest bathroom."

"What about it?" My patience has grown thin when it comes to the handicapped accessible tub. Derrick promised me over and over it's on the way.

He clears his throat. "It's not coming."

"What do you mean it's not coming?"

"My guy thought he could get me one, but he can't."

I rub my temples. "I asked you repeatedly to tell me if this was going to be an issue. I could have ordered one two weeks ago, but you insisted your guy would come through." The volume of my voice steadily increases. "What am I supposed to do now?"

Derrick slumps. His hands hiding in the stomach pouch of his grey hoodie. "I called another one of my buddies. He can get me one, but it will take a week."

186

"A week?!" Derrick recoils. "We put everything on hold in there waiting for that damn tub."

"I know, I'm sorry."

I walk past him toward the kitchen. I set my purse down on the new island and search for my cellphone. How does it fall to the bottom every time?

My hand shakes as I type my passcode. I try to steady it, but the tremor won't stop. I set my phone down for a moment. I am unsettled by my tremor coming back, but I have to keep moving.

"What else needs to be done?" I ask Derrick.

"Almost everything is done except for the bathroom. I promise you Abby, we will bang it out once the tub comes in."

"You also promised me a tub," I snap at him. I pick up my phone again, but my hand is still shaking. "Shit."

Derrick steps closer to me. "Abby, are you okay?"

I squeeze my eyes shut. "I'm sorry for snapping at you. I've had a rough couple days and I haven't gotten enough sleep. I'm sure you will do all you can to meet the deadlines."

"I will. I swear."

I watch my hand trembling on the countertop. "Everything will be fine."

Am I talking to Derrick, or myself?

***

"Thank you for seeing me on such short notice."

I'm sitting in Dr. Harris's office twenty-four hours later. I somehow got in to see her the day before New Year's Eve.

"My nurse told me you sounded very concerned about the return of your initial symptoms. I wanted to see you as soon as possible. What's going on?"

I tell her about my hand tremors.

She glances through her notes. "The last time I saw you, the tremors were under control. Have you continued taking the medication?"

187

"Yes. Every day."

"No breaks? No accidently forgetting to take a dose?"

"No. I take it every morning with breakfast. I even have an alarm on my phone to remind me."

"Have you changed your diet or environment in any way?"

"Not really. I have a new house, but I was in it before the meds. I'm working out more, but my diet hasn't changed."

"How about stress? Have you been under a lot of stress lately?"

I snort. "Yes. My whole life is stress."

"Would you say you're under more stress now than in the recent past?"

"Yes. My job has been very demanding the last few weeks. Plus, I worked extra hours for a holiday event." I pause then add, "And I'm fighting with my mom."

She frowns. "I'm sorry to hear that. The holidays should be a happy time."

Dr. Harris has me go through the usual routine. I walk a straight line for her and touch my nose. She does the knee reflex test and checks my pupils. She holds my hand for a moment, hoping to feel one of the tremors. Of course I don't have one.

She slides her chair back. "Here's what I think. By your own description, your life has been stressful lately."

I nod.

"Stress can do a lot of things to your body, including triggering your MS symptoms."

"So my tremors are back because of how busy I've been?"

"Kind of. It has more to do with the chemical reaction stress can cause, as well as the anxiety associated with stress. There's a reason doctors tell their patients to stop and relax every now and then. Your body physically needs a break too, not just mentally and emotionally."

"What can I do about it?"

"For the moment, I'll give you a steroid shot and call in a prescription for additional steroid pills. I'll warn you, it's a lot of pills."

"How many?"

"Ten a day."

My jaw drops. "Ten? A day?"

She nods. "Yes, ten. Preferably with a meal."

"For how long?"

"You'll do ten for five days, then I'll ween you off of them."

"Will that stop the tremors?"

"Hopefully. But you also have to rest. I want you to take off for a few days."

"I can't do that," I protest. "We're too busy."

Dr. Harris looks me in the eyes. "Abby, this is your health. Do you want the tremors to stop?"

"Yes, of course."

"Then you need to stop. You need to relax and decompress. Okay?"

I deflate. "Okay."

"Good. I'll have my nurse Nancy come in and give you the shot. The pills should be ready by the time you get to the pharmacy. Call me if there's any issues."

"Thanks Dr. Harris."

She stands and squeezes my shoulder. "You're fine Abby. Don't worry about this. Temporary relapses are common."

My concern slips out. "What if it's not temporary?"

"If I'm wrong, and this is not a temporary relapse, we'll figure something out. There are other options. But let's not put the cart before the horse. I'd bet my house this is temporary."

"Okay," I say softly.

"Have a good New Year's Eve, but don't party too hard," she teases before she leaves.

That won't be a problem. I have zero New Year's Eve plans. Elle invited me to her family's annual party, but I'm not up to it. I'd rather lay on my couch and eat ice cream.

I wince when Nancy gives me the steroid shot a few minutes later. "Will I feel like Wonder Woman?"

She laughs. "Probably not, but you'll feel better." She jots down notes in my chart. "Temporary relapse, huh?"

"Dr. Harris thinks so."

"Dr. Harris knows her stuff. If she says it's temporary, it's temporary."

Nancy's reassurance makes me feel a little better, but it fades when I call Elle.

"Four days? You sure you don't want more time off than that? It sounds like you need at least a week."

Elle's concern makes everything seem worse. She's usually so light and carefree. "I can't take off more time than that. Four days should give me plenty of time to relax and catch up on sleep."

"You sure?"

"Yes."

"If you need more time, just say the word," she insists. "I can cover for you. Lord knows you covered for me after the Jackson incident. Let me repay the favor."

"Four days is plenty."

"Promise you'll tell me if it's not?"

"Yes, I promise."

After convincing Elle I will do nothing but sleep and binge-watch Netflix for four days, I stop by the pharmacy to pick up my medications. I also grab snacks while I'm there. The less I need to go out, the better.

Oscar looks at me like "What are you doing here?" when I get home. I'm usually gone this time of day.

I pet his head. "Get used to it. You're going to see a lot of me the next few days."

I change into leggings and a hooded sweatshirt. I surf the channels for a good show, then kick up my feet and eat the spaghetti bowl I picked up from Piada on the way home. Let the lounging begin.

Chapter Eleven

It's been less than twenty-four hours into my self-imposed relaxation and I'm bored. Laying on the couch for four days sounds fun in theory, but I'm not loving it.

I got up this morning and made what I consider a gourmet breakfast – bacon, eggs, toast, and coffee. It's usually a bag of mini muffins or a protein bar. After cleaning my mess, I moved on to the boxes in what should be my formal dining room.

I open the first box and immediately shut it when I see the stack of photos on top. Pictures of my childhood that once brought a smile to my face will only make me sad today. I don't need to see the fake happiness on my dad's face, or the frilly dresses my mom made me wear to events better suited for my pink overalls.

To the basement it goes, along with three other boxes filled with mementos from high school and college. My basement is a little creepy, cinderblock walls and concrete flooring, but it is clean. I came down here with a broom and vacuum the first day I moved in to get rid of the spider webs.

I admire the new empty spot in my dining room. I'm making progress! I'm about to dig into another box when a tremor shoots through my hand. Is this the universe telling me to sit my butt down?

Pouting, I plop down on the couch and check my cellphone. I smile when I see a text from Dean.

Any big plans tonight?

Nope. Going to relax at home.

Isn't Elle throwing a big party?

Crap, I did tell him about that.

She is, but I'm not going. Not feeling well.

193

I'm sorry to hear that ☹ What's wrong?

Should I tell him the truth? Or play it off? I don't want to talk about it, but I don't want to lie either.

> *My neurologist recommended that I take it easy for a few days because some of my symptoms returned. No biggie.*

I wait for a response, but I don't get one. I sigh and put my phone down. New Year's Eve and I'm spending it alone on my couch. Even worse, time is crawling. It's only noon. How is that possible? I'm never going to make it.

I check my phone one more time before heading upstairs to take a shower. No response from Dean. Oh well. He likely got distracted by his family.

But when a few hours pass and still no response, I start to worry. Did I scare him off? Surely not, right?

Then why did he disappear on me? He always says "good-bye" or "later" when something comes up. He just dropped off the face of the Earth.

Fucking MS. Why can't my life be normal? This disease sucks. I'm stuck at home because of it, and now I'm scaring off a guy I really like. For a moment, I kick myself for telling him. I should have blamed a virus or something. But then I'd have the guilt hanging over my head. Plus, if he can't handle my MS, I need to know.

Elle calls to check-in a while later. "You aren't unpacking boxes are you?"

"No." This isn't a lie. I stopped unpacking boxes hours ago.

"Don't make me come over there," she warns.

"Alright, alright. I unpacked a few boxes earlier, but I'm camped out on my couch. I'm pretty sure my ass will be imprinted on this cushion."

She laughs. "You sure you don't want to come over tonight? I'll pick you up."

"Nah. A party requires putting on something other than leggings, and that seems like too much work."

"Call me if you change your mind. I'll keep my drinking light just in case."

"Drink all you want chica, I'm staying home tonight."

She sighs. "I feel bad you're alone on New Year's Eve. You want me to come stay with you?"

"No, no, no. Have fun."

Despite my conversation with Elle, and my insistence that I'm fine, I wonder if I should get up and get dressed. Sitting here alone on New Year's Eve can't be a good idea.

"Whoever you kiss after the ball drops is the person you want to bring into the new year with you the most," my dad told me when I was six years old. This little nugget has stuck with me through the years. While I acted like it's no big deal to be alone on New Year's Eve, how will I feel when that ball drops and I'm by myself?

I almost have myself convinced to get dressed and ready to go when my doorbell rings.

Elle!

I jump up and swing my front door open. "I told you, I'm..." I stop short. It's not Elle. "Dean?"

I blink a few times to make sure I'm not seeing things. He's wearing his black basketball pants with the baby blue swish and a grey puffer jacket. His nose and cheeks are pink from the winter wind, and snowflakes melt in his hair.

Wow. He's so cute.

He smiles wide. "I hope you don't mind me stopping by unannounced. Again."

Why does he always show up when I look like crap? My hair is once again in a sloppy bun and I am sans makeup.

"Aren't you supposed to be in Florida?" I ask stupefied.

"I couldn't miss the snow." He shivers. "Mind if I come in?"

"Oh, duh, sorry." I step to the side. "Come on in."

Dean steps across the threshold. "Is it okay if I set this on your coffee table?"

195

I notice for the first time he is carrying a white box. "Sure. What is it?"

"Entertainment."

I raise an eyebrow. "What kind of entertainment?"

"The best kind." He opens the box and takes out a game console.

"Video games?" I giggle.

"Not just any video game, it's *Operation New World 2*."

"The brand new one? The one that's not even out yet?"

"That would be the one." He walks over to my television and unravels the console's cables.

"My stepbrother would die if he knew I have *Operation New World 2* in my possession."

"Oh, I'm not giving it you," Dean informs me. "It's the prototype. We have to play it to see if there are any glitches."

"So you're putting me to work?"

He grins. "Something like that."

I watch with amusement as he hooks everything up. "You want a drink or a snack? I have a closet full of goodies."

"Whatcha got?"

"Everything from potato chips to Little Debbie snack cakes. Pick your poison."

"Do you have any pretzels?"

"Coming right up."

I grab the pretzels off my kitchen counter and two bottles of water from my fridge. My heart warms when I walk back in the living room to see my cat rubbing against Dean's legs as he stands in front of my TV making sure we're good to go.

"Your cat likes me," he says with a smile. "What's his name?"

"Oscar."

Dean reaches down and scratches behind Oscar's ear. "Hi buddy."

196

Why is a man being nice to my cat so hot?

"Water work for you?" I ask as I set down our snacks.

"Yep, perfect." He hands me a game controller. "You ready for this?"

"I have no idea what I'm doing, but yes. I'm ready to kick some butt."

He smirks. "You're too cute to kick butt."

"Oh yeah?" I nudge him with my shoulder. "We'll see about that."

***

"Take that you alien scum!" I drop my controller. "Boom! Level cleared."

Dean nods, impressed. "Nice work. Maybe we need to make this game harder."

"Just admit it. I'm a badass."

"You are a badass." He smiles, then checks his watch. "It's 11:00, want to switch over to live TV?"

"It's 11:00?" I look out the window. Yep. It's pitch black out there. "How did that happen?"

"You got sucked into the video game vortex."

"Apparently." I stand and stretch. "You like grilled cheese?"

"Yes. Why?"

"I can make us sandwiches real quick."

"Sounds great." He extends his arms to the sky and yawns. "I didn't realize how hungry I am until we stopped playing."

"Video game vortex got you too, huh?"

We walk into the kitchen and Dean butters the bread while I find the griddle and cheese.

"Colby jack work for you?"

"Yep. It's one of my favorites. Scientists have found that the chemicals released while you eat cheese are akin to the effects of street drugs." He pops a piece of cheese in his mouth.

I laugh. "That explains a lot."

While our sandwiches are getting nice and toasty, I ask Dean the burning question. "Why are you really here?"

"I told you, I had to see the snow."

"You left the Florida sunshine for snow?"

"Yep." He pops another piece of cheese in his mouth.

I put my hand on my hip. "Okay. Out with it."

"What?" he asks innocently.

"Is there a work emergency you need to handle?"

"No."

"It's okay if you left your vacation early for work. I'm a workaholic too, ya know."

He shrugs. "I wanted to keep you company."

I glance over at him, spatula in hand. "You didn't have to do that, but I really appreciate it."

"I didn't want you to be alone."

I flip our sandwiches. "Because it's New Year's Eve?"

"That's part of it."

"What's the other part?"

He rubs his chin, taking his time to answer. "I remember what it's like to feel crappy and stuck in the house." He grins. "I wanted to introduce you to video game therapy."

I smile. "Video game therapy is pretty amazing."

We're silent for a moment, then he offers to take over. "I should be the one cooking for you."

"I'm fine. I just have to take it easy for a few days."

"What did the doctor say?" When he sees my hesitation, he adds, "We don't have to talk about it."

"No, it's okay. She thinks it's a temporary relapse. It can happen when you're under a lot of stress, and work has been really stressful lately. Plus, I'm going through some stuff with my mom."

198

"I'm sorry," he says, his eyes sincere.

"It's so frustrating." I set down the spatula. "Most days I can act like I'm not sick. I mean, I'm not. I'm fine. But then this disease inside me takes me down without notice."

He nods. "I understand. I used to wake up every day wondering if this will be the day the cancer comes back."

"Oh Dean..."

"It's better now, but every once in a while the thought pops back into my head. Usually on days when I'm feeling under the weather. Is this it? Is the cancer back?"

I consider his words. "I suppose I'll be like that too, even if it's a cold. I'll wonder if it's a product of the MS."

"Hopefully the time off will get you back on track."

"That and the steroids I'm on."

"You're on 'roids? Sweet!" He does his best Arnold Schwarzenegger impression. "You will be jacked and stacked." He flexes his arm, his bicep bulging through his long sleeve t-shirt.

I bat my eyelashes a few times. What was he saying?

When I gather my wits, I grab plates from my cabinet and flip our sandwiches onto them. "You want applesauce?"

He raises an eyebrow. "Applesauce?"

"Yes, applesauce." I open my fridge and take out two single serving cups of applesauce. "You're never too old for applesauce."

We watch Carson Daly stand in the middle of Times Square and summarize the past year while we eat our sandwiches. It's effortless. Comfortable.

"What were you doing last year on New Year's Eve?" I ask.

"I was in Florida with my family. We rented a houseboat and watched fireworks. How about you?"

"I was at Elle's parents' house. They have a game night until the countdown."

"Sounds fun."

I nod. "It is."

"Not as fun as *Operation New World* though," he jokes. He stands and takes our dirty dishes to the kitchen. I hear him open my dishwasher and put them inside for me. "Want anything to drink?" he calls out.

"No, I'm good. Take whatever you want."

He strides back in a moment later, a new bottle of water and a bag of chips in his hand. "I couldn't help myself. I love potato chips."

I laugh. "No problem."

There are plenty of seating options in my living room, but Dean takes the seat next to me on the couch. I don't mind at all. In fact, I love it. It also doesn't bother me when he puts his arm around my shoulder when he's done snacking on chips. I instinctively lean against him.

It's incredible how natural this feels. I don't care that he's seeing me in my pajamas with zero makeup and my hair looking a mess. I don't care that I'm missing Elle's party, and he doesn't seem to care that he isn't on a boat watching fireworks in warmer climates.

When the countdown starts, we both stand and yell along with the crowd. The anticipation of those final seconds builds inside me. We shout, "One!" and watch the ball drop. Confetti showers the mob of people in Times Square. Frank Sinatra sings "New York, New York" and the camera zooms in on couples giving each other their New Year's Eve kisses.

Dean steps in close, his eyes smoldering. "I have a confession to make."

My body temperature rises. "You do?"

"There is one other reason I came to see you." He pulls me in and plants a kiss on my lips.

Electricity surges through me. I wrap my arms around him, holding on tight for what may be the best kiss of my life. I've had New Year's Eve kisses before, but nothing like this. His lips are soft and warm, the faint taste of applesauce lingering on them. I

200

part my lips to allow his tongue to pass through, lost in the moment.

Too soon, he dips me dramatically and makes me laugh. He stands me up straight, still holding me close.

He smiles. "Definitely worth flying home for."

I blush, not quite sure what we do now. I'm a smidge disappointed when he pulls away. I wouldn't mind a few more kisses.

He wiggles a game controller. "Want to play another round?"

I smile. "Sure."

An hour later, the day catches up with me. "I think I'm done," I tell him, "but you can keep playing."

"Nah, that's okay. We can call it a night." Dean turns off the game and switches my television back to its normal setting.

I lean against him and he puts his arm around me. "Thanks for coming over tonight. I had a lot of fun."

"Me too."

"Can I ask you a favor?"

"Sure."

"Will you stay the night?" I glance up at him, worried he won't like my suggestion.

He rubs my shoulder. "If you want me to, I'll stay."

"I want you to stay."

I lead the way up the stairs and we climb into my bed. Without having to tell him, he understands that I'm not looking for sex. I'm looking for some old-fashioned cuddling. I pull the covers over us and roll to my right side. He snuggles in close behind me and drapes his arm over my body. I doze off within minutes, comforted by his presence. Safe and secure in his arms.

***

"What do you mean you slept together?" Elle asks the next day when she stops by.

"I mean, we slept together."

"No hanky panky?"

"Nope."

She frowns. "That's incredibly disappointing."

"We did have an amazing kiss last night."

"And then?"

"We played video games." I pour milk into a bowl of cereal. "I'm sure it sounds lame, but it was fun."

"What about this morning?"

I think back to waking up next to Dean. His hair tousled from sleep, nice and warm under the covers. I smile. "He gave me a kiss good-bye before he left for work."

"That's it?"

"It was a sweet kiss," I argue.

"Blah."

I giggle. "Sorry to disappoint you."

"I'm trying to live vicariously through you. You need to get more action."

"Why don't you get some action of your own?"

"Not interested."

I finish chewing my mouthful of Lucky Charms. "Let me know when you are. Dean knows someone he thinks will be a good fit for you."

"Oh really?" She raises an eyebrow. "Who?"

"His accountant."

She rolls her eyes. "So another boring guy who will lay next to me in bed, but not feel me up?"

I throw a rainbow marshmallow at her.

She chucks it back. "I'm only teasing Abby. Dean sounds like a great guy."

"He is."

"When will you see him again?"

"He's coming by tomorrow night."

202

"For more gaming action?"

"Maybe." I clean out my bowl and put it in the dishwasher. "Can we talk about work now?"

Elle shakes her head. "Nope. No work talk. You're on vacation."

"Will you at least tell me when Derrick gets the tub?" I plead.

"I will update you on the tub. That is all." She stands and grabs her purse. "I gotta roll. I'm meeting the Shephards at the office in half an hour."

"Do you have the plans I put together?"

"Yes. I downloaded them to my tablet. We're good to go."

I smile. "Thanks for doing this. I really appreciate it."

"No problem." We walk toward the front door. "What are your plans for today?"

"I have no idea."

"A new season of *Grace and Frankie* is on Netflix," she suggests.

After Elle leaves, I ponder what to do. I have the whole day to myself. I consider working out, but that's probably too much given the doctor's orders. The sun is shining, maybe a walk is in order. I bundle up and walk a big circle through my neighborhood. The fresh air feels good.

Once my nose is frozen, I head back home and take a shower. I'm back to square one. Netflix? Unpack a couple boxes? Or…should I play some more *Operation New World 2*? Dean will appreciate me continuing to test the prototype, right?

I turn on the game console and grab the controller. There's nothing I won't do to help a friend.

***

"You've been practicing, haven't you?" Dean playfully accuses when he stops by.

"Maybe just a little."

203

It's day three of my "relaxation vacation" and I'm psyched to have company. Especially this particular guest.

He smirks. "Just a little?"

"Okay, maybe a lot," I admit.

"Good! This is exactly why I brought it over. Had any issues?"

"Nope. Not unless kicking ass is an issue."

He laughs. "How quickly the padawan becomes the master."

"Don't *Star Wars* reference me, Mister. You still owe me a movie date."

"Indeed I do. Want to go now?"

I shrug. "Sure. I just have to put on some makeup."

He raises an eyebrow. "Why? You look great."

"The only place I go without makeup is the gym." I expect him to tell me I'm being ridiculous like some of my exes, but he doesn't.

"Okay. I'll check the times while you get ready."

I jog up the stairs and do my quickest makeup routine. Powder foundation, a dab of bronzer here and there, mascara, and lip gloss. I flip my hair upside down and tease it for volume. I change out of my hoodie and into a nice sweater, and exchange my Uggs for my tall brown leather boots. I spritz perfume on my neck and wrists before putting my favorite watch on.

Ten minutes later, I'm downstairs and ready to go.

"You look great," Dean compliments me. He leans in close. "Smell great too."

I blush. "Thanks. Is the movie playing tonight?"

"Yep. Next showing starts in half an hour. I think we can make it."

"Absolutely." I grab my coat and scarf. "You want me to drive?"

"No way. You're on vacation. I'll drive."

"My own personal chauffeur."

He wiggles his eyebrows. "Just one of my many talents."

The January air is crisp when we step outside, but it doesn't bother me a bit. I'm happy to get out of the house. I smile when he opens the car door for me.

"Thank you." Always so chivalrous.

"What's the last movie you saw?" Dean asks as we drive to the theater.

"Wow, it's been a while. I haven't had much time to do fun things."

"Me neither," he admits.

It takes me a minute to come up with the answer. "*Jurassic World*, the newest one."

He whistles. "That has been a while."

"How about you?"

"I just saw *Frozen 2* with my niece, but before that, it was *Avengers: Endgame*."

"You watched *Frozen 2*?" I ask with a grin.

"What Katie wants, she gets."

"How old is she?"

"Five."

"That's a fun age. My niece is only six months old."

"She'll grow fast. Seems like yesterday Katie was six months old."

"How often do you get to see her?"

"I go down to Florida three or four times a year. I make sure I take Katie out for some Uncle Dean time. Usually ice cream and a movie." He laughs. "Although she did convince me to take her to an American Doll store a few days ago. That set me back a pretty penny."

"I bet." I glance over at him. "It's great you spend time with her. I want to do the same with Rosie as she gets older."

"You mentioned you have a stepbrother, any other siblings?"

205

"Nope. How about you?"

"Just one brother. He's two years older than me."

"Do you get along?"

"Yes. He's one of my best friends."

"Nice! When I was younger I wished I had a sister. But then I met Elle, and she filled that gap for me."

"She seems like a wild one."

I laugh. "She can be. She was in rare form at the Christmas party. Oh, and I told her about your friend. She's not quite ready to date yet, but I think she's close."

"Maybe we can go out as a group. Blind dates are so awkward."

"Agreed. That's a good idea." I remember the tickets Mrs. Warner gave me. "Are you a Blue Jackets fan?"

"I don't catch all of their games, but I go to half a dozen a season."

"Mrs. Warner gave me VIP suite tickets for a game in two weeks. Want to go?"

He glances at me, his brown eyes sparkling, then focuses on the road. "Of course."

I realize with a mix of excitement and trepidation that I like making future plans with Dean Porter. I like it a lot.

Chapter Twelve

"Do you think there's room in the living room for a sectional?"

Pam and I are furniture shopping. My relaxation vacation has been over for almost two weeks and I'm back in the saddle. The time off was good for me. I caught up on sleep and was able to mentally sort out everything that's going on in my life. The tub arrived for Pam's condo, thank God, and everything is complete save for a few items. Now we have to fill it with furniture.

"You definitely have the space. This one reminds me of the leather sofa you sent me a picture of last week."

She nods. "Yes, it is very similar. I like the look of it."

"It's very sophisticated."

"I want comfortable though too. It comes across cold."

"We can bring in soft fabrics to warm it up. Here, let me show you." I search the showroom for throw blankets and pillows to demonstrate what I mean. I find the perfect cream-colored cotton throw and soft tan pillows.

Pam's eyes light up. "I see what you mean. I love it!"

We walk around the furniture gallery picking out a coffee table and a reading chair. We mix and match the colors and materials because she doesn't want her home to be monochromatic. We also choose bar stools for her kitchen island, and a runner for the hallway.

While we're picking out a bedframe, she brings up the app. "How are things going with Illing It?"

I stop myself from telling her that's not the app's name. Mostly because I still don't know what I want to call it. "It's in the final stages. Dean and his crew are finishing up their new video game, but he'll focus on the app again soon."

"Are you having a launch party?"

"A launch party?"

She nods. "Yes. An event celebrating the day you launch the app."

"We haven't talked about it. Do you think we should?"

"Yes. Bring as much attention to it as you can. How are you advertising it?"

"Um, I don't know that either."

"How do you expect people to hear about it?" Her question is an innocent one, no judgment in her voice.

"I haven't thought about it to be honest. This all happened so fast and on a whim. I suppose Dean and I need to talk about marketing."

"There's so many apps out there. You have to come up with a way to stand out."

"May sound too simple, but what if we dropped fliers off at medical centers? Get in front of the people who would use it the most."

"I like that. Pharmacies and clinics could be a good place too."

"True. I'll talk to Dean and see if his marketing team would be willing to float a few ideas."

"How about this?" Pam offers. "Tell me when your launch date is, and I'll announce it on air and on my social media pages."

My jaw drops. "You would do that?"

"Yes. Your app has the potential to serve a great purpose. People need community. And people also need a reliable source of information. I try to be that person when it comes to news and other current events. So I will absolutely support your efforts to be that source in a different arena."

I'm dumbfounded. "Wow Pam. I don't know what to say."

"You don't have to say anything. You do, however, have to help me pick out a bed."

***

208

When Pam and I wrap up at the furniture gallery, I debate whether I should stop in to see Dean. His office is only five minutes from here. Are we at the "drop in" stage of our relationship? He's stopped by my place unannounced and it doesn't bother me.

We've hung out several times over the last two weeks. The *Star Wars* movie was a hit for the both of us, hockey was an absolute blast, and we beat *Operation New World 2*. Sure Dean made the game and knows all the ins and outs, but a win is a win.

It's 4:30 p.m., which means most of his employees will be out of there in half an hour. I decide to take a chance and drive to his office.

Seth greets me with a smile when I walk in. "Hey Abby!"

"Hi Seth. How are you?"

"I'm good. And you?"

"Doing well. Is Dean available?"

"I don't know, you tell me – is he available?" Seth bats his eyelashes.

I smirk. "Is he on the phone or in a meeting?"

"No, he's not."

"Great. Thanks Seth."

"Later Abby."

How does Seth know Dean and I are more than business associates? Dean must have mentioned it to him. Despite their very different personalities, Dean told me he and Seth are good friends.

The thought of Dean telling Seth we're dating makes me smile. If Dean is telling people about me, he must be serious about us.

Dean's door is already open. I peek inside and see he's watching *Sports Center*. Phew! I'm glad I'm not interrupting anything.

"Knock, knock."

He jumps up off the couch when he sees me. "Hey! This is a nice surprise."

"My turn to pop in and see you."

"I like it." He pulls me in for a quick kiss. "What brings you this way?"

"I was furniture shopping with Pam at Froman's. It's just down the street."

"I know that place." He motions toward his desk and lounge area. "I got this furniture there."

"Really?"

"Yep. I saw their sign when I drove by, pulled in, picked out a few things..." he slaps his hands together "and wham! Fully furnished office."

I giggle. "Sounds like you put a lot of time and effort into it."

He grins. "It was an excruciating ten minutes."

I plop down in one of his office chairs. "Pam got me thinking about advertising for the app."

"She did?" He sits in the chair next to me and turns it sideways so we can talk.

"Yes. She asked when our launch date is. I told her I don't know. Then she asked what types of marketing we're doing, and I told her I don't know that either."

"My guys say it will be ready in two weeks. They're testing it to make sure there are no issues. They'll also put it in front of a focus group if we want."

"Do you think we should do that?"

"For an app?" He shakes his head. "I don't. The consumers are the ultimate focus group. They'll let us know what they do and don't like. Then we change it accordingly."

I tell him about the idea I had for fliers and Pam's willingness to discuss it on air and her social media pages.

"Wow, that's nice of her."

I nod. "Agreed. Should we do more than that?"

"I'll talk to marketing. My guess is they'll recommend ads on social media and in the app store."

"But all of that costs money."

"Good thing I have money, huh?"

"I don't want you to spend your money."

"Why?"

"It's not right."

He takes my hand. "Abby, I want to see this app work. It's our brainchild. I will do what I can to make it successful. This means a lot to you, and it means a lot to me."

"Are you sure? It doesn't feel right."

"Does it help to know it will be a tax write-off for the company?"

I laugh. "Well, when you put it that way…"

He rubs my palm with his thumb. "Let me do this. Okay?"

I nod. "Okay."

He leans back in his chair, the matter settled. "What do you want to do tonight? There's a really good…" Dean is interrupted by shouting in the hallway. "What the hell?"

We exchange a glance as Seth yells, "You're not allowed in here anymore! Your office is empty!"

Before I can stand from my chair, a man charges in, Seth trailing right behind him. I begin to panic, but then I realize I know our intruder.

"Jackson?!" Dean and I say at the same time.

Jackson looks terrible. His hair is a mess. His button-down shirt is crumpled and untucked from his khakis. His eyes are wide and wild.

Dean jumps up. "What are you doing here?"

"I want my stuff," he growls.

"Your stuff?" Dean crosses his arms. "I emailed, called and texted you about your stuff weeks ago. You never responded."

"What-the-fuck-ever man, just give me my stuff."

"We packed your belongings and put them in storage. There are several boxes. Give me your address, and I'll mail them to you."

"Yeah, right. I want them now."

"No," Dean says, jaw set. "You need to leave."

Jackson stumbles forward, then catches his balance. He points his finger at Dean. "Give me my stuff, or I'm calling the police."

Dean shrugs. "Go ahead. In fact, Seth, why don't you call them for us?"

"Will do." Seth turns and takes off for his desk.

"Jackson? Are you okay?" I ask from my seat.

He notices me for the first time. He narrows his eyes, his drunken mind trying to catch up. "Abby?"

I give him a little wave. "Hi."

"How's that slutty friend of yours?" he sneers.

My jaw drops. "Don't you dare call her that! You're the one who got caught with another woman."

"Yeah, but, she was cheating on me while I was out of town."

I stand, fists balled at my sides. "She never, ever cheated on you. She loved you. Don't try to make yourself look better by making shit up."

He rubs his chin, an odd expression on his face. I've never known Jackson to be a drinker. Despite my anger, it's shocking to see him this way. "You know, I need to get my stuff from our condo."

"Don't bother, it's gone," I tell him.

Rage crosses his face. "Gone? What do you mean, gone?"

"I donated it."

"You what?!" His nostrils flare and he comes toward me.

I take a step back, my heart racing. He's pissed.

"That's enough!" Dean grabs Jackson's right arm and pins it behind his back. He turns Jackson's body and pushes him out the door.

212

"Lay off man!" Jackson protests. "That fucking hurts!" Jackson's efforts are in vain. Dean is much stronger than he is.

Dean doesn't let go, he keeps pushing Jackson down the hallway. "It's time for you to leave."

I trail behind them, watching in wonder as Dean manhandles a grown man like he's a ragdoll.

Dean looks over his shoulder at me. "Call Elle. Make sure she knows what's up."

Good point.

Elle, who is infamous for not answering her phone, actually picks up after the third ring. "Hey lady!"

"Where are you?" I ask without returning her greeting.

"At home. Why?"

"You need to leave, now."

"Uh, o-kay."

"For real, you need to leave."

"Why? I'm in my comfy pants."

"Jackson is here."

"Jackson? My ex, Jackson?"

"Yes! What other Jackson do we know?" She's not getting it. "Do you still have the key to my place?"

"Yes."

"Put on some shoes, and meet me there."

"What the hell is going on?"

"Your ex is drunk and pissed off. He could be heading your way."

"Where are you?"

"Dean's office."

"Why is Jackson at Dean's office? I'm so confused."

"He came to get his things."

"Oh."

213

"Which means he could be heading to you."

"Ohhh." Finally, it's sinking in.

"I told him I donated his stuff, and it pissed him off even more."

"Smooth move Ex-lax."

I roll my eyes. "I'm not playing around. He's drunk off his ass. He's acting insane. You don't want anything to do with it. Trust me."

"Okay, fine. I'm getting off my couch."

"Good. I'll see you in a few."

Dean walks in as I'm ending my call with Elle. "He's gone."

"He isn't driving, is he?"

Dean shakes his head. "No, his Uber was still outside. The driver said the next stop is the airport. I told him to call me if they go anywhere else."

"Good idea. Elle is on her way to my place now."

"Does Jackson know where you live?"

"No. He hasn't been to my new house."

Dean sits in his desk chair, exhaling a deep breath. "Phew. That was crazy."

"What was he doing here? He told Elle he was moving to Texas. Or at least I think it was Texas…"

"He was rambling on and on about how he made a huge mistake. The new girlfriend broke it off with him when she realized he didn't have as much money as she thought."

"Nice."

"He'll try to win Elle back."

"It won't work."

Dean raises an eyebrow. "You sure about that? I've seen a lot of people get back with exes who didn't deserve second chances."

"She won't. She's done." I frown. "I suppose I should head home. I'm sorry."

"For what?"

"We were about to make dinner plans."

"It's okay. We'll go out another night."

"Want to come by later?" I ask hopefully.

"I'd love to, but Elle should stay the night with you. Just in case."

I sigh. "True."

"Have a girls' night. Pizza, ice cream," he smirks, "pillow fights."

I laugh. "In lacy lingerie, right?" I walk behind his desk and lean down to give him a kiss. "I'll catch up with you later, k?"

"Sounds good."

Driving home I realize I already miss Dean.

***

"I can't believe he was drunk."

"As a skunk." I hand her a slice of the pizza I picked up on the way home.

"That's so weird. He hardly ever drinks."

"I know. He was wasted though. He probably passed out in the back of the Uber.

"What is he doing in Columbus?"

"I asked the same thing." I grab a slice of pizza for myself and sit at the island next to Elle. "Apparently, the new woman dumped him."

Elle nearly chokes on her bite of pizza. "Already?"

"Yep. She thought he was rich. When she realized he isn't, she was out the door."

"Seriously?"

"That's what he told Dean."

She sits quietly for a moment, then breaks out into laughter. "Oh my God. Karma is such a bitch sometimes."

"Indeed."

"Did he ask about me?"

"Um, kinda."

"Kinda?"

"Well, I think he meant you when he asked how my slut friend is doing."

Her jaw drops. "He called me a slut?"

I nod.

"What an asshole!"

"He tried saying you cheated on him first."

"He did not!"

"Yeah, he did. Don't worry, I set him straight."

Elle puts her pizza down, staring off into the distance. "I can't believe he said that. Why would he say that?"

"To make himself look better. So he can play the victim."

Tears well in her eyes. "Why does that hurt the most?"

"No one believes him," I say softly. "The only people who heard him say it were me, Dean, and Seth."

"Yeah, but if he said it to you guys, he's probably telling other people too."

"So?"

"So?! Everyone will think I'm a cheater."

I shake my head. "No they won't. No one who knows you will believe it for a second."

"I bet his parents do though. They never liked me."

"Who cares if they believe him? You never have to see them again."

"I should call them," she says with conviction. "Let them know what a dick their kid is."

"They'll never believe you. You'd be wasting your time. People believe what they want to believe."

She frowns. "I know. It just sucks he feels the need to drag me through the mud when he's the one who cheated."

216

"What will you do if he calls you?" I ask, thinking of Dean's question earlier.

"I won't answer."

"Dean's pretty sure Jackson will reach out to you."

"How long did Dean talk to him?"

"Long enough to drag him out of the building and push him into the Uber."

Elle grins. "He dragged Jackson out?"

"Yep." I wipe pizza grease off the corner of my mouth. "I'm about to say something inappropriate."

"Oh." She wiggles her eyebrows. "Do tell."

"It was really hot."

She laughs. "Did you get all hot and bothered?"

"Holy cow." I fan myself. "He's usually so polite and sweet, which I love. But seeing him grab Jackson like it was nothing and take control, phew baby." I crinkle my nose. "That's anti-feminist, isn't it?"

"He was showing you another side of him. The side that will protect you and stand up for you. That's hot. You want to know your partner has your back."

"You make it sound so mature. I was practically drooling."

Elle pours a can of Pepsi into a glass of ice. "Have you two done the deed yet?"

"No, not yet."

"What are you waiting for?"

I shrug. "Not sure exactly."

"Are we beyond kissing?"

"Yes. We explored a little."

"Have you seen what he's working with?"

I laugh. "I felt it, once."

"Ugh! You're killing me Abby."

217

"It's killing me too," I admit, "but I don't want to rush things. We're having fun going at our own pace. It's nice to date someone who isn't putting up a front to get in my pants."

Elle de-greases her new slice of pizza with a napkin. "I'll take it slow when I start dating again. It'll be weird being with someone other than Jackson."

"It will be strange at first, but you'll get used to it."

Later that night, lying in bed, my mind wanders to my potential first time with Dean. Will it be clumsy and awkward? Or will we be in sync? Vegas odds are on clumsy and awkward, but it makes me smile anyway.

***

"Where do you want this box?"

Dean is holding a large box labeled "extra throw pillows".

"Basement."

"If all the boxes are this light, we'll be done in no time."

"You're not that lucky."

After spending the night last night, Dean offered to spend his Saturday helping me finally complete the moving process. I suggested we go out, but he picked up a box and asked which way to head.

"You'll feel so good when this is done," he insisted. "I'm not a neat freak by any means, but I've noticed when my house is clean and organized, I feel lighter."

"Whatever Marie Kondo," I teased.

"I have no idea who that is."

We've only been working for an hour, but there is already a substantial difference. Most of the boxes are basement-bound, filled with things I don't use on a daily basis. Evidenced by the fact that I haven't opened them since I moved in.

I follow Dean down the steps with another light box. This one labeled "winter clothes". It is actually filled with clothes I haven't fit into since college, but I'm not ready to part with them.

218

"Want to see something funny?" I ask when we stack our boxes in the corner.

"Sure."

I pull out the box with my old photographs and school yearbooks. We sit on the floor going through everything. I hand him my fifth grade picture. "Check out this hot mama."

"Aww, you were so cute."

"Wasn't I though?"

"Still are," he says with a wink.

I show him my old spelling bee trophies and academic awards. I even bust out the book I wrote in second grade. I giggle as I read it out loud to him. To Dean's credit, he is either genuinely interested or good at pretending he is.

"I wish I had my old stuff here so I could show it to you. It's all in Florida." He helps me put my mementos back in the box. "Maybe you can fly down there with me sometime."

I meet his eyes. "I'd love that."

He smiles. "You might see my house in Florida before you see my place half an hour away."

I laugh. "I know. We always hang out here."

"You want to go see my place now?"

"Now? As in, right now?"

"We don't have to. I'm not sure what your plans are for the day."

I raise an eyebrow. "When do I ever have plans?"

"Let's go then." He extends his hand and helps me stand.

"Can I change out of this dusty outfit first?"

"Of course."

I run upstairs and freshen up. I change out of my pajamas and into jeans and a striped sweater. I wash my face and put on my basic makeup. I brush out the tangles in my hair and throw on a pair of ballet flats.

I skip down the stairs. "I'm ready."

219

Dean, who is lounging on my couch petting Oscar, looks up from his cellphone. "I have an idea."

"Okay."

He hesitates, then asks, "Do you want to stay the night at my place?"

I shrug. "I can if you want me to."

"Tomorrow is a Sunday, so we can stay up late watching movies and sleep in."

"Sounds good to me. I'll pack an overnight bag."

I jog back up the stairs and process Dean's invitation. Why was he nervous about asking me to stay the night? Did he think I would say "no"? He's stayed here half a dozen times, why would I turn down his invite?

I pick out a cute purple tank top with the words "Sweet Dreams" written across the front and the matching shorts. I also grab a comfy hoodie in case it's cold in Dean's place. I grab a pair of skinny jeans and a shirt for tomorrow along with clean undies and a bra.

Next stop is my bathroom. I pack my makeup remover and my meds. I forego bringing my makeup bag. Sounds like we'll be lounging at his place most of the time, so I won't need it. My hairbrush, toothbrush, and deodorant finish off my packing.

A stray thought dances through my mind as I make sure I have everything I need. What if tonight is the night?

I stop dead in my tracks and sit on the edge of my bed. Is that why he was nervous when he asked me to stay over? It will be our first night at his place. Maybe the change of venue makes the event more special.

Holy crap!

I'm not sure how to feel about this. I'm excited, nervous, and scared at the same time. Things are good with us. In fact, they're amazing. What if we aren't compatible in that way? It will ruin everything. On the other hand, I'm ridiculously attracted to him and I don't know how I've been able to hold out this long. There's no way we aren't compatible in that arena. No way.

I take a deep breath to calm myself. I can't walk downstairs a frazzled mess, he'll know something is up. Besides, I'm probably overreacting and reading too much into it.

"I'm really ready this time," I announce as I walk downstairs.

"Awesome. You want to grab a bite to eat on the way?"

"Yes, I'm starving. I worked up an appetite with all that heavy lifting."

He laughs. "How does Spaghetti Warehouse sound?"

My eyes widen. "Oh my gosh, I love Spaghetti Warehouse."

"I had a feeling you might."

We bundle up and Dean carries my bag to his SUV. Like he always does, he opens my car door for me before putting my overnight bag in the backseat. Ever the gentleman.

Despite my nerves about what may or may not happen at Dean's place, our conversation takes off. It's just so easy with Dean. Time flies when I'm with him. Before I know it, we're in the Spaghetti Warehouse parking lot. My stomach growls when I catch a whiff of the Italian yumminess cooking inside.

We split a trio – lasagna, manicotti, and spaghetti with meatballs. I eat until I can't take another bite.

"Any room for dessert?" our waiter asks.

"No," Dean and I answer at the same time.

"How about a cannoli or a slice of cheesecake to go?"

I raise an eyebrow at Dean.

He smiles. "We'll take two of each, please."

I giggle when the waiter walks away. "You know me too well."

"Oh, did you want something? Those are for me," he teases.

I groan as I get in the car a few minutes later. "I really outdid myself this time. I may have to unbutton my pants."

Dean laughs. "Does this mean you aren't up for a cruise around COSI?"

"COSI?" I haven't been to the COSI museum in years. I glance out my window. "It is just across the street, isn't it?"

Dean nods. "They have a deep sea exhibit this month I want to check out."

"Let's do it. We're right here, might as well."

I check the closing hours on my phone as Dean drives over to COSI's lot. "They're open for another three hours. We have plenty of time."

We walk through the dinosaur exhibit on the way to the deep sea attraction. I gaze up at a full-size skeleton of a tyrannosaurus rex.

"Bizarre to think one of these guys could have stood in this spot, isn't it?" Dean asks.

"Yes. Very."

We take our time weaving through the hall, watching the short educational videos and pressing all the buttons to hear what scientists believe the dinosaurs sounded like. I smile listening to the passing children "ooh" and "aah" over the fossils. Dean holds my hand the entire time, his warm fingers entwined with mine.

We forego the "Under the Skin" exhibit. The placard outside warning guests that there are actual cadavers behind the closed doors turns me off.

"No thanks," I tell Dean when I see it, "but I'll wait out here if you want to go in."

"That's okay. I'd rather go to the ocean."

"Wow," I murmur when we go "Under the Sea".

The museum has essentially become a temporary aquarium. Huge fish tanks fill the exhibit rooms from floor to ceiling. Neon jelly fish dance in one tank, while sharks circle their space in another. We touch sea urchin, starfish, and sting rays in the open tank. Dean laughs when I make fishy faces at the clown fish, and teases me when I crinkle my nose at the electric eels.

"I ate eel once."

I fake gag. "Eew."

222

"It was a dare back in college. I didn't want the guys to think I was a wuss, so I took a bite."

"How was it?"

"I threw up the next morning," he says matter-of-factly, then grins.

I laugh. "No thanks. I'll stick with chicken."

I'm having so much fun. I feel like a kid again. We take seats on a bench across from the largest tank in the exhibit and sit quietly, watching the fish swim by. It's cathartic.

Too soon, an announcement comes over the PA. "Attention COSI guests. It is now 5:45 p.m. and the museum will be closing in fifteen minutes. Please make your way toward the exits."

I frown. "5:45 already?"

Dean stands and extends his hand. "We can come back again. The exhibit will be here for two more weeks."

We walk toward the exit, stopping every now and then to catch a quick glimpse of a display. Seeing the sign for the restrooms, I politely let Dean know Mother Nature calls. I'm only in the bathroom a few minutes, but when I come back out, Dean has a gift shop bag in his hand.

"I couldn't resist."

I smile wide when I open the bag. It's an adorable stuffed animal version of a clown fish. "It's so cute!" I make fishy faces at it like I did the real ones.

Dean laughs. "That right there is exactly why I bought it."

"Thank you." I kiss his cheek. "I love it."

On the drive to Dean's house, I realize I know nothing about it. "Where do you live?"

"New Albany."

"Nice! New Albany has grown a lot the last few years."

"It has. I like my neighborhood, but I'm not sure how long I'll stay there."

"Why?"

"A lot of big corporations have moved in. Which means more traffic and more people. I'd rather live somewhere a bit quieter. I don't like a long commute."

"Understandable. How long have you had your place?"

"Five years."

I pause dramatically. "You have a Batcave, don't you?"

He laughs. "I wish."

"You are a lot like Bruce Wayne. Rich, hot, athletic."

"You think I'm hot?" he asks, giving me a sideways glance.

"Uh, yeah. Have you seen yourself?"

"I see myself as the dorky computer guy. Not the hot guy."

"Why can't you be both?"

He smiles. "Touché."

He turns into a quiet subdivision a few minutes later. I'm surprised when I recognize one of the homes. "Wait a second...I've been here before."

"You have?"

"Yes. I worked on Mrs. Hanna's kitchen two years ago."

"Mrs. Hanna? I don't know her."

"She lived in that house over there." I point to a two-story cape cod.

He shakes his head. "Sorry. I've never met her."

Dean drives deeper into the subdivision, taking me to a section I didn't explore when I was working with Mrs. Hanna. I wish I had. These homes are gorgeous. Unlike some subdivisions, the houses are not lookalikes. They each have unique styles, but were built with the same attention to detail.

I laugh when we pull into Dean's driveway. "You live in a craftsman too?"

He smiles. "Funny, right?"

"Yours is a hell of a lot nicer than mine, but yes."

"What are you talking about? Your house is great."

"I love my house. Don't get me wrong. But it's not...this..." I wave my hand in the direction of his home. "Your house is my house on steroids."

Dean's house is twice the size of mine. The exterior is a soft grey with white stone accents. The pillars and woodwork are ornate and beautiful. I'm tempted to turn my house into a mini version of his. I can't wait to see the inside.

Dean pushes the button for his garage and slowly pulls in. I'm surprised when I see a matte black Ducati parked in the space.

"You have a motorcycle?"

"Every once in a while I need an adrenaline rush." He turns off the car. "Want to go for a ride?"

"In January? No thanks."

Dean's all black motorcycle was a preview of his home's color scheme. A sleek black marble countertop plays off his white kitchen cabinets and white marble tile flooring. Stainless steel appliances, an espresso maker, and a massive island I could sleep on add to the kitchen's opulence.

His living room is an upscale bachelor pad. Black leather couches, a massive television, surround sound, and a console holding every gaming system made. The guest bathroom is all white with grey accents and an elevated glass bowl sink. Everything is modern and sleek, exactly what you expect a tech guru's home to be.

"You're making me nervous," Dean says from behind me.

"Me? Why?"

"I see you assessing my place with your home decorator's eye."

I laugh. "I can't help it. It's awesome."

"This part of my house is for show. My basement is where the fun is."

He takes me downstairs to his game room. Foosball, ping pong, and billiard tables take up half the space. The other half is filled with old-school arcade games.

225

"Mrs. Pacman!" I exclaim.

"Want to play?"

"Yes!"

Dean turns on Mrs. Pacman and we play a few rounds. He beats me easily, but it's still fun.

"How about dessert?" he suggests when we're done playing.

We take a cannoli and a slice of cheesecake to share. Dean turns on the TV and we settle on his couch. We peruse our options for our movie marathon and ultimately settle on *Ghostbusters*.

"I'm an 80's movie junkie," I confess. "I could watch them over and over again."

"I love Bill Murray. I can watch anything with him in it."

The sugar from the desserts keeps me going through the first movie, but by the time we're halfway through *Ghostbusters II*, my eyelids are heavy.

Dean notices I'm not as energetic as I was earlier. "You want to call it a night?"

"I'm sleepy, but you can stay up."

"Nah, we can finish it another time." He grabs my overnight bag and shows me to his bedroom. "I hope you'll be comfy in my bed."

"I can sleep anywhere. I'm sure your bed will be just fine."

He flips on the light and I marvel at his room. "Wow Dean, this is amazing."

It isn't what I expected at all. I thought it would be modern lines and a slick mix of black and white like the main area of his home. But this is completely different. The walls are painted a subtle tan instead of white, and the flooring is a light hardwood. It has a beach house feel, but somehow maintains masculinity.

I turn my attention to the bed. The bedding is a white down comforter with no throw pillows. I'll have to do something about that. I have a five throw pillow minimum. The headboard and bed frame are like nothing I've ever seen before, and that's saying something. It takes me a second to realize what it is.

226

"Is that driftwood?"

"Yes. I miss the beach. Ohio is great, but being landlocked sucks. I wanted this room to remind me of the ocean."

"It works. My first thought was beach house."

The master bathroom follows the beach theme. It is mostly light blue with white accents, but the glass shower is another surprise. Instead of tile, the walls are covered in sea glass. Bright green, blue, white, and brown glass stones shine under the overhead lighting.

"Did I do good?" he asks.

"This is awesome. I may have to steal this idea from you."

"I'll take that as a compliment." He sets my bag down on the counter. "I'll give you some privacy."

He steps out of the bathroom and closes the door behind him. The bathroom is pretty clean for a single guy. I would speculate that he cleaned before he invited me over, but his shaving cream and razor are out on the counter. There are a few stray hairs in the sink from the last time he shaved, but nothing atrocious.

I use the bathroom, change into my pajamas, brush my teeth, and remove my makeup. My thoughts about Dean's agenda for the evening tickle the back of my mind, but I don't feel the nerves I had earlier. This feels like any of our evenings together. Relaxed, comfortable, completely at ease.

I find Dean sitting on his bed taking off his sneakers when I walk out of the bathroom. He smiles. "You look cute."

"Aww, thanks."

He takes his turn in the bathroom and I crawl under the covers. I assume he sleeps on the same side of the bed as he does when he's at my house. I glance around his room again, noticing little details I missed when I first walked in. He doesn't have art on the walls, but he does have a surfboard leaning in one corner. It's orange and yellow paint is peeling in the middle, as if it's been used.

Dean steps out of the bathroom in nothing but his boxers. I've seen him this way a dozen times, but it still takes my breath away.

He has an amazing body. I can tell how much time and effort he puts into maintaining his physique. I'm so glad he isn't one of those guys who tries to show it off. Not because I would get jealous, but because he isn't obsessed with how he looks.

He flips off the overhead light. Moonbeams stream in from the windows, casting a light on Dean as he climbs in bed.

"Are you sure you're real?"

He chuckles. "That's an odd question."

"You're the perfect person. You can't be real."

He leans in close. "You want to hear something funny?"

"Of course."

"I was just thinking the same thing about you."

"Really?" My heart kicks into overdrive. The energy around us is humming.

"If I wasn't real, could I do this?" He kisses me with his soft lips.

I smile when he pulls away. "I need more evidence."

He kisses me again, this time deeper, more intense. My hands wrap around his shoulders, pulling him against me. I don't want him to stop. And he doesn't.

Chapter Thirteen

"What?!"

People sitting at the surrounding tables in Panera all turn to look at me and Elle.

I slump down, shading my eyes with my hand. "Elle, can you quiet down please?"

"When did this happen?" A piece of tomato falls out of her sandwich, as if it is also shocked by my news.

"Saturday."

"Saturday!" More looks.

"Yes, Saturday," I say in a hushed tone, hoping it brings her down a notch.

"It's Monday and you're just now telling me?"

"I was with Dean all day yesterday. This is the first chance I had to tell you."

She raises an eyebrow. "All day, huh? Saturday night must have been good."

I blush.

"You ho," she says with a smirk. "Good for you. Safe for me to assume you aren't going to give me details?"

"Yep."

"You're no fun," Elle pouts.

I change topics. "How do you feel about a double date this weekend?"

"With the numbers guy?"

"Yes."

She shrugs. "I don't know."

"Come on. It will be fun."

"Where are we going?"

"We were thinking Dave & Busters. We can eat and then goof around."

"That's fine. The noise of the games will block out his voice."

I laugh. "If you don't want to go, just say so."

"No, I need to get back on the horse." She takes a sip of her iced green tea. "It's been so long since I went out on a first date."

"I know. It stinks. But he could be a great guy."

"Aww, it's so cute. You're so positive and upbeat since you found your manicorn."

"My manicorn?"

"Yes, a unicorn among men."

I nearly spit out my water. "Oh my gosh, that is hilarious."

"He is though! Dean is perfect for you."

"You'll find a good guy too."

"I'm not so sure. I'm not the best at judging character."

"You have a shitty ex. We all do. It's not your fault he was a jerk."

"I must be getting older because the bad boys have zero allure to me now. I finally figured out that the bad boys stay bad boys."

"Truth."

Elle picks at her potato chips. "When I was younger, there was so much appeal to the idea of a bad boy falling so in love with me that he changes his ways. That shit doesn't happen."

I consider her observation. "It may happen when we're young because we all grow up. But at our age, we are who we are."

"Nicely put Kesha." She stands. "You ready to get out of here? I need to go shopping for a new outfit if I'm hitting the town this weekend."

***

"Do we really have to get up?" I whine.

I'm snuggling with Dean in my bed the following Saturday. It's nice and warm under the covers and I have no desire to move.

"Unfortunately, yes."

"You sure you want to run the gauntlet with me today?"

"The gauntlet?"

"Lunch with my dad and stepmom, then the double date with Elle and Tom."

Dean laughs. "Two relationship testers in one day. That is brutal."

"See? Let's stay here instead."

Dad called a few days ago and asked if I would meet him and Samantha for lunch at First Watch.

"Maybe you can bring that boyfriend of yours with you."

"I'll ask him, but he may have to work. The new game is keeping him busy."

When I asked Dean, I gave him an out if he wanted to take it. "I know you're really busy working on *Operation New World 2*, but my dad asked if you would like to go to lunch with him and Samantha on Saturday."

"Sure, that sounds great," he said without hesitation. "I'd like to meet them."

Aren't guys supposed to be wary of meeting the family? Not Dean. Maybe he really is a manicorn...

After some gentle prodding, Dean convinces me to get up and get ready. "We can shower together to save time," he suggests.

I'm suddenly wide awake.

Lunch with my parents goes well. They love Dean, I can tell. He doesn't put on any airs for them, he's his laidback and comfortable self the entire time. Samantha nearly swoons when he tells them about his volunteer work at the children's hospital, and Dad talks his ear off about boating when he finds out Dean is from Florida.

"He's a keeper," Samantha says when we walk to the ladies' room together.

231

"He's great, isn't he?"

"He's so handsome, and well-spoken, and he can't keep his eyes off you. He's over the moon for you."

"You think so?" I ask with a smile.

"Yes! There's a certain way a man looks at a woman he's in love with." She pauses. "I don't know how to describe it, but you know it when you see it."

I know the look she's talking about. The one a happy groom gives his bride as she walks down the aisle. The one Frida Kahlo described when she said, "Take a lover who looks at you like maybe you are magic."

"I like him a lot," I confess to Samantha. "More than anyone I've dated before."

"Good! I'm keeping my fingers crossed for you two."

I'm happy to see Dad and Dean were able to keep their conversation going while Samantha and I were gone.

"Your dad was just telling me about their recent trip to Aruba."

Samantha's face lights up. "Oh, it was wonderful! Did he tell you about scuba diving?"

"Not yet," Dad responds.

"I've never been scuba diving before, and my word!" Samantha launches into her story.

Dean and I exchange a glance and a small smile. He rubs my shoulder before resting his hand on the back of my chair. The first relationship tester of the day is a huge success.

***

After a nap and a change of clothes, Dean and I pick up Elle for our double date. She's wearing a pair of skinny jeans with a black sweater and a new pair of navy blue and black suede high-heeled booties she bought at the mall the other day. I smile when I see she is wearing eyeliner and mascara, she's going all out.

Dean jumps out of the car to open Elle's door for her.

"You didn't have to do that," she insists as she steps inside.

232

"I'm doing it on behalf of my friend," Dean explains. "Tom isn't here to do it for you."

I turn sideways in the passenger seat so I can compliment Elle. "You look fantastic!"

"Thanks. I wasn't sure if the booties were too much."

"Not at all. You look perfect."

Elle buckles her seatbelt and takes a deep breath. "I'm nervous."

"Don't be. Tom is great," Dean assures her.

"He's your friend, you have to say that."

"Does it help to know he texted me saying he's nervous too?"

"He did?"

"Yes."

"What's his story? Why is he single?"

I'm curious to hear the answer to this myself.

"Similar story to yours actually. He was engaged to his college sweetheart, but two months out from the wedding she found someone new."

"Yikes."

"He was pretty torn up about it for a while. He's dated here and there, but no good matches."

"How long ago was the breakup?" I ask.

"Let's see…it was around the time we moved into the new office, so close to two years ago."

Elle whistles. "Two years is a long time to be single."

"It is, but he wasn't interested in going on dates with women who weren't a good match."

"What makes you think he'll like me?"

I glance over my shoulder. "Who wouldn't like you?"

"He is a fun loving guy. If he was at Mrs. Warner's party, he would have been up there singing with you. But he's also serious about his career, and is a great friend. All qualities you have."

We arrive at Dave & Buster's ten minutes early. Elle and I get a table while Dean hangs back for Tom.

Elle grabs the beverage menu. "I need a drink."

I laugh. "It's going to be fine. Just be yourself."

"I feel like I'm sixteen and waiting for Ben Cardinal to pick me up."

Elle has her back to the entrance, so she doesn't see Dean and Tom approaching. "They're coming," I whisper as discreetly as I can. "You can thank me later."

Tom is tall with dark hair and blue eyes. Elle is a sucker for blue eyes. He and Dean are laughing as they walk toward the table. Elle and I both stand as they approach. I watch Elle's expression as she turns to see Tom for the first time. She plays off her awe well. I glance at Tom and he seems pleased to meet my best friend.

Dean handles the introductions. "Tom, this is my girlfriend Abby. And this," he turns to Elle, "is her friend and business partner, Elle."

Tom extends his hand to me first. "Abby, so nice to finally meet you."

"Likewise."

He shifts his attention to Elle. "Sorry they're putting you through this. I'm Tom."

Elle laughs as she returns his handshake. "Nice to meet you."

Dean winks at me as he takes his seat. "Has the waiter been by to order drinks?"

"Not yet."

As if on cue, our waiter shows up with dinner menus. "The special tonight is two for twenty. You get an appetizer to share, two dinners, and a dessert for two."

Elle bats her eyelashes at Tom. "Want to share?"

And just like that, Dean and I are on our way to passing the second relationship tester of the day.

***

234

"I'm exhausted." I belly flop onto my bed.

Dean yawns. "Me too. I didn't think we'd be out until 1 a.m."

"Me neither. I can't remember the last time I shut a place down."

"Elle and Tom hit it off." Dean climbs into bed beside me.

I roll over onto my back. "I'd say so. Hopefully your friend is trustworthy enough to drive my friend home."

"Tom is one of the nicest guys I know. She's in good hands."

"Maybe Tom is her manicorn," I muse out loud.

"Her what?"

I explain Elle's term to him.

He chuckles. "So I'm your manicorn?"

"Don't worry, it won't be your pet name."

He leans on his elbow, gazing down at me. "How tired are you?"

I smirk. "Why do you ask?"

"No particular reason." He runs his fingers along my arm. "Just curious."

"I could be persuaded to stay awake a bit longer."

"Oh really?" He kisses my neck, sending heat waves through my body. "Does this help my case?"

***

I'm floating in the night sky, my pink dress billowing behind me. A huge smile on my face as I drift amongst the stars. A comet whirls by me, its light and heat warming my skin. Suddenly, a loud ringing fills my ears and disturbs my peace.

"Abby...Abby..." a deep voice whispers.

I turn away from the voice, wanting to continue my journey through space. The ringing noise sounds again, shaking the stars and planets around me.

"Abby...Abby..." the voice more insistent. "Someone is at your front door."

Huh?

My eyelids flutter and Dean comes into focus. "Good morning sunshine. You want me to answer your door?"

I rub my eyes. "What time is it?"

"It's 10:30 a.m."

"10:30? For real."

"Yes. This is the first time I've slept past eight since college."

I throw the covers back and walk over to my window. I'm not expecting anyone. I pull back my curtain and see a car in the driveway behind Dean's SUV. My heart sinks.

"Shit," I mumble under my breath.

"Who is it?"

"My mother," I sigh.

"The family introductions continue," he says with a smile.

I frown. "Actually, I'd prefer it if you stay up here. Is that okay?"

"Of course." His expression has changed to concern. "Are you okay?"

"As you know, my mom and I didn't leave off on great footing the last time I saw her. I doubt she's here to play nice."

"Tell you what, I'll hop in the shower to give you some privacy. If you change your mind and want me to meet her, I'll jump out and get dressed. If not, I'll stay in the shower until you tell me she's gone. Or until the water turns cold."

I give him a soft kiss. "Thank you."

He heads for the bathroom while I head for the steps. The pit in my stomach is heavy. I'd hide in the basement and not answer the door if I thought I could get away with it. But my car is in the driveway. She knows I'm home.

I take a deep breath before opening the door. There stands my mother in all her glory. She's in her standard outfit of white blouse and black pants, her white and black checkered pea coat buttoned

236

to the top. We haven't spoken a word yet and she already looks annoyed.

"Mom, what are you doing here?"

She pushes past me into the house. "I saw a strange car in your driveway." She looks me up and down. "What are you wearing?"

"They're called pajamas, Mom. Why were you driving past my house?"

"I drive by every now and then to make sure you're alive."

I roll my eyes. "Someone will call you if I die."

"I'm not so sure. You and your father aren't great communicators."

I ignore her dig and cut to the chase. "Why are you here?"

"I told you, I wanted to make sure you're okay."

"As you can see, I'm fine. You can go now."

"Well how am I supposed to know? You never call me."

I sigh. "I'm not doing this with you right now."

"Doing what?"

"I'm not having this conversation. The one where you try to make me feel like shit and a bad person."

"I don't do that," she protests.

I avoid the urge to push back. That's what she wants. "Mom, I'm not doing this today. My boyfriend's here, and I'm not in the mood."

"Your boyfriend?" she asks surprised.

"Yes Mom, my boyfriend. You may find this shocking, but men are actually attracted to me."

She pulls at the collar of her coat and lowers her voice. "Does he know about your disease?"

"Yes," I say through clenched teeth. "He knows everything about me."

"Does he know you may not be able to have children?"

My temperature rises. "First of all, that's not true. Second, we haven't talked about it. And third, it's time for you to go."

"So pushy. I'm just trying to give you advice."

"Seriously? You've destroyed every relationship you have, and you want to give me advice?"

My comment stings. She flinches, then regains her composure. "That's big talk from a girl who can't keep a man longer than a couple months. Don't bother introducing me to this one. He'll be out of the picture soon anyway."

"Get out," I hiss.

Seeing my anger, she backtracks. "I'm simply saying…"

"Get out," I repeat. "Now. And don't come back unless you're invited."

She tilts her chin up, the telltale sign she's about to unleash more bitterness. "Some daughter you turned out to be. Are you sure your illness isn't messing with your brain?"

I cross my arms. "In fact it is messing with my brain. Slowly eating at it as we speak. Funny thing is, I'm thinking clearer than I ever have."

She stares at me a moment, her eyes narrowing. She turns for the door and pulls it open. She's about to step out, but she can't resist the urge to get the last word.

"Call me when you come to your senses." She turns in a dramatic huff, finally stepping across the threshold and onto the front porch.

I stomp toward my front door. "Do me a favor, hold your breath until I do."

I slam the door and lock it. I hear the thud of her boots as she descends my porch steps. I lean my back against the door and take deep inhales through my nose. Her car roars to life outside and her engine revs as she backs out.

I close my eyes and fight the tears that threaten to spill. Why does she have to be like this? What have I ever done to deserve her hatred?

I push myself off the door and trudge up the stairs. Steam billows around me when I open the bathroom door. Dean sees me through the glass stall door.

"Hey, how did it go?"

"Not good." I close the toilet lid and slump down. "I told her to get out, then slammed the door in her face."

Dean shuts off the water and steps out. He grabs a white towel off the rack and starts drying off. If I wasn't so pissed, I'd offer to help.

"You want to talk about it?"

"She's so damn mean to me."

"Worse than Thanksgiving?"

"Yes."

"Ouch." He crouches down in front of me, the towel wrapped around his waist. "It's not your fault. It's not even about you. It's about how unhappy she is with her life."

"My mind knows that, it does. But every child wants her mom to love her. It hurts when she treats me like this."

He takes my hands. "I'm sorry Abby. You don't deserve it. No one deserves it. Here," he stands and starts the shower water again, "take a hot shower. I'll get dressed and make breakfast."

I hug him before he leaves. "You're amazing. Thank you."

"Just one question."

"Okay."

"Lucky Charms or Frosted Flakes?"

***

"Your mom's a whore."

"Elle!"

"Actually, I take that back. She might be nicer if she was a whore. Your mom's a prude."

"Gross. Can we please talk about something else?"

"Fine."

"Here are the plans I drew up for the Donaghue's basement."

Elle plops down on the couch in my office and scans my drawings. "This is great. They'll love the Jack and Jill bathroom."

"I think so too. Their teenagers may not like sharing a bathroom, but at least they'll be able to have their own bedrooms."

"Is there space for a pool table?"

"A pool table?"

Elle nods. "Mr. Donaghue emailed me this morning and asked if we can add a pool table."

I open the Donaghue's file on my computer and look over the measurements. "There should be room in the southeast corner."

"Great! I'll let him know."

We move on to the Thoman's master bathroom. "They want a sauna installed where the master closet is, and they want us to break out the wall between their room and the guest room to steal space for a new closet."

"A sauna?" Elle asks.

"Yes. They vacationed in Finland recently and Mrs. Thoman swears it helps with her chronic sinus infections."

"Do we know anyone who installs saunas?"

"Derrick says he has a guy who can do it."

"The same guy he got Pam's tub from?"

I groan. "Don't ever say the word 'tub' to me again."

"Speaking of Pam's place, when will it be done?"

"Derrick is putting in the finishing touches this week. She's moving in next Thursday."

"Wow, I can't believe it's almost done."

"I'd celebrate, but we're too busy." I check my watch. "I have to go. I'm meeting Dean and his team to go over the final version of the app."

"Nice! When is the launch date?"

"We haven't set it yet, but soon."

"You know what's strange?" Elle stares off into space, lost in thought. "You met Dean because of Jackson, so I guess my relationship with him was worth it."

"If things pan out with Tom, you have Jackson to thank for that too. You never would have met Tom without Dean."

"True," she agrees, her eyes shining.

"How did your evening with Tom end?"

"He walked me to my front door and gave me a sweet good-night kiss."

"Aw, that's so cute."

"It was." She blushes, something Elle never does.

"You like him, don't you?"

She nods. "I do. We're going out again Friday night."

It makes me happy to see my best friend happy, especially after what she's been through. I hop in my car and drive to Dean's office. Seth greets me with his usual smile and directs me to the back conference room. Everyone is set up and ready to go, the main screen of the app displayed on the large television.

"Hi everyone! Sorry if I'm late."

"You're not late," Dean assures me. "We finished our last meeting early."

I hang my coat on the back of my chair and take a seat. "I'm excited to see it."

Dean points his remote at the screen, and a guiding arrow pops up. "First stop, Lovesick." He clicks on the Lovesick logo and a new screen appears. "We're logged in as Megan."

Megan smiles. "I created my profile this morning. I told the app about myself and my ideal partner."

There are several photos of people I don't recognize on the screen. "Who is everyone else?"

"We recruited family and friends to join," Dean explains.

"They're already on the app?"

"Technically yes, but they can't use it yet. We enabled it long enough for them to download it and register."

"Gotcha."

The next feature they show me is Sick & Inspired. I'm surprised to see there are entries here as well. "Are these real stories, or are they for testing purposes?"

"Real stories." Dean clicks on the first entry. "Our guinea pigs shared their experiences without us asking them to, they did it on their own."

The title of the entry he selected is, "I Still Buy Bras."

Brian, one of the members of our think tank, speaks up. "That's my aunt."

> *I had a double mastectomy last year. I will eventually get implants, but I'm waiting for my skin to completely heal. In the meantime, I bought silicone fillers to wear in the cups of my bras. I have always loved shopping for lingerie, and I'm not going to stop now. Cancer may have changed my body, but it didn't change me.*

"Wow Brian, your aunt is incredible."

He nods. "She is. She went through chemo like a champ."

"How is she now?" Dean asks.

"Great. She follows up with her doctor every few months and is doing well."

Dean clicks on the next one, "I Ain't Got Lyme for That."

> *For me, the worst part of Lyme disease was the time period I went with no diagnosis. Several doctors told my parents my symptoms were psychosomatic. They blamed my extreme fatigue and physical symptoms on depression and anxiety. They made me feel like I was crazy. I would lay in my bed and cry all day. I had to take a semester off from college because I wasn't physically able to get out of bed without assistance. I thought my life was over.*
>
> *My mom never gave up though. She finally found a specialist who was willing to listen. He immediately*

242

recognized my symptoms as characteristics of Lyme disease. Within a week of being on the antibiotics I was better. It was like someone flipped a switch. I am concerned about a relapse, who wouldn't be, but I have my life back. And at least I know what it is now.

The biggest lesson I learned: it's your body. Don't let someone, even a medical professional, tell you what you instinctively know is wrong. Don't give up looking for answers. The right treatment is out there.

"When I first got sick, I thought I might have Lyme," I tell the group. "Its symptoms can be similar to MS."

Melissa, another member of our think tank, raises her hand. "It's mine."

"It is?" I ask shocked. I never would have guessed Melissa has Lyme disease. She's so vibrant.

"Yes. It was hell on Earth. I'll do anything I can to help someone through that experience."

The rest of the walk through goes well. In fact, it's fantastic. I can't wait to watch the app grow as more and more people join.

"What's the proposed launch date?"

Dean looks around the group, then back at me. "We're thinking two weeks from today."

I nod. "Okay. I'll see Pam next Thursday. She'll spread the word."

"We have one hundred members right now, just from our family and friend guinea pigs." Melissa slides a list to Dean. "We have fifty more that are willing to sign up if we give them access."

"What about an event to spread the word?" Brian suggests.

"It's too late to plan a launch party," I say with a frown. "But what about if we have an event in the spring?"

Dean rubs his chin. "I've been thinking about a 5k. We could collaborate with Children's Hospital and bring in a big crowd."

We kick around a few more ideas, but it's getting late. Dean thanks everyone for their time and I make sure I let them know

243

how much I appreciate everything they've done. I stay behind and look through the app one more time.

"You like it?" Dean asks.

"I love it. I'm blown away."

"Good." He leans down and kisses my forehead. "I like it when you're happy."

I turn off the TV. "What's on the agenda for this evening?"

"Dinner. Some movie watching. And if I'm lucky, a night of sleep next to my girlfriend."

I smile. "Your house or mine?"

"If you pick up dinner, I'll run home, grab a change of clothes, and meet you at your place."

"Sounds good." I stand and put on my coat. "Why don't you leave some things at my place? This way you won't have to run home on the nights you want to stay with me."

"You don't mind if I take up some of your closet space?"

"No, not at all."

"Awesome, that will make things easier. You should do the same. Have some of your things at my place too."

I nod. "Okay. Will do."

I'm smiling like a goofball on my drive home. Dean wants to have stuff at my house! I'm going to have stuff at his house! We've graduated to the "toothbrush phase" of our relationship. I call Elle to tell her the news.

"Already? Wow! Good for you."

"I know it's soon, but we get along so well."

"These things aren't measured in time."

"Well that was very Hallmark Channel of you."

She laughs. "You're both smart people. You won't rush into something you're not ready for."

I make two stops for dinner. I order Indian food for Dean and get Thai for myself. The restaurants are right next to each other, so the pickup is quick and easy. I beat Dean to my place, and take the opportunity to change out of my dress and heels and put on more comfortable clothes.

While I'm in my closet, I move a few things around so Dean has room on one of my hanging racks. I also clear out one of my dresser drawers so he can put things in there as well. The process makes me happy. I was the cautious one in my previous relationships. I enjoy my space and free time, and never liked the thought of sharing it with someone.

But it's different with Dean. He isn't intruding upon my life. He doesn't expect me to change anything about myself for him. He encourages me to pursue my career goals and doesn't get upset when I need to work late. He has his own ambitions, and doesn't expect me to sacrifice any of mine so he can achieve his.

"Hello?!" Dean calls out when he walks in the front door. "Anyone home?"

"Upstairs!"

He walks in the closet a minute later. "Whatcha up to?"

"I made space for you."

"Nice!" He hangs the t-shirts and sweatshirts he brought with him in the open spot. He puts a few pairs of boxers and socks in the drawer I emptied for him, and his toothbrush now sits next to mine in the holder.

We chow down on the food I bought, each stealing a little from the other, and watch a few episodes of *First Time Flippers*.

"If we ever flip a house together, we're hiring someone to hang the kitchen cabinets."

Dean laughs. "No doubt. Would you ever flip a house?"

"I kinda do that every day. Just for other people."

"True. You want to flip one with me?"

I'm surprised by his question. "As an investment?"

"No. For us."

"To move into?"

He nods. "Not right now, of course. But sometime in the future."

245

"Could be fun," I reply, despite the growing trepidation in my stomach.

As thrilled as I was about making space for Dean in my home, the thought of selling our houses and living together gives me pause. Later in bed, after Dean's passed out, I stare at the ceiling and do what I do best – overthink. Why did his question bother me so much? Because it's so soon? Because buying a home with someone is a big commitment? Or is it something else?

I roll to my side and gaze out my bedroom window. I've never seriously considered a long-term future with someone. The closest I came was my boyfriend right after college. We dated for a year, but I wasn't convinced we would be a good married couple. I ended it when he criticized my work schedule and told me I should work for a design firm as opposed to starting my own business.

That's not the issue with Dean. I can see us being happy into the indefinite future. I envision us growing older, and the dream fades. I see Dean being healthy and active, while I slowly deteriorate. First a cane, then a walker, then a wheelchair. My body giving out on me quicker than it should.

What if the meds don't help me? I've already had a reoccurrence of my symptoms. What if I need assistance with everyday activities? That will hinder Dean. It will slow him down. He has so many plans, a lot he can share with the world. He doesn't need an anchor at home holding him back.

My emotions ran the gamut today. A few hours ago I was ecstatic, now I'm deflated. The gentle rhythm of Dean's breathing is the only sound in the room, but my fears are deafening.

***

The next morning, I go through the motions with Dean.

"Are you feeling okay?" he asks over breakfast. He woke up early and made scrambled eggs and bacon.

"Yes, why?"

"You're quiet this morning."

"Sorry, I'm thinking about my appointments today."

246

"You have a lot going on?"

"Yes. Three client meetings. How about you?"

"Another trial run of *Operation New World 2*. Then a meeting about the next game."

"The next game?"

He nods. "We're working on a concept for a new series. I want it to be geared toward the preteen and teen group. They need a new and challenging game series that isn't violent."

"Like Mario was?"

"Yes, exactly." He puts his dishes in the dishwasher and kisses the top of my head. "I'll see you later."

"Okay." My smile fades when he's out the door.

Once I'm at the office, I push my personal issues to the back of my mind and focus on work. My appointments go well, I book all three projects. We are now calendaring jobs three months out. The clients don't seem to mind the wait, but I need to talk to Derrick about getting additional contractors and workers to help.

At 6:00 p.m. my phone buzzes with a text from Dean.

In the mood for Mexican tonight. You up for it?

I strum my fingers on my desk. For the first time since I met him, I decline a night with Dean.

I think you were on to something this morning – I'm not feeling so hot. I'm going to have some soup and get in bed early tonight. Raincheck?

Because he's Dean, he offers to help.

Do you need me to bring you anything?

I sigh. I am such a bitch for lying to him.

No thanks. I'm leaving the office now. I'll catch up with you tomorrow.

My message nips a potential visit from him in the bud. I want to be alone tonight.

I drive home and watch TV in a zombie-like state. I'm seeing the images, but not absorbing them. I make myself eat soup just

247

so I can tell myself I didn't completely lie to Dean. I fall asleep on the couch and trudge up to bed an hour later.

I wake to a message from Dean asking how I'm feeling. I tell him I'm feeling a little better and plan to test the waters by going in to work. I'm not sure if I want to see him today, and this message will give me an out either way.

Work again serves as a distraction and I fully engross myself in it. I eat lunch at my desk and finish the mock drawings for all three of the new clients. I'm dreading my usual post-work text with Dean. Do I want to see him?

As much as I'd love to be in his arms, I put him off again.

> *Still not feeling great. More soup and sleep is needed. I hope your day went well.*

A few minutes later, I get a response.

> *So sorry to hear that. I miss you, but I want you to feel better. Get some rest.*

I spend the evening at home feeling crappy and have a night of restless sleep. I toss and turn, the empty space next to me cold and depressing.

I get out of bed well before my alarm and arrive at the office an hour earlier than normal. I'm already in the middle of a project when Elle walks upstairs.

"You're here early." She sits on my couch.

"I had trouble sleeping, so I came in."

"Guess who I ran into last night at Kroger?"

"Who?"

"Dean."

I sit straight up. "You did?"

"Yes. I went out with Tom for dinner and swung into Kroger on my way home. Dean was in the coffee aisle. Imagine my shock when he told me you've been sick the last couple days."

My heart stops. "What did you tell him?"

248

"I played along. Told him I've covered appointments for you."

I let out a sigh of relief. "Thank you."

She purses her lips. "What the hell are you doing?"

"What do you mean?"

"Don't play dumb with me. Why are you lying to Dean?"

I examine my pen cap. "I need space."

"Space for what?"

"You wouldn't understand."

She crosses her arms. "Try me."

"He mentioned buying a house together."

"And?"

"That's it."

"You were psyched to tell me he's leaving stuff at your house. What's the big deal?"

I slam my pen down. "The big deal is I'm not a normal person."

"Come again?"

"I have MS, Elle. It's not a good idea for him to plan a future with me."

Her jaw drops. "Are you kidding?"

"No."

"I suppose I shouldn't be in business with you anymore either then, huh? You should just close yourself up in your house now and be done with it."

I sigh. "Like I said, you don't understand."

"If Dean is in a car accident tomorrow and is paralyzed from the waist down, would you walk away from him?"

"Of course not."

"So why would he do the same to you?"

"It's different," I argue. "The odds of me having a disability are a lot greater than him getting in an accident."

"You never know what life will bring Abby. That's what a relationship is. Weathering the storm. Enjoying the sunny days, and fighting like hell together against the hurricane. You have no idea if your disease will progress, and yet you are willing to destroy your relationship with Dean over it."

"Dean's a good guy. He'll feel obligated to stay with me."

"Have you considered that if, and I mean *if*, your disease progresses, he'll stay with you because he loves you?"

I rub my temples. "I need more time to think about it."

"You need to stop thinking about it!" Elle raises her voice. "That's your fucking problem. You're thinking about it too much."

Tears form in my eyes. "I love him, Elle. I don't want to hold him back."

Elle's glare softens. "At least give him the chance to make the choice for himself. You'll regret it if you don't."

"I know."

"You're my best friend. It's my job to tell you when you're fucking up. And you're fucking this up, big time."

"You're right. I can't keep lying to him." I stand and grab my purse. "I'm going to see him now."

"Good. Let me know how it goes."

My hands shake as I drive to Dean's office. I ignored his good morning text earlier. I didn't know what to say. I still don't know what to say, but I have to stop running. I have to face him.

Seth is on the phone when I walk in, but gives me a thumbs up as the go ahead. Everyone is at their desks, computers fired up and energy levels high. One of the techs is reviewing a scene from *Operation New World 2* I recognize from when Dean and I were trying it out. It looks much sharper now.

Dean's door is closed when I round the corner and I consider bailing out. Instead, I take a deep breath and knock on the door.

"Come in!"

I slide the door open tentatively. "Hey."

He jumps up from his desk and walks toward me. "Hey! I was starting to get worried about you. I hadn't heard from you." He gives me a hug. "How are you feeling?"

"I'm okay."

"What's up?" His brow is furrowed. He's on to me.

"Can we sit down?"

"Sure."

We head for the couch near his television and sit side by side. "I have a confession to make."

"Okay…"

"I'm not sick. At least, not physically. But I was under the weather."

"Under the weather, how?"

"I was upset about something. I needed time to think it through."

He frowns. "Why didn't you just tell me?"

"I don't know."

"So you lied?"

I fidget. "You can call it that if you want. I went home and went to bed early both nights. I needed the time and space."

"I wish you would have just said so." His frown deepens. "I don't like that you weren't forthcoming with me."

"I'm sorry. I've never been in this type of relationship before. This is the first relationship I've been in where my partner wants to have difficult conversations with me. The guys I was with before avoided them at all costs."

"And that's why you're not with them anymore."

"I know, I know."

"What did you need time and space to think about?"

"We need to have a really serious conversation, but I don't know where to start."

He softens and scoots closer. "Whatever it is, it's okay. We need to talk about what's bothering you."

Tears spring to my eyes. "I'm sorry. I'm sorry if I hurt your feelings. That's the last thing in the world I want."

He rubs my back.

"The truth is, it scared me when you mentioned getting a house together."

"Ah, too soon?"

"It's not that. I really want to. I would love to live with you. I miss you when we're not together."

"Then what is it?"

I squeeze my eyes shut, then force myself to open them and meet his gaze. "It's not fair to you."

His eyes widen. "What's not fair?"

"I could end up in a wheelchair Dean. I don't want to be a burden on you."

"Abby, I don't care about that."

"I know you don't, but I care about it. I want you to have a full and happy life."

"I am happy. I have a full life. But that's only if you're in it."

"I don't want to hold you back." I start sobbing, I can't help it.

He pulls me in tight. "You listen to me Abigail Henry. I want you when you're healthy. I want you when you're not healthy. I will carry you to the top of Kilimanjaro on my back if I have to. I'm all in with you. We are a team."

I'm letting it all out. All my fears and hesitations. "What if I can't have children?"

"Then we don't have kids."

"Are you sure you're okay with that?"

"First of all, I don't know if I want kids. Second, I have children in my life in other ways. My niece, your niece, and the kids I volunteer with at the hospital. If we decide we want children of our own, we talk to your doctors about it, or look into adoption."

"It's more complicated with me."

"Are you kidding? Everything with you is easy."

I smile. "I mean life decisions are harder with me because of my health."

"We can't predict the future, Abby. So let's just live today, and enjoy what we have. We can spin scenarios forever, but at the end of the day, I'm going to pick you every time. Every single time."

"Are you sure?"

"I've never been more sure of anything."

I gaze up into his eyes. "I love you."

He wipes a tear from my cheek. "I love you too. Nothing will change my mind about that."

I lean my head against his chest, comforted by his arms and the sound of his heart beating. Relief floods my veins. I did it. I confessed my biggest fears. And he didn't walk away. He pulled me in.

I close my eyes and relish the moment. For the first time in my life, I understand what it means to be madly in love with someone.

Chapter Fourteen

It's move in day – for Pam.

All her furniture is in place and I've left no stone unturned. The condo looks gorgeous and I couldn't be happier with the way it turned out. The white marble tile sparkles, the countertops gleam, the tub in the guest bathroom is perfect, and the custom bookshelf/entertainment center turned out better than I hoped.

"You did an amazing job Derrick."

He smiles. "We had some bumps along the way, but we made it."

"Indeed," I say with a laugh. "You ready to do this all over again?"

"Yes. I'll be on the new jobsite Monday. Until then, I'm taking the rest of the week off."

"You should. You deserve it."

"If there's nothing left to do, I'm starting my vacation now."

"Before you go, there's something I want to talk to you about."

"Okay."

"We have several jobs lined up, and I have more clients coming in this week. Do you have another crew we can use? We're already scheduling three months out, I'm not sure clients will wait much longer than that."

"Actually, my cousin is a contractor too. His team may be able to help us out."

"Really? Do you have pictures of projects they've done, or client references?"

"Not handy, but I can get them. I've seen their work, they do a good job."

255

"It would make me feel better if you supervised his crew for a while. Maybe not all day, but stop in to check on them. At least in the beginning."

He nods. "Understandable. I'll talk to him and let you know."

"Great!"

Derrick glances around the condo, his hands on his hips. "This may be our best job yet."

"I think so too."

He extends his hand. "Once again, thanks for the work Abby."

"You're welcome. And thank you for putting up with me."

Derrick takes off and leaves me to do the walk through with Pam. I stare out her massive windows and watch pedestrians on the streets below. It's a warm day for February, and people are out enjoying the sunshine while it lasts.

I turn when the elevator doors bing behind me. Pam steps out, her mouth open.

"Wow Abby, this is amazing!"

"Do you love it?"

"Yes! Do you know how hard it was to not sneak in here last night?"

I laugh. "Come on, let me show you around your new place."

Pam helped me pick out most of the furniture and accessories, so there are no huge surprises. Nevertheless, she gushes over each room.

"This is the first home I've had where I feel like it's completely mine. Does that make sense?"

"Yes. That's the beauty of starting with a fresh canvas. It can be anything you want it to be."

"My mom is going to love the guest bedroom. The bathroom for her is perfect. Thank you."

"You are so welcome. I hope you're happy here."

She smiles ear to ear. "It's not L.A., but this feels like home."

I show her a few odds and ends – how to work the remote for her bookcase, which switches do what, and where we hid the pamphlets for her new appliances.

"All the warranty information is with the instructions if you ever need it. Plus, I have copies scanned into your file if you misplace them."

"You have everything covered."

"I try."

"How are things going with the app?"

I'm glad she asked me about the app. I was wondering how I would sneak the launch date into our conversation today. "We're launching it Friday."

"This Friday?"

"Yes."

"Did you decide to do a launch event?"

"Dean reached out to the other members of the Children's Hospital board, and we're collaborating with them to sponsor a 5k in April."

"Why so late?"

"We figure we'll get a bigger crowd in April because the weather will be nicer. Plus, it gives us time to work out any bugs with the app."

"I see." Pam takes out her phone. "I'm emailing the producer right now to have him add this to Friday morning's broadcast. I'm not working on air yet, but he'll do this for me."

"Really? That would be great!"

"Send me a picture of the app's icon, and I'll post it on my social media accounts."

"I'll have Dean send it to you this afternoon." Before I can thank her, she continues.

"I'll be on air by the time your 5k comes around. I'll hype it once you have the date set in stone."

"You have no idea how much this means to me. Thank you."

She slips her phone into her coat pocket. "You helped me find a fantastic doctor for my mother, you did a wonderful job turning my empty shell of a condo into a comfortable place, and you're a great person on a mission to do good work for others. It's the least I can do."

After promising Pam a five star dinner for her efforts, I head back to my office. It's a tremendous relief to have Pam's condo off my plate. I constantly worried something would go wrong. I can't put myself through that again. I have to trust the process and realize I can handle whatever is thrown my way.

I smile when I see Elle's car parked outside our work home. "Knock, knock," I call out when I walk in.

"In here!" she yells from her office.

I let out a sigh of relief when I flop down in the chair opposite her desk. "Pam's condo is officially done."

She claps. "Yay!"

"How's your day going?"

"Good. I met with Ted and Jane Wilson."

"Remind me who they are."

"Basement mother-in-law suite."

"Ah, right."

"They love your idea of adding a walkout in the southwest corner. I warned them it could get pricey because of the landscaping that needs to be done outside, but they don't care. They want it. They aren't thrilled about the wait though."

"I talked to Derrick about that today. His cousin is a contractor and may be able to help us."

"Excellent!" She shuffles papers on her desk. "Also, I spoke to our accountant."

"Ugh. I forgot it's that time of year."

She nods. "He gave me the checklist of what we need for our taxes."

"I have most of it saved already. It won't take long."

"Enough work talk. Do you and Dean have plans Friday night?"

"It's our launch date for the app."

She slumps. "Oh, right."

"That's in the morning. We should be able to go out in the evening. Why? What's up?"

"Tom and I are going to the Blue Jackets game. Would you and Dean like to join us?"

"I'll ask him, but I'm guessing he'll be up for it. Have you and Tom seen a lot of each other?"

She snickers.

"I mean dates Elle, not literally."

"We've been out a few times."

"And?"

"He's a nice guy. I get the sense he's ready to settle down."

"Is that a good thing or a bad thing?"

She crinkles her nose. "I'm not sure yet. I don't want to play around, but I'm not rushing into anything either."

"Understandable. Jackson burned you pretty badly."

"He did. I need to be careful and not carry that into a new relationship. Especially with a great guy like Tom."

"Have you been reading relationship books lately?"

"No. Why?"

"You had excellent relationship advice for me the other day, and now you're being very mature about healing before diving headfirst."

She blushes. "Okay, fine. I read *Love Bandages*, the book by Dr. Quartz."

"Dr. Quartz? The lady on late night infomercials?"

"That would be the one."

I giggle. "She seems like a whack job, but if it helps, it helps."

"I hate to admit it, but it did. She made me realize my relationship with Jackson was lacking for a long time. He shouldn't have done what he did, but I understand why he did it."

"Because he's a dick?"

"Yes. He's a dick, and I was never willing to admit it to myself. I held on because I wanted the comfort and routine."

"Wow, I don't know how to handle this new, mature version of you."

"Oh, don't worry," she says with a smile, "I'm still your foul-mouthed friend who embarrasses you on a regular basis."

I smile. "Good. I wouldn't want it any other way."

***

"We have less than twenty-four hours to launch, Abby. We need the name."

"Illing It has grown on me. Plus, you have everything ready to go. It would be more work for your team to change it."

Dean raises an eyebrow. "Are you sure? You've been pretty vocal about how much you don't like it."

"I'm sure."

"We can change it down the road if you think of something you like better."

"Is it a good idea to change the name once it's up and running?"

He shrugs. "Once the app gains traction and has a following, no. But it would be okay to change it in the early stages."

"How many people do you think will download it?"

"No clue. It's hard to say. We purposely didn't run a huge marketing campaign for it because we want to see how the audience reacts."

"Right. I just hope it's not a flop."

"Look at it this way, if we help one person, it was worth it."

260

I smile. "True. In some ways, we already have. A few of your team members were able to share their stories with us, and we're doing the 5k."

The next morning, I watch the morning news while I get ready. I clap when I hear the anchor plug our app.

"Dean!" I bust into his bathroom to find him drying off. Oh my... what was I saying?

"What's up?"

I clear the dirty thoughts from my mind. "They just hyped our app!"

"Nice!"

"Is there a way to track how many people sign up?"

"The app store will let us know." He kisses my cheek as he walks by. "These things take time. We'll check it tonight."

By the time we get home from the Blue Jackets game with Tom and Elle, I'm bursting at the seams.

"I need to know! Tell me!"

Dean laughs. "Okay, okay. I'll check it." He logs into the program and smiles. "One thousand and two."

"Is that good? I mean, it sounds good."

"If it was a commercial app, we'd be disappointed. But for an app like ours, I think it's great."

"I'm logging on to see if people joined the groups."

He takes my cellphone out of my hand. "Why don't we go to bed instead?"

"I'm not tired."

His eyes smolder. "Neither am I."

Oh my...

***

"Stand up and walk to the door for me. Walk the straightest line you can."

261

Dr. Harris is looking especially sharp today. Her black dress and pearls remind me of Audrey Hepburn in the *Breakfast at Tiffany's* poster. Replace her pen with a cigarette holder and she'd be the perfect stand-in.

"How have you faired on the medication?" she asks when I sit down. "Still going well?"

"Yes. No issues."

"Any return of your symptoms?"

"No, not since the last time you saw me."

Dr. Harris jots down notes. "That was the end of last year, correct?"

"Yes."

"So four months with no symptoms at all?"

"Yes."

"Hard to believe it's April already, isn't it?" Dr. Harris asks with a smile.

"Definitely. The year is flying by."

I'm waiting for her to get to what I really want to hear – the results of my MRI. Believe it or not, six months have passed since my initial diagnosis. Dr. Harris wanted me to get an MRI to see if the meds are doing what they're supposed to be doing. After this, I'll get an MRI annually.

"I reviewed your scan." Dr. Harris turns to face me. She smiles. "Everything looks the same."

"No changes?"

"No changes." She shows me a screenshot on her laptop. "The spots aren't larger than they were before."

I breathe a sigh of relief. "Thank goodness."

. "Hopefully this is the worst it ever gets for you."

"That would be amazing."

"We'll keep our fingers crossed, and your meds in your system," she says with a wink.

262

"I've seen commercials for a new medication. It said you only have to take it twice a year. Are any of your patients on it?"

"I had a few patients try it. They're three months in to the first dose. We're monitoring them closely to see how they do. I don't want to change your meds just yet. You're doing well on them, and I'm still testing the waters with the new medication."

"Makes sense."

"I'll keep you posted." Dr. Harris stands and extends her hand. "I'll see you in six months for a check-up."

"Thanks Dr. Harris."

"Oh," she says just before she steps out of the room, "I love the app."

"You've seen it?" I ask surprised.

"One of the nurses showed it to me. I saw your picture on the front page. I loved your testimonial about MS and your temporary relapse."

"You did?"

"Yes. I've told a few patients about it. Good job."

I am stunned. If Dr. Harris has heard of the app, and her patients are talking about it, it's really taking off. I've seen the numbers grow the last two months, but I lost touch with the fact that those numbers are people. Real people like me.

I call Dean on my way to the office. "Dr. Harris knows about the app!"

"She does?"

"Yes, and she's telling patients to check it out."

"While I'm glad she's spreading the word, I'm only concerned about one of her patients right now."

I laugh. "Sorry, I was excited."

"Do you want to talk about your appointment? We don't have to if you don't want to."

"My MRI showed no progression!"

I hear him breathe a sigh of relief. "That's great news."

"It is."

"We should go out tonight and celebrate."

"We can't. We have to be up early for the 5k in the morning."

"Fine, we'll celebrate tomorrow night. If we're not too tired."

"That's a big if."

"Your place or my place tonight?" he asks.

"Umm, we've done my place the last two nights. Let's crash at your place."

"Sounds good. I'll grab Chinese on the way home."

I hang up with Dean and call my dad. He is thrilled to hear my news.

"What a relief!"

"Definitely." I change the subject. "Are you coming to the 5k tomorrow?"

"Wouldn't miss it. Samantha and I are only walking it though. My body gave up on running a long time ago."

"That's fine. There will be a lot of walkers."

"Is it okay if Austin and Kelly come?"

"Of course!"

"Austin may bother the crap out of Dean," Dad cautions. "Make sure you prepare him."

"I've warned Dean that Austin has a man-crush on him."

"A man-crush? I think Austin may be in love with him."

I giggle. "See you in the morning. Love you."

"Love you too sweetheart."

I call Elle next.

"That is fantastic news! Woo hoo! Party at my house."

"No parties. 5k tomorrow, remember?"

Elle groans. "Why did I let you talk me into getting up early on a Saturday?"

"Because I'm your best friend and you love me."

"Oh yeah, right," she says with zero enthusiasm. "I'll see you in the morning."

I beat Dean to his place and lounge on his couch. I take stock of my current life situation. My business is taking off, the app is doing well, I have an amazing boyfriend, a ride or die bestie, and wonderful parents in my dad and stepmom. My health is steady and my stress levels are down.

For a moment I consider calling my mom. I haven't spoken to her since I kicked her out of my house. My aunt called me a couple weeks ago to spill the tea.

"Your mother told me you two aren't talking."

"She's right, we're not."

"She also said you kicked her out of the house."

"Yes, ma'am."

My aunt laughed. "She must have really done it this time. I don't know how you've put up with her for so long. She tried telling me your new boyfriend brainwashed you, but I know better than to believe anything she tells me."

The conversation with my aunt reminded me that Mom isn't on my side. She lives on an island all her own. Despite this, I feel obligated to let her know I'm okay. Why is that? I'm sure it's an urge I'll fight my entire life. I lived through the cycle for so long, it will always be a part of me.

Instead of reaching out to my mom directly, because no good will come of it, I send my aunt a text letting her know my results. She'll appreciate me keeping her posted, and I'm sure she'll tell my mom she heard from me.

I smile when I hear the garage door open. All thoughts of my mom disappear. It's time to hang out with my man.

***

"Holy crap! This is insane," Elle exclaims when she finds us the next morning in the 5k crowd. "We're parked in another area code."

I'm happy to see Tom is with her. It wouldn't surprise me if they have the toothbrush conversation soon.

"Isn't it great?" I beam. "There's almost two thousand people here."

Tom scans the crowd. "Impressive."

"The Children's Hospital did a great job spreading the word."

Dean returns from the signup table and hands me my runner's bib. "You're lucky number 777."

"What do I win?"

Elle pins her bib to her shirt. "Leg cramps and dehydration."

"You didn't have coffee this morning, did you?"

She sticks her tongue out at me in response.

Dean pins his bib on. "I just talked to the head of oncology. He asked if we would consider creating an Illing It app for kids."

"Really?"

"Yes. He said kids are on their parents' phones all the time while they wait for appointments, or have treatments."

"True. I haven't thought about that before."

"Me neither. He said the hospital is willing to create kid friendly videos explaining illnesses, treatments, and medical lingo for us to use."

"That would be awesome. We should do it."

Dean nods. "I agree. I'd like to create kid friendly games for it as well."

I smile. "I love it. We'll have all age groups covered. Each with their own unique experience."

Before we can discuss the idea further, I spot my dad and Samantha. I wave to catch their attention. When that doesn't work, Dean starts waving his hand in the air as well. Dad finally spots us.

I give him a big hug when he reaches me. "You made it!"

"We walked a 5k to get here, but we made it," my dad groans.

Samantha smacks his arm playfully. "It was three blocks."

I glance over her shoulder. "Where are Austin and Kelly?"

"They're on their way. They'll meet us at the finish line. I told them we can grab a bite to eat after the race. I hope you don't mind."

"Not at all."

The MC walks out on the temporary stage built at the start line. "Good morning everyone!"

The crowd cheers in response.

"We're about to start the race. Before you take off, I want to thank the sponsors of the event – The Columbus Children's Hospital and the new app Illing It. The app was created for people with chronic illnesses. Please check it out and show them some support. Now get your butts to the start line!"

Our group moves along with the crowd and waits for the gun to fire. I glance over at Dean and take his hand.

"You ready to run this race with me?"

He smiles. "You know it."

Acknowledgements

There are several people in my life dealing with chronic illnesses. Some of them autoimmune disorders, others chronic pain. I have an incredible amount of respect for people who deal with lifelong illnesses and do so with a smile on their faces. They seem to truly understand that we have one life to live, and regardless of the obstacles, we must make the most of it.

As always, I am forever grateful to my friends and family. My son is growing up before my very eyes and I hope I'm showing him no dream is too crazy.

I lost my Pekingese and writing buddy Duke last summer. After some hesitation, I was introduced to a Pekingese puppy who my son and I named Remi. We adore him. He reminds me that even after loss, we should seek out happiness.

I'll be forty in a few weeks, and as I approach the final days in my thirties, I feel incredibly grateful. I spend my time doing things I absolutely love doing and share it with people who love me and want the best for me. I've found my niche in the world, and I hope in some way it brings joy to others.

To my readers, wow. I still can't wrap my head around the fact that people read my books. If you want to interact with me, you can find me on Facebook – Neva Rae Bell or on Instagram - @Neva_Bell_Books. Remi and I can also be found doing silly things on tiktok - @nevabellbooks. If you're not on social media, you can reach me via email at NevaBellBooks@gmail.com. Just don't send hate mail. It hurts my feelings, and I don't do well with criticism ☺

Thank you again for spending time with me. You'll never know how much I appreciate it.

The Neva Bell Library

Romantic Comedies
Love & Omissions
The Sleeping Arrangement
The Things We Don't Say
Abigail Henry Feels Fine

The Branded Series
Branded
Torn
United (Coming Soon)

Poetry Collections
Wildflower
Dandelion
Venus Flytrap
Orchid
Tiger Lily
Daffodil
Daisy
Dragonfly
Wasabi
Symmetry
Lion Tamer (coming Summer 2021)

Allie Hayes Titles
Restless
The Perfect Cure
Naughty Girl Poems

Learn more at www.nevabellbooks.com

Made in the USA
Monee, IL
02 June 2021